*"Chad, mee̶̶̶
Hannah sai̶̶̶*

He stared at the baby and the sparse-haired, drool-covered little imp stared back, chattering as if saying something directly to him, then holding out the toy she chomped on in his direction. He swallowed hard, his heart expanding, surging against the bands he'd wrapped around it so long ago. Her large eyes were open, so trusting, her cheeks flushed, her entire face animated.

Chad awkwardly moved to accept the offering, only it appeared she hadn't meant for him to take it, merely to feel it. When he released the slobbery rubber, she gave a peal of laughter then stuck it back in her mouth.

A grin edged its way across his face and he swore he could feel one of those intangible bands in his chest snap and begin to unravel.

Now there was no doubt in his mind that Bonny was *his*.

Dear Reader,

As the air begins to chill outside, curl up under a warm blanket with a mug of hot chocolate and these six fabulous Special Edition novels....

First up is bestselling author Lindsay McKenna's *A Man Alone,* part of her compelling and highly emotional MORGAN'S MERCENARIES: MAVERICK HEARTS series. Meet Captain Thane Hamilton, a wounded Marine who'd closed off his heart long ago, and Paige Black, a woman whose tender loving care may be just what the doctor ordered.

Two new miniseries are launching this month and you're not going to want to miss either one! Look for *The Rancher Next Door,* the first of rising star Susan Mallery's brand-new miniseries, LONE STAR CANYON. Not even a long-standing family feud can prevent love from happening! Also, veteran author Penny Richards pens a juicy and scandalous love story with *Sophie's Scandal,* the first of her wonderful new trilogy—RUMOR HAS IT... that two high school sweethearts are about to recapture the love they once shared....

Next, Jennifer Mikels delivers a wonderfully heartwarming romance between a runaway heiress and a local sheriff with *The Bridal Quest,* the second book in the HERE COME THE BRIDES series. And Diana Whitney brings back her popular STORK EXPRESS series. Could a *Baby of Convenience* be just the thing to bring two unlikely people together?

And last, but not least, please welcome newcomer Tori Carrington to the line. *Just Eight Months Old...* and she'd stolen the hearts of two independent bounty hunters—who just might make the perfect family!

Enjoy these delightful tales, and come back next month for more emotional stories about life, love and family!

Best,
Karen Taylor Richman
Senior Editor

Please address questions and book requests to:
Silhouette Reader Service
U.S.: 3010 Walden Ave., P.O. Box 1325, Buffalo, NY 14269
Canadian: P.O. Box 609, Fort Erie, Ont. L2A 5X3

Just Eight Months Old...

TORI CARRINGTON

SPECIAL EDITION™

Published by Silhouette Books

America's Publisher of Contemporary Romance

With warm gratitude we dedicate this, our first Special Edition, to Karen Taylor Richman and her own special "addition." We'd also like to thank Kim Nadelson and Debra Matteucci for their initiative and limitless help.

The pleasure's all ours!

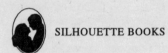 SILHOUETTE BOOKS

ISBN 0-373-24362-6

JUST EIGHT MONTHS OLD…

Copyright © 2000 by Lori & Tony Karayianni

This edition published by arrangement with Harlequin Books S.A.

® and TM are trademarks of Harlequin Books S.A., used under license. Trademarks indicated with ® are registered in the United States Patent and Trademark Office, the Canadian Trade Marks Office and in other countries.

Visit Silhouette at www.eHarlequin.com

Printed in U.S.A.

TORI CARRINGTON

is the pseudonym of husband-and-wife writing team Lori & Tony Karayianni, who have been cowriters for nearly as long as they've been a couple. They describe their lives as being "better than fiction." Despite their different backgrounds—Tony was born near Olympia, Greece, and raised in Athens, while Lori is a native of Toledo, Ohio—their shared love for romance and travel allows them to constantly redefine what follows "and they lived happily ever after." In their books you'll see Tony's keen eye for plotting and hunger for adventure, and Lori's love for vivid characters and the fundamental ties that bind us all. Along with their four cats, they call Toledo home, but also travel to Athens as often as they can.

This talented writing duo also writes for Harlequin Temptation under the Tori Carrington pseudonym. Lori and Tony love to hear from readers. Write to them at P.O. Box 12271, Toledo, OH 43612 for an autographed bookplate.

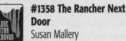

Chapter One

The dog days of summer in New York City held little appeal for Hannah McGee. Never mind the bittersweet memories they brought drifting back. The heat and humidity wreaked havoc on her pale, lightly freckled skin and turned her brick-red corkscrew curls into a Panama hat of frizz.

Standing on the sweltering asphalt, she closed the car door then wiped at a one-inch spot on her vest, a little memento her eight-month-old daughter, Bonny, had bestowed upon her that morning. Giving up, she pulled the vest closer to her torso, the weight of the stun gun she called The Equalizer and a small canister of pepper spray she had tucked into a belt just inside the waist of her gauze skirt reassuringly familiar. For the past few years she'd never needed anything more to protect herself. Which was good, because even when she was a NYC police officer, she'd never much liked carrying a revolver.

After today she wouldn't need any of this paraphernalia at all.

Still, goodbyes were something she'd never much liked. Saying adios to rusty rental cars, meals caught on the run and chasing bail-jumpers wasn't that big a deal. But bidding adieu to her boss, Elliott Blackstone, was going to be a little bigger. She'd worked with him for the past three years. In an indirect way, he'd made it possible for her to switch career paths to trade in her bounty hunter title for that of private investigator. After today, that'd be official. She eagerly looked forward to planting her feet firmly on that new path just as soon as she closed the gate to this one.

She pulled open the glass door to Blackstone Bail and Bonds and welcomed the swell of cold, air-conditioned air that swept over her.

Five minutes later, she wondered if the obstacle that had just plopped down in the middle of her path came any larger—and that by no means referred to Elliott's considerable size.

"I can't pay you, Hannah."

Elliott Blackstone hovered somewhere in his mid- to late-forties, his passionate dislike of parting with anything green that had a picture of a president on it one of his defining traits. She understood this about him. In fact, after the first few occasions, she'd come to look forward to their little tugs-of-war. But this wasn't the usual Elliott pleading poverty even though his posh office could easily match that of a banker. No, Hannah had the piercing sensation he was serious.

"El, I'm already late picking up Bonny because you sent Jack Stokes out on the same run. Can't we just finish up here and call it a day?"

Blackstone cleared his throat. "Where is Stokes, anyway?"

Hannah remembered the dim interior of The Bar in South Jamaica, Queens, where she had picked up bail-jumper Eddie Fowler an hour before. "Probably still handcuffed to a bar rail. Unless someone took pity on him." She smiled. "Though that's highly unlikely."

Elliott tugged a handkerchief from the front pocket of his silk-blend suit and mopped his forehead.

Hannah glanced at her watch, then sat in the visitor's chair opposite him. "Okay, why don't you start from the beginning."

He fell silent for a good thirty ticks of the antique grandfather clock in the corner. "You know I wouldn't mess you around on something like this, Hannah. I always pay you on time." He sighed.

But this time was different. She'd just completed her last run and her new business waited. She needed the money now.

"El—"

He shifted his bulk in the leather chair. "You been watching the news lately?"

"I haven't turned on the TV or picked up a newspaper since last week." She wanted to add it was because she was setting up her new business in a rented office downtown, but didn't. "Are you telling me you did something newsworthy and I missed it?"

Elliott laughed without humor. "No, not me. Two of my clients." He regarded her as if gauging her disposition then pursed his fleshy lips. "Would you mind if I introduce someone else into our discussion? There's someone else waiting in the connecting office. Someone I need on this case as much as I need you."

Case? Before she could ask him what he meant, he got up then crossed to open a door. "I think it's safe."

The moment the visitor strode into the room, Elliott's warning made sense.

Oh, yes, the obstacle in her path could get bigger. And had. By two times.

Hannah looked at the man who had walked out of her life fifteen months ago without a second glance. The man she had loved and wanted to marry. Only it wasn't Chad Hogan who had needed Blackstone's warning. Chad had nothing to fear from her.

She, on the other hand, had everything to fear from him.

Chad's gaze slid over her body, making her skin grow markedly warmer. Her vest and skirt more than adequately covered her, but the open way Chad looked at her made her feel as if she wore very little.

Elliott stepped between her and her ex-partner. "I know this must come as a shock, Hannah. But I think once I explain, you'll understand why I flew Chad in from Florida."

She barely heard Elliott's words. She swallowed back a year's worth of memories, hardly aware of the interrogation-like silence that had settled over the room.

"I can't believe you did this, Elliott." Hannah's voice sounded like it had spiraled from the bottom of a barrel.

"Listen to me for a minute," he pleaded. "I need you both—"

"I think you need your head examined," she snapped. Reluctantly she looked at Chad, as if silently asking him to confirm her assessment of the situation. When he spoke, the deep timbre of his voice was as powerful as his presence. "You look great, Hannah."

That was the last thing she'd expected him to say.

Through the door to the reception area, Hannah overheard someone arguing with the receptionist. In a corner of her mind that still worked, she distantly realized it was Stokes.

Elliott sighed. "Why don't I leave you two alone to iron out your differences, huh? I've got to go straighten out…whatever is going on outside."

The door closed behind Elliott. Like a spinning carnival ride, the room seemed to grow distinctly smaller. The distance Hannah stood away from Chad seemed to lessen by inches, though neither of them had moved. Chad was gazing at her with that…look. That half-lidded look that said so much, yet promised so little.

"How are you doing, Hannah?"

She absently rubbed the goose bumps spreading over her skin. "Doing? I'm fine, I guess. You?"

Often, she'd wondered what she would do on the off chance she ever saw Chad again. She'd rehearsed what she might say. Or rather, what she wouldn't say. But now…now she realized all her preparations were for naught. Nothing could have prepared her for facing a man who commanded a room merely by standing in it. And time certainly hadn't changed that trait, even if he displayed some other more noticeable changes.

"We never were very good at small talk, were we?" She thought she detected a measure of uneasiness in his question. Chad, uneasy? She walked to the wet bar in the corner of the office, needing to put distance between not only her and Chad, but between the present and the past. She picked up a delicate porcelain cup and poured herself some coffee, the shaking of her hands preventing her from pouring more than an ounce.

"I think any kind of verbal communication was a problem with us." She took a deep sip of the hot liquid, barely recognizing it was bitter.

Fight or flight. Hannah's heart beat double-time. She recalled the term she learned at the academy. Fight or flight was the immediate reaction you experienced when faced with a difficult and/or dangerous situation.

And despite the time that had passed, the emotions that had dimmed, the obvious and inconspicuous changes in each of them, Hannah wished for the world that she could take flight.

"So..." She clutched her purse closer to her side. Where was Elliott? Her gaze flicked to the desk, the bookcase, anywhere but Chad's face. Still, time and again it wandered to forbidden territory.

The filing cabinet...Chad. Had the slight crinkles around his eyes deepened, intensifying the mercurial gray of his eyes? The picture on the wall...Chad. Was that a little gray in his sandy brown hair, adding a hint of the distinguished to his rugged appearance? The closed window...Chad. Oh, God, why did he have to look at her that way?

Flight.

"Look, Chad, I don't know what Elliott had in mind, but..." But what? Did she tell him she was hanging up the "out of business" shingle as far as skip-tracing went? Did she share that tomorrow she was going to open the doors to Seekers, a business they had once planned to run together? Or did she tell him she couldn't possibly work with him because at a baby-sitter's house in Brooklyn Heights waited her eight-month-old daughter. A child he didn't know existed.

His daughter.

She chewed on the soft flesh of her bottom lip. "Why don't you go ahead and hear Elliott out? I'm overdue for a vacation anyway." Liar, she called herself. She moved to leave.

Chad stepped forward and grasped her wrist. She faced him, her heart surging up into her throat. "Hannah, I..."

She swallowed with difficulty, her gaze fastened on his mouth, waiting for the rest of his sentence to emerge, sure she wouldn't hear it over the rush of blood past her ears.

He suddenly dropped his hand, then straightened. "You don't have to leave. I'm the one real good at walking out, remember?"

She did remember. All too well. But why did she get the impression that wasn't what he'd wanted to say? "Walking really isn't the word for it," she found herself whispering. "You ran. So fast you would have thought I was threatening a death sentence instead of proposing marriage."

Chad stuffed his hands into the pockets of his well-worn jeans. "I see you haven't thought about this as much as I have. Not that I blame you. If our positions were reversed, I'd probably have forgotten me the instant the door catch slipped home."

Inexplicable tears burned the back of her eyes. She would never have expected this from him. She didn't quite know what to do with this kinder, gentler Chad Hogan.

"Maybe you're right, Chad. Maybe I haven't thought about it much." She slowly drew her shaking fingers through her hair, then dropped her hand to her side. "Anyway, none of that makes any difference anymore, does it? Things have changed, Chad. Everything has changed."

She grasped the door handle.

"Has it, Hannah? Because from where I'm standing, it doesn't look like much has changed at all."

If you only knew.

"Hannah...I made a commitment to you. We lived together for over a year. Certainly I get points for that."

"Yes, Chad, you do. And when combined with your other scores, you're way in the hole." She cleared her throat. "You know, once I believed we had a future together. I even believed you loved me. But it was nothing more than wishful thinking, wasn't it?"

His gaze was intense. "Wishful thinking? Is that how you see our time together? Wishful thinking?"

Hannah tried to deny the ribbons of memories that unfurled in her mind. Images of him training her up close and personal in the finer points of skip-tracing after she'd quit the force and Elliott had matched them up. The long, intense way he used to watch her before they got involved. Their first, hungry kiss and the countless stolen moments thereafter while they chased bail-jumpers across the country. Their uncomplicated lifestyle, until—

Hannah shivered. Until she got pregnant.

"Look, just because my idea of commitment wasn't the same as yours doesn't mean that we can't work on this case together," he said.

A spark of disappointment mixed in with the pain already pressing against her chest from the inside. "Don't try to fit what happened into one little sentence, Chad. Things between us were more complicated than that."

He took a step toward her, bringing him altogether too close. He gently curled his strong fingers around her arm. She swallowed hard, the clean, warm smell of his flesh filling her senses, her pulse drumming loudly in her ears. His attention lingered on her mouth and she caught herself running her tongue over her lips.

Oh, it had been so very long since she'd kissed him. Felt the dark intensity of his touch. For one long, desperate moment, she wanted to feel it again. To turn the hands of time back to when his mouth was hers to claim. When she'd have willingly given everything that was hers over to this man whom she had loved as deeply as she'd known how.

But she'd learned how fleeting that type of passion was. And realized it wasn't what she wanted anymore. Wasn't what she needed. If, indeed, she had ever truly wanted it for herself. She'd always longed for more. And it was for that reason their relationship failed.

Curiosity lay in the depths of Chad's eyes as he moved closer still. A tiny cry erupted from Hannah's throat, her traitorous body responding to the physical need vibrating through her at the feel of his body against hers, chest to chest, hips to hips.

She tugged herself free from his grasp. "No," she whispered.

She quickly turned away, seeking to put not only physical distance between them, but emotional. And the only way to do that was to leave.

She opened the door to find Elliott standing there waiting for her.

Hannah tried to navigate her way around him. "Sorry, El, but I can't do this."

"Wait a minute." Elliott's thick hands grasped her shoulders, holding her in place. "I didn't call you two here because I had some illusions about you reconciling. I did it because I need you. It's your business if you don't want to tell him—"

Fear eclipsed Hannah's confusion. In a moment's span Elliott could upset fifteen months' worth of rebuilding. She shook her head as inconspicuously as possible.

Elliott sighed. "Anyway, that's your business." He dropped his arms but refused to let Hannah pass through the doorway. "If you walk out of here, McGee, Blackstone Bail and Bonds will cease to exist."

Elliott glanced over his shoulder at the receptionist in the outer office, then stepped inside, closing the door after himself. "Look, just listen to me. There could be a great deal of money in it for you. Enough for you to...see through your plans more solidly."

She remained silent.

He stared down at something he held in his hand. "Here, my secretary took this call for you." He handed her a small slip of paper. She read it, then slid it into her skirt pocket. Elliott glanced at Chad. "Hogan, why don't you and I go outside and give Hannah a few minutes to think?"

Chad brushed her as he passed. Heat rippled over her skin. It wasn't fair that after so much time, after all that had happened between them, she should still be so powerfully attracted to him. Or maybe it was because so much had happened between them that her body took on all the characteristics of a blanket longing to cover him.

The door closed after Blackstone, and Hannah found herself alone. She tugged the message from her pocket and crossed to the phone. The door opened again. Her stomach tightened, but when she turned, it wasn't Chad staring at her from the doorway, it was Jack Stokes. Her anxiety melted into exasperation.

The bounty hunter was attractive what with his craggy, blond good looks. But at the moment, men in general didn't appeal to Hannah.

She replaced the telephone receiver.

Stokes quickly closed the door. "Hey there, Hannah, luv, remember me?" The Australian held up his right wrist where her handcuffs were still solidly attached to his wrist.

Hannah closed her eyes. This wasn't happening....

"I owe you big-time for this one, McGee," Stokes said in his heavy accent.

"Yes, well, if you had been a little nicer to me, you wouldn't be sporting that particular bit of jewelry, would you, Jack?"

"You always were a piece of work, Hannah."

"I'm really not up for this." She dug in her skirt pocket, then gave him the key to the handcuffs.

He made a show out of unlocking himself. "Tell me, Hannah, what's our old pal Hogan doing back in town?"

Ah, now she knew the real reason he'd sneaked into the room. And sneak was exactly what he'd done because Hannah doubted time would have dulled Chad's dislike for the wily, easygoing Aussie.

"That's something you'll have to ask him," she said, pretending a nonchalance she didn't feel.

Jack stepped a little closer, turning on what Hannah knew was his best charm. Only it had never really worked on her. "Come on, luv, you can be straight with me. What's Blackstone up to? Tell me and I'll call it even."

"Even?"

He tossed her the cuffs.

Hannah tucked them into the holder on the back of her concealed belt. "I really wish I could tell you, but I don't know what Elliott's up to."

"Come on, McGee. Admit it, you wouldn't tell me if you did know. Which leaves us off at the same place we started, doesn't it?"

"Which is?"

"I owe you one."

Finally, the door closed behind him and Hannah leaned against the desk and rubbed her forehead. What, exactly, did she do to deserve today?

It seemed that no sooner had the door closed, it opened again.

She glanced at the message in her hand, then at Elliott Blackstone. While she didn't think she'd ever completely recover from the shock of seeing Chad again, now that she'd had a little time to collect her thoughts, she couldn't help wondering how much money was involved. Start-up costs for Seekers had drained more of her savings account than she'd expected. Then there was the plumbing that needed to be replaced; wiring that needed to be brought up to code. If this trace was as important as she was coming to suspect, then it could mean some much-needed earnings.

"Give me five minutes, Hannah. That's all I ask." A breath expanded Elliott's cheeks.

She caught herself absently running her fingertip along the name listed on the phone message then nodded.

Elliott immediately seemed to relax as he said, "Okay. Two weeks ago I extended bail to two people. Normally that wouldn't be important, but one thing makes these two different from the rest. Enough that they made the news." He paused for a moment. "Money."

Hannah tried to concentrate. To forget Stokes had thrown down a professional gauntlet she had no intention of picking up. To wipe from her mind that Chad waited on the other side of the door. "You deal in five-and-dime cases, Elliott. Small time."

"Normally, yes, but no one else would take these two, so I made an exception."

She latched on to the critical tone in his voice. "Who are they?"

"Two employees of PlayCo arrested for grand larceny."

"Grand larceny?" She pushed her hand through her hair. "PlayCo's a toy company. What did they take? Mickey Mouse's pants?"

Shaking his head, Elliott tried for a smile, and failed miserably. "I wish it were that simple. My brother-in-law is the attorney for these two. I made bail as a favor to him. They were due for a preliminary hearing this morning and...well, you know the rest."

"How much do you stand to lose?"

Elliott swallowed visibly and named an amount.

Hannah dropped her arms from where they were crossed over her chest. She didn't know what shocked her more: the reappearance of Chad in her life or Elliott's atypical behavior. She decided Chad definitely came out a painful first.

"Like I said, it was a favor." Elliott glanced at his recently chewed fingernails. "Look, I could go on all day about how this was a first offense. About how they had worked for the company for ten years and all that, but I won't." He paused. "The fact is I put up the bond and they skipped."

Hannah drew in a deep breath and slowly let it out, trying to come to terms with everything that had happened in the past ten minutes. Ten minutes. Six hundred seconds. Such a short time, really. A short time she was afraid would affect every minute of her life thereafter.

Elliott wasn't joking when he said he was in danger of closing down. If made to pay the amount of the bond, not only would his office be history, but Elliott himself would probably be paying off the debt for his next two incarnations.

"Why call Chad in?" She recrossed her arms over her chest.

"He's the best there is, aside from you." His expression was earnest. "Hannah, I need every ounce of manpower I have for this one. I swear, if I lose this place you might as well dig a hole for me six feet under. And don't think I'm exaggerating. As much as I complain and manipulate, this business is my life." Elliott shifted uneasily. "So...what do you say? Will you postpone your plans for Seekers and take this last one on?"

Hannah thought about her daughter, the cost of the day-care center she'd wanted to enroll her in and the one she'd chosen instead because it was more reasonably priced. If she succeeded in this trace, she'd be able to afford to send Bonny to the other one...plus a whole lot more.

"Does it mean working with Chad?"

Relief colored Elliott's ruddy features. "That's up to you."

"You have files on these guys?"

He pushed a thin manila folder across the desk. "Here. Only they're not both guys." Hannah looked at him. "One is a woman."

"What is this?" She examined the single sheet of paper in the file. The application form was skimpy at best, half the blanks left empty.

"Like I said, this was a favor."

"Yes, you said that. What did you do? Just sign the bond without the normal paperwork? This isn't like you, Elliott."

"Believe me, if I had known this was going to happen, I would have got more."

"It says here that the jumpers put their houses up."

"Expensive houses, too. The only problem is they're

mortgaged to the hilt. Not worth the dirt they're built on to me.''

"I don't know, El..." She stepped away from the desk and chairs, pulling down the front ends of her vest. "Finding these two would be like finding—"

"I know, I know. Like finding needles in a haystack the size of Europe.''

Accepting the case meant more than postponing the opening of Seekers. It meant working with Chad again. A very risky prospect indeed. She wouldn't even consider working against him. She might be afraid of what the man could do to her personal life, but she wouldn't make the mistake of misjudging his professional talent.

She slid her hand into her pocket, fingering the message inside. Anyway, maybe it was time Chad knew the truth. The thought alone choked off her breath.

"Exactly how much money did you say there'd be in it for me?'' she asked.

Elliott named an absurdly high figure.

"I'm in.''

"Good.'' Elliott leapt to his feet. "You have four days.''

"Four days?''

"If you don't bring them in within four days, you miss out on the money and I lose my business. Hell, I'm lucky the judge even rescheduled the hearing.''

Four days wasn't much time, Hannah thought. That came out to two days apiece to find each bail-jumper.

"No problem.''

Chapter Two

Heat pressed in on Hannah from all sides as she left Blackstone Bail and Bonds. But the external heat didn't concern her half as much as the emotions expanding inside her. She drew to a stop, as much to adjust to the change in temperature as to face Chad where he leaned against the building.

It was like someone had clipped an image from her memory and pasted it right in front of her: his right shoulder casually propped against the brick of the building; his hands stuffed into the pockets of his faded jeans; his legs crossed at the ankles, emphasizing the dusty cowboy boots he always wore.

Even as she compared him to the image, she noticed some changes that didn't match up. Details that went beyond the physical.

When she'd known him before, there had been a sadness about him, a grief she'd later learned stemmed from the death of his wife and child in a car crash he'd refused to go into detail about. Now? Well, now he looked…more distant, somehow. Harder.

"Elliott really bought himself one this time, didn't he?" Chad's gray eyes focused on the cars streaking by on the ten-laned Queens Boulevard. "What was he thinking?"

The sun slowly sank behind the western skyline. Hannah gazed at it, then at him again. "Obviously he wasn't."

Hannah walked toward the battered Ford LTD. Chad picked up his duffel bag and followed, grasping on to the passenger's door handle at the same time she opened the driver's side. Her hand froze on the hot metal.

"Where are you going, Chad?" Her voice came out little more than a whisper.

"With you, of course."

Her stomach plunged to her feet. "I don't recall inviting you."

He squinted at her against the sunlight. "Since you agreed to take the case, I thought we'd be working together. Are you saying you want to go out on your own?"

She wondered why her throat suddenly felt like sandpaper. "And what if I am?"

"I know you better than that. We each know exactly what the other is capable of. I'm certainly not interested in working against you."

Hannah recognized her own thoughts only minutes earlier.

Chad drew in a deep breath and slowly let it out. "Look, I just got in from Florida and took a taxi from the airport. If you want me to catch another one, let me know."

Hannah remained silent, half tempted to take him up on his offer. She could do without him slipping back into her life right now. She wanted, needed time to grow accustomed to his being back, even if it was only in an official capacity.

But time was something she didn't have. Besides, she suspected no amount of time would lessen the empty ache in her chest...or change the reality standing in front of her in the shape of Chad Hogan.

She leaned against the car.

"Okay, Chad, I'll work with you." She ignored his probing gaze. "But it doesn't mean side by side, night and day. I just mean I won't work against you."

He spread his hands on top of the roof and drummed his thumbs against the hot metal. "You're telling me aside from sharing information, you would rather not lay eyes on me. Is that it, Hannah?"

"Yes." She gripped the door handle again. The squealing of tires ripped through the thick air.

She spotted the rusted monster of a car bearing down on her a nanosecond before Chad clutched her wrists and hauled her toward the curb and into his arms. She stared at the darkly tinted windows of the Monte Carlo as it sped down the street, the back end fishtailing as it turned right at the first intersection.

"Damn New York drivers," Chad murmured, his breath disturbing the hair over her ear.

Tugging her gaze away from the empty street, Hannah became instantly aware of her position in Chad's arms. She shivered at the solid feel of her breasts against his chest, took a breath of the familiar, tangy smell of his clean skin, wriggled to free herself from the hot, electric touch of his hands against her back.

"Let me go, Chad," she whispered, uneasy with the knowing shadow in his eyes.

He released her.

Hannah turned on watery knees and got in the car. She watched him stow his duffel in the back then climb in next to her.

"Where did you get this rust bucket?" he asked.

If the heat outside was stifling, the stagnant air inside the car was even worse. Hot sweat trickled between Hannah's breasts even as awareness continued to surge through her veins from their brief contact.

He ran his hand across the dust-covered dash. "A rental?" he asked.

She nodded. "I had to, for conspicuousness' sake. I was just about to take it back in exchange for my own."

Chad's face was unreadable in the fiery hues of the setting sun. "You kept the Alfa?"

Longing swelled in her stomach. She had not forgotten the Alfa Romeo had been a thirtieth birthday gift from him. She turned the key in the ignition. The only gift he had given her during their two years together. An expensive gift—not only for the money, but it had been one of many things that had cost them their relationship.

"Yes, I kept the Alfa," she said quietly.

She stared ahead at the sparse traffic.

"Uncle Nash says my old room over the dry cleaners is empty, so let's head there." Chad's voice cut through the thick air. "We'll pick up some Chinese and—"

Hannah shifted the car into drive. "I am not going to Coney Island with you, Chad." She pulled away from the curb, then remembered she hadn't intended to take him with her.

"You're being unreasonable, Hannah. You lived there…we lived there together. You're as familiar with the place as I am. All I'm suggesting is we get out of this heat and get an early start in the morning. The last thing on my mind is getting you into bed.''

She took a corner a little too quickly. ''Interesting you should say that. It's one of the things you were very good at,'' she said quietly. ''Look, Chad, there's no going back. Not to Coney Island. Not to the way things were between us, either professionally or personally.''

Despite her argument, the months they'd been apart began to fade into the background, leaving her feeling insecure and defensive. Which didn't make any sense, really. She and Chad were no longer a couple. They no longer shared the same apartment. Their lives were completely separate. Still, that didn't change the fact that one important thing connected them and always would.

Bonny.

Gripping the steering wheel, she concentrated on this important detail.

''I have something I need to do,'' she said. ''If you want me to drop you off, let me know. If not, you're welcome to come along for the ride for now.''

''I'll come along for the ride.''

''And after that, you're on your own. Right?''

''Right.''

Something in Chad's voice compelled her to look at him. She winced at the shuttered expression he wore.

''Why don't we forget about the past and start from scratch, okay, Hannah? I don't need the hassle any more than you do. We're both adults. Why don't we approach this like the professionals we are and forget the rest?''

Her hand shaking, she switched on the radio, the

only part of the car that worked properly. The interior filled with the neutral sound of country music.

What would he say when he found out a reminder in the shape of an eight-month-old little girl made it impossible for her to forget?

Chad studied Hannah from beneath half-closed lids, then pulled at his collar. It was hot. But whether his new sense of discomfort had to do with the August heat or how right Hannah had felt in his arms again was unclear. He glanced at her slender ankles visible below the hem of her gauzy skirt, then budged his gaze up her long, almost too slim body to her blue, blue eyes. Everything about her spoke of freshness, strength and a love for life.

Face it, Hogan, you missed her.

While the admission didn't come easily, he'd always known Hannah struck an unnamed chord in him. He watched the freckled backs of her hands as she gripped and released the steering wheel, and fought the urge to reach out, take one of those hands in his. It had taken a lot to walk away from her nearly a year and a half ago. But he'd had no choice. She had made that clearer than a Florida sunrise. He forced his glance away from where the humid breeze stirred her curly red hair. Why did he feel like someone had just taken a paintbrush to his gray, cynical life? And why did he feel that her vital presence was exactly the reason he had to freeze her out?

Because, he told himself, whatever primal urges made him ache to touch her, to lose himself in the taste, the feel of her, he couldn't risk letting her in again. She had come too close the last time.

The moment he met Hannah nearly three years ago he knew he'd end up hurting her, but had been helpless to stop himself. He recognized instantly that the qualities that drew him to her would be the very traits that would eventually push them apart. Hannah demanded everything from life—and she'd expected everything from him. Only she hadn't known that he no longer had everything to give.

The way he saw it, their breakup had been inevitable. It had never been a question of "if" but of "when" and "how." He knew from the outset that Hannah would one day finger him for the fraud he was. Would notice his shortcomings and boot him out of her life. What he hadn't banked on was that her rejection would cut so deep. Or that his hurting her would hurt him so much it was painful sometimes to breathe.

During his self-exile in Florida he had hoped his absence would help heal Hannah's wounds. He had also sought forgiveness for having hurt her. From the sea where the Gulf met the Atlantic in the Keys, and from the vodka bottles that never had anything to give beyond illusionary escape. Each and every day he pushed himself to the limit in his two-bit assignments in order to feed his untouched savings account, and each and every morning when he awakened, he found himself more restless than before. He had moved his secondhand trailer from seacoast town to town, concentrating on local skip-traces and collecting license plates from uninsured vehicles for twenty bucks a pop. He had searched for a peace that proved as elusive as the answer to why his wife and son had been torn from his life four years ago, before he even met Hannah.

No, he had nothing left to give Hannah...except his apology. And he'd been offered the perfect opportunity to give it to her when Elliott called him that morning.

Hannah pulled into the no-parking zone outside the central Queens police station and turned off the ignition. Chad knew it was where she had served five years as a NYC police officer.

"I thought we were going to pick up the Alfa," he said.

Hannah let herself out of the car and Chad followed. He tried not to watch her, appreciate the way she moved, the way she walked. He tried harder still to ignore the fear she tried to hide. He'd expected several reactions from her, but fear wasn't one of them. Hannah had never been afraid of anything. Was it fear of him? Possible, but not probable. All he knew was he didn't like to see the emotion coloring her eyes when she looked at him, which wasn't often.

"We are," she replied. "Right after I find out what the police have on these bail-jumpers."

"Hey, McGee!" the uniformed officer at the front desk greeted Hannah as they entered. "What brings you back to this part of town?"

Hannah stepped up to the desk and smiled. "Slumming it, I guess, Smitty."

The fifty-some-odd-year-old officer eyed her. "Slumming it! You're a real barrel of laughs, McGee."

Chad noticed the way Hannah relaxed, appearing comfortable with the precinct banter she must have mastered during her stint as a police officer. Much more comfortable than she was with him.

"Is Schindler around?" she asked.

The officer moved a hand to his right.

"Just where he always is. Guy should have gone home hours ago. I think he'd die without those blasted files."

She moved through the throng of people toward the records room, barely noticing that Chad had a difficult time following. Hannah greeted a few detectives as they slid through yet another room.

"Here we are." Hannah stopped outside a plain wood and smoked glass door marked Records—Do Not Enter and knocked.

"Can you get into hot water for this?" Chad asked as she opened the door.

"Don't let the sign scare you. I think more people enter because of it."

She peered around a series of metal shelves. "Schindler?"

There was a long silence, then a short, brawny man stepped from between two of the metal monsters overburdened with worn manila folders.

"Hannah, is that you?"

She leaned closer to Chad. "The running guess around the precinct is Danny Schindler lifts file folders in lieu of weights in his spare time."

Chad got a whiff of her skin. She never had idea one how much her nearness affected him while they were together. The passage of time told him she still didn't have a clue. It was the innocent smiles, the innocuous comments, the spontaneous touches that always got to him more than any obvious overtures. Then again, Hannah was obvious about nothing but her opinion. And she'd welcome his reaction—innocent or otherwise—as much as she'd welcome a bad sunburn on her fair skin.

"Hey, Danny, I see you're still buried up to your neck in files," she said, oblivious to Chad's thoughts. Which was just as well. If she caught a hint of what was going on in his mind, she'd likely push him into a taxi the instant they hit the street again.

"Yeah, well, you remember how it is. A crime a second and all that. Someone has to keep track of them all."

Schindler scrutinized Chad as Hannah introduced him.

Chad crunched the clerk's hand in his, giving the muscle-bound geek a once-over before Schindler turned back to Hannah.

"Tell me you're not still living the life of a bounty hunter."

"Bail enforcer," Hannah corrected.

"Then this is more than a I-was-in-the-neighborhood-and-thought-I'd-stop-by visit, isn't it?"

She appeared slighted. "Now, would I be so crude as to use our friendship for my own professional gain?"

The smile never wavered from Schindler's face. "Every chance you get." He dropped the files he held to his overloaded desk. Chad watched one slip toward the edge then fall to the floor. He didn't move to stop it. "What can I do for you, Hannah?"

"What have you heard on the two arrested at PlayCo?"

"The team that unofficially skipped bail from Lower East?"

"That's them. I need whatever L.E. has on them. Can you handle it?"

"There is nothing I can't handle, you know that."

Schindler picked up the telephone and called what Chad guessed was his fellow records clerk at the Manhattan precinct.

"Danny and I go back a ways," Hannah quietly explained.

"So it seems." Chad settled his weight more evenly as he listened to Schindler persuade the person on the other end of the line to fax him the information.

"What are the odds on them having something we

can use?'' Chad asked, shifting through the files strewn across the desk.

Hannah closed a file he had opened. ''Better than average. I'm sure PlayCo kept files on them. Whatever was in them was no doubt turned over to the police.'' She tried to take another folder from him but he refused to let it go. She sighed. ''Would you quit? We could get in enough trouble as it is.''

Chad opened the file and scanned the contents. ''You didn't seem too concerned before.''

''That's because I'm used to being in trouble with the hierarchy of this precinct.'' She pressed her index finger into his chest. ''You, on the other hand, could very well be arrested for just being in this room.''

Chad gazed at her finger, then slowly followed it up to her face. The finger against his chest grew suddenly hot. She quickly removed her hand.

''It might be an enjoyable experience. Provided you're in the cell with me,'' he said.

''It took a little doing, but Janice promised to fax the records right over,'' Schindler said, hanging up the receiver. As he spoke, a telephone rang in the corner and the fax machine sprang to life. ''And here they are now.''

The three of them watched the information roll in. The physical data sheets listed Lisa Furgeson as a thirty-five-year-old female with blond hair and blue eyes, five feet, six inches tall, one hundred and thirty pounds. Eric Persky was a thirty-eight-year-old male with light brown hair and green eyes, six foot two, two hundred and fifty pounds. Grainy black-and-white copies of pictures followed.

''Thanks, Schindler.'' Hannah pulled the last page from the holder, looking to where Chad gazed over her shoulder. It took all of his restraint not to curve his arms around her waist and pull her against him, just as he used to do, back before—

He took a step backward, barely aware of putting distance between them. Her closeness reminded him of times he had no right remembering. He watched Schindler offer Hannah a manila folder to put the fax in. Her hands shook as she put the flimsy paper into the file folder. Apparently she was as aware of their closeness as he was.

"It's a start." Chad concentrated on something other than the shadow of fear in her wide blue eyes. "Mug shots, charges...." He reached around her, turning the top of the folder open, careful not to touch her as he did so.

Hannah moved farther away from him. He dammed the groundswell of emotion her rejection aroused.

"I've...I've got to make a phone call." She hurried away from him and toward Schindler's desk a few feet away.

"Be my guest," Danny offered. "You need anything else, give me a yell. Oh, and I think that it goes without saying, but this little...transaction stays between us, okay? The last thing I need is Marconi coming down on me." He grinned. "I think that's the last thing you need, too."

"You can say that again."

The records clerk disappeared between the towering metal shelves. Chad turned his attention back to Hannah. She tugged the slip of paper Blackstone had given her from her pocket and started dialing a number. Chad rubbed the back of his neck, easing the tension bunched there. Who had left her a message at Elliott's office?

"Hi, it's Hannah," she said into the receiver, turning away from where he looked on.

The familiarity of her tone didn't sit well with Chad.

Had she become involved with someone else since their breakup? He stiffened, something similar to jealousy burning through him. He wanted to take the receiver from her pretty little hand and hang up on whoever was on the other side of the line. Instead, he shoved his hands into his jeans pockets.

"I see," Hannah said into the phone. Chad slowly stepped around the other side of the desk, watching her brows draw together. What? Trouble in paradise? Good.

She caught him watching her and turned quickly away. "Okay. I can be there in a couple hours. Is that all right? Good, I'll see you then."

We'll see about that, Chad thought, his jaw so tight he couldn't say a word if he wanted to.

"Who's Marconi?" Chad asked as they left the precinct.

Hannah vaguely noted the sun had set, but the air showed no sign of cooling. Not unlike her skin, which still tingled from Chad's nearness in the records room.

It wasn't fair that she should still be so attuned to Chad's emotions, feel so much for him. But if there was one thing she learned very early on—a point proved time and again since—it was that life wasn't always fair.

"He's the precinct captain." She glanced back at the plain, stone building. She had once wanted nothing more than to follow in her father's policeman's footsteps and become a cop. What she hadn't counted on was Victor Marconi being just as determined to see her off the force.

It was easy to remember Uncle Vic's face when he'd told her, "Your father and I went back to Hell's Kitchen, Hannah. He was more than my partner, he was my best friend. You were your daddy's little girl, and you'll remain so in my eyes.''

"I am not a girl, Victor. I'm a woman.''

Mickey D. McGee was the only person who remained untarnished and uncorrupted in Hannah's heart and memory, unlike the other men in her life. His strength had been equaled only by his faith in a Catholic God that had comforted him after his wife's death following the birth of their only child. A God she hadn't been able to turn to when her father was shot and killed in the line of duty when she was only eighteen.

"Your father turned in his grave the day you showed up here for recruitment, Hannah,'' Uncle Vic had told her.

"My father trained me to be a police officer from the time I could walk. Far from turning in his grave, I bet he would have been proud.''

Now Hannah forced her gaze away from the precinct doors and the uniformed officers going in and out. It had taken Uncle Vic years to do what he promised mere weeks after he was promoted from commanding sergeant to captain: He'd made her quit.

Victor Marconi, whom she hadn't talked to since leaving the force, was just another ghost from the past she'd just as soon avoid right now. She looked at the other. Chad Hogan openly returned her gaze.

She opened the car door and slipped behind the wheel. "I think it's a good idea for you to catch a cab from here, Chad.''

"You want to talk about something?''

He got into the car after her and she started it. "About what?''

"About what you were thinking just now.''

Puzzled, she sat concentrating strictly on her

breathing for a scant moment. "Victor Marconi is more than the captain of the precinct. He was...um, my father's partner. Up until the night Dad was killed in the line of duty." She handed him the manila folder.

Chad took the data and put the file aside without opening it. "You told me your father died, but left out that it was in the line of duty."

She swept her hair back from her forehead. There were a lot of things she'd left out. And one of them was across the river now, waiting to be picked up. "Despite the history between Marconi and me, or maybe because of it, he won't hesitate to have us both arrested if he finds—"

"You didn't respond to my comment, Hannah."

She pulled away from the curb. "Maybe because there isn't a response." She looked at him. "When we were together we were either working, arguing or...making love. There wasn't much time for anything else." She turned her head away from him to gauge the traffic.

The silence in the car was strained until Hannah pulled up to the Ugly Duckling rental agency that owned the rust bucket they sat in. Which was just as well because it took Hannah as long to regain control over her emotions. In the back corner of the lot, the red Alfa's waxed hood shone under a security light.

"She looks good," Chad murmured.

She led the way up to the small shack where she traded keys with Frank, a skinny punk rocker wearing untied combat boots and a chain connected from nose to ear. Within moments she and Chad stood on either side of the gleaming Alfa Romeo. He stared at the For Sale signs in the back windows.

"You're selling her?"

"Uh...yes." Hannah felt as if she had betrayed him

in some way with her answer. Despite the car's role in their breakup—she'd wanted a ring, he'd bought her a car—she had grown attached to the Alfa. In an odd way it served as a concrete reminder that Chad had cared about her in his own way, even if it wasn't the way she needed him to care about her. She avoided his probing gaze. He didn't have to know that with the money she would get from Elliott for this trace, she'd be able to afford to keep it and pay the sky-high insurance premiums.

She disarmed the alarm and slid into the driver's seat, not objecting when Chad tossed his duffel into the back and entered the other side. She pressed a button and the canvas top folded back. She stared up at the ribbon of star-filled sky visible between the towering buildings.

"I used to pass this car every day on the way to Blackstone's before I..." His voice drifted off. "It had your name written all over it, Hannah. It still does."

Hannah sensed his gaze on her profile and slowly looked at his finely etched face, features she had once memorized with her hands and mouth. She wondered at the changes there. They were harder somehow. More skeptical. Her gaze flicked over his thick brows and his eyes. Gray eyes that hinted at a smoldering fire, rimmed by thick, dark lashes. Her attention focused on his mouth. That enticing, teasing, infuriating mouth that had once brought her more happiness than a hundred star-filled nights. And had made her hurt more than she would ever tell him.

"You never said that."

Chad's lips played at a crooked grin, turning the right side of his mouth up just enough to make his emotions known. "There was something about the—" he stretched his arms, his right one going out over the

side of the car, his left finding the back of her seat
"—about the freedom of it that reminded me of you."

His strong fingers sought and found the back of her
neck. Hannah tensed.

"I saw you in it. Hood down...red hair flying around
your face." Chad's voice lowered to a provocative
hum, his fingers doing interesting things to the sensitive
nerve endings at the base of her neck.

Hannah laid her palm against his chest. She might
be having trouble with her heart, but she was grateful
her head was still screwed on tight enough to stop herself from making the same mistake twice.

"Please, don't, Chad. We're not teenagers at a drive-
in movie. Things have changed. Everything has
changed."

He stared at her. "That's the second time you've
said that."

"Yes, well, that's because it's true. And you'll find
out why soon enough." Oh, yes, he'd soon find out.
And the instant he saw sweet little Bonny's face, she
had no doubt he'd beat a retreat faster than his last one.

"These changes...they wouldn't happen to have
anything to do with the phone call you made back
there, would they?" he asked.

She dragged her gaze down his face, then back up
to his eyes again. "Yes, Chad. Yes, they do."

Chapter Three

Hannah pulled up outside Eric Persky's Forest Hills house on Juno Street and shut off the engine. She took in the large, Tudor-style structure.

"Are you sure this is the place?" she asked.

Chad checked the file Elliott had given her with the one Schindler provided. "This is it."

"For some reason I have a feeling this case isn't going to be as easy as I thought," she said.

"Sure it is." He stepped out and stared through the open window. "You planning to wait here?"

"No." Hannah let herself out of the car. The day's events seemed to have happened months ago instead of hours. Not only had Chad sauntered back into her life—something she had yet to fully deal with—but vivid, tender memories of her father had flooded back with disturbing clarity. Hannah longed to sit on the couch with eight-month-old Bonny, three dozen Oreos with the double stuffing, a couple of boxes of animal crackers, the remote control, enough formula to fill the pantry and a gallon of chocolate milk and forget the world existed until she felt ready to deal with it. Which might be never. The only problem was the world wouldn't allow it. Not when the four-day time constraint on apprehending Eric Persky and Lisa Furgeson was quickly ticking by. And not when Chad stood watching her, his gaze making her want to concentrate on everything but the case.

She halted directly in front of the house, staring up at the handsome structure. Chad stepped beside her. Hannah tried to ignore how striking he looked with the night's shadows shading the solid planes of his face. The interior of the house was dark, but to make sure no possible visiting relatives or other live-ins were home, Hannah pressed the lighted doorbell and listened to the chime echo inside. She didn't worry that it was ten o'clock and the neighbors might be watching. As far as anyone was concerned, she and Chad were just friends paying a visit. Besides, Hannah didn't plan to be there long enough to raise much suspicion. She rang the doorbell a second time.

"Do your thing, Chad." She moved aside and held open the outer storm door so he could bend over the lock on the heavy wooden door. He quickly manipulated the small metal tools he slid from his back jeans pocket until the door opened inward. Hannah waited for an alarm, but none sounded. She didn't find it unusual. The police had probably been tramping through the house all day and had switched it off.

"All yours." Chad pushed the door open.

Hannah passed him. "Haven't lost your touch."

He gently caught her arm. "Haven't I?"

Tiny little butterflies fluttered in her stomach, both at the feel of his hand against her skin and the sober look on his face. Why did she get the impression he wasn't talking about the case anymore? And why did she want to forget Persky and Furgeson even existed and start making some sort of sense out of what was and wasn't happening between her and Chad Hogan?

He briefly closed his eyes, then used his grip to steer her into the large foyer.

A shadow moved to Hannah's right. Chad must have seen the same thing because he reached around her and closed the solid front door, shearing off the outdoor security light that silhouetted them like targets.

"What's going on— Oh!" Chad propelled her off to the side of the foyer. She slowly backed away, her heart thudding painfully in her chest. Where did Chad go? She couldn't see a thing.

Something moved. Hannah slipped The Equalizer's charger on and held the stun gun tightly in her hands. There were two shadows. She gained her night vision and made out the shapes of two men near the door, apparently looking for her and Chad. Speaking of Chad...

"Where'd they go?" one of the guys whispered.

"How the hell should I know? Why don't you turn on your flashlight?"

There was a rattling sound. "The batteries must be dead."

Hannah crouched lower. The two men spread out. Hannah backed up farther until she bumped into something hard and warm. She gasped.

"Quiet," Chad whispered, gripping her hips.

Hannah's stomach contracted, the most intimate part

of him pressing against her bottom. She tried to wriggle from his grasp.

"I don't like this," one of the other men said. "What if they're cops?"

The second guy hurried past, then doubled back.

"Would you just stay still." Chad's warm breath filled her ear.

"Yeah, you're right," the other guy said. "Let's get out of here. I don't think what we're looking for is here anyway."

Chad finally pulled away from her. Relief swept over Hannah, strong and complete, leaving a sense of exposure in its wake. "Stay here."

"Where are you going?" Hannah whispered, clutching the stun gun with shaky hands.

Chad rounded her and rushed full steam toward the two men as they opened the front door. He hit one in the back of the knees, sending him hurtling onto the front steps.

"Chad!" Hannah rushed forward. Chad jerked to look at her. The free man hit him in the back of the head with his flashlight. Chad stumbled slightly, then leaned against the wall for support.

The first man grabbed the second and they disappeared through the door.

Stuffing her stun gun back into her belt, Hannah rushed to Chad.

He shrugged her hand from his arm. "What were you doing, Hannah? I thought something had happened to you when you yelled out like that."

She tried to gather her wits around her. Her fear for his safety had distracted him and given the other guy an open opportunity for attack. She had meant to spare him pain, instead she had caused it. A stupid mistake.

But his name was out before she'd had time to consider the consequences.

Chad hurried to the door. Hannah followed. She barely made out the two shadows running through a shrub-darkened lawn two houses away.

"Great, just great." Chad closed and locked the door then flipped a switch to his right. A car-size chandelier filled the foyer with its bright, blinding light. He softly muttered a curse.

Hannah reached out, then stopped, unsure if it was a good idea to touch him. If ever touching him again would be a good idea. Still, it was her fault he'd been clobbered with a flashlight. She reached out again, ignoring his curious stare, half expecting him to push her away.

She carefully probed the back of his head with her fingers, ignoring the clean softness of his sandy brown hair, and the memories that rushed back at seeing her fingers entangled in the thick mass. Her breath snagged in her throat.

"I thought so." She located the marble-size bump at the base of his skull and found the blow hadn't broken the skin. "You'll live." She tugged her hands away from him and refused to meet his gaze.

His first question echoed through her mind. What were you doing, Hannah? And what had she done? Never in her years as a cop, then as a skip-tracer, had she put someone else in danger.

She tried to shrug off her uneasiness, but it wasn't easily dismissed. Instead, she turned from him and examined an overturned vase. If she couldn't explain to herself what had happened, how was she supposed to explain it to him?

"At least they didn't find whatever it is they were looking for," she said.

"Yeah, them and about three other search teams."

Hannah glanced around the ransacked foyer and the many rooms that snaked off it. "Well, since you're probably not up to that staircase, why don't you take the first floor?"

"You're a real hoot, McGee." Chad massaged the back of his head, his gaze still questioning.

Hannah quickly scaled the stairs to the second floor. Maybe it wasn't too late to back out of this case. Just hand the information over to Chad, and wave at him as he drove off into the night.

Coward.

She glanced around the second floor hall. Only that morning she hadn't had any problem taking on Eddie the Snake *and* Jack Stokes. So what was it about being with Chad again that made her act like somebody's...mother.

"Oh God," she muttered, the impact of her thoughts hitting home.

She hurried down the hall, thrusting aside the unwelcome insight and trying to focus on the case.

Who were the two men they'd run into and what exactly had they been looking for? She'd have to take a look at the data Schindler had given her. See what Persky and Furgeson were accused of stealing and whether or not the police recovered it. She didn't think the information would help her find either of them, but it might give her an idea how deep a hole they had dug for themselves.

She turned on the overhead light and sifted through a bureau in the master bedroom. The bottom drawers held nothing of use, unless you were a six foot two,

two hundred and fifty pound man. Hannah rummaged through socks, T-shirts and long johns. She pulled a pair of the latter out. If this was any indication of how big the man was, she and Chad had their work cut out for them.

She closed the drawer in exchange for one of the top ones.

"Gambling chips."

Hannah stared at the array of blue and red discs. Closer inspection told her they were from Atlantic City. Not unusual for a New Yorker, except Persky seemed to be a regular visitor. Faded matchbooks were also scattered among the drawer's contents. Hannah picked them up one by one, only to toss them back. There were a few from different casinos, but the majority were from one in particular. She picked up the older-looking of the matchbooks. She was searching for any sign of a phone number, a name, anything that would give her an idea where Eric might be. Granted, she could be jogging down the wrong avenue, but it was worth a try. Clichés were clichés because they happened so often.

She was getting nowhere quick when she opened one with faded blue ink on the inside cover.

Hannah leaned against the bureau, holding the book up to the light.

"Find something?" Chad stepped through the doorway.

Hannah glanced at him. "You're not done down there already?"

"Gone through every drawer, every cupboard, and looked under every seat cushion." He displayed envelope-size pieces of paper. "The only articles worth anything were in his desk. Our friend likes to keep old bills for comparison.''

Hannah looked up from where she stared at the matchbook, catching the thoughtful, unguarded expression on Chad's rugged face. A sense of the familiar wound through her. For a moment she was reminded how well she and he had worked together brainstorming ideas for Seekers. She absently rubbed at the stain on her vest and tugged her gaze from his.

''Are there any phone bills?'' she asked.

Chad sifted through the pile in his hands. ''Visa, MasterCard, gas company...here we go.'' He held a bill out to her. ''A love note from old Ma Bell, herself.''

Accepting the itemized bill, Hannah continued to manipulate the matchbook. ''Can you make this out?''

Chad looked over her shoulder. Every muscle in her body tingled in alert. With barely a hesitation, he said, ''It's a girl named Rita Minelli's phone number.''

Hannah dropped her hand to her side. ''I've been trying to read this thing for five minutes and you take one look and tell me exactly what it says?''

Chad grinned at her. ''I've copied a few numbers on matchbooks in my time.'' He took the number from her.

Hannah didn't need the reminder of how uncommitted his lifestyle was. ''Very funny.''

He examined the matchbook. ''There's no area code.'' He flipped it over and stared at the cover. ''Atlantic City.'' Chad tossed the matchbook on top of the bureau, pulling the next drawer open. It yielded a handful of photographs. He silently thumbed through the photos. There was one of Eric Persky standing with Lisa Furgeson and another colleague inside what Hannah guessed to be PlayCo's factory.

The next picture was of the house they were in. Placing that one under the others, Chad stared down at another.

"Do you think that's the woman in the matchbook?" Hannah asked.

The photo was of Persky and a woman. A pretty brunette in her early- to mid-thirties.

"If it is, the number isn't local." Chad pointed to the smock the woman wore. "I know that outfit. It's one cocktail waitresses wear."

"It's almost too simple."

Chad slipped the photo of the woman and the one of Eric and his colleagues into his front pocket. "What makes you say that? Chances are the woman in the picture was a one-nighter. Or they broke up months ago and she hasn't seen him since."

"My instincts tell me the name on this matchbook and the woman in the picture are one in the same. If we find her, maybe we'll find Persky," Hannah said. "Crooks are rarely as clever as they make them out in movies."

"And if we find Persky, hopefully he'll lead us to Furgeson."

"That's right. If Persky is with some woman in Atlantic City, then chances Lisa Furgeson is with him are slim."

Chad eyed the cracked concrete sidewalk that separated him and the car from a four-story walk-up in Brooklyn Heights. After leaving Persky's, he'd suggested they hit PlayCo next to see what the company's personnel records held on the two bail-jumpers. But Hannah had driven them here instead, saying she had something to do first. Chad tapped the face of his watch for the third time, remembering the call she'd made at the police station. Could she be in there explaining things to the man who had replaced him?

A possessiveness he hadn't known he was capable of burned through him. Certainly he hadn't expected Hannah to wait around for him.... Or had he? Is that the real reason he didn't hesitate when Blackstone gave him the perfect excuse to come back? He stared at the back-lighted screen door. If subconsciously he had entertained ideas of rekindling his relationship with Hannah, he suspected they were about to be squashed.

"Come on, Hannah," he muttered, resisting the urge to lean on the horn.

He had half a mind to barge in there and drag her out caveman-style. The impulse stunned him. He shifted on the leather bucket seat. He and Hannah had happened a long time ago. She had every right to go on with her life...didn't she? But no matter how logically his mind argued the point, his gut told him he wanted her, boyfriend or no boyfriend.

He reached for his duffel bag in the back. His hand bumped hard plastic and he twisted to stare at a large, gaily colored object fastened to the back seat. He didn't know how he'd missed it before. Maybe because he'd been focused on other things when he'd first put his duffel on the floor. Perhaps because he'd sat in the passenger's seat up until then, narrowing his line of vision when he got in and out of the car.

What was Hannah doing with a child's car seat fastened in the back? Just how far had this new relationship of hers progressed? He hadn't noticed a wedding ring. Then again, he knew better than anyone that appearances were deceiving. She'd been driving a sputtering old rust bucket when they met up outside of

Blackstone's. He knew she didn't have any siblings, so a young niece or a nephew was out. Even if she'd had one, he doubted she'd keep a seat in her car—

Door springs squeaked, interrupting his rapid-fire suppositions. Breaking his gaze away from the object that posed so many questions, he turned his head to find Hannah coming out of the house—and his head filled with even more. He stared at the bundle she held in her arms. His throat tightened painfully, his breath froze in his lungs, and every curse he sought scrambled beyond his grasp. Hannah awkwardly opened the passenger door and released the seat so she could push it forward.

Chad sat staring at her from where he'd moved behind the steering wheel.

"Come on, sweetie, stop wiggling so Mommy can get you into your seat," Hannah said.

It dawned on Chad that she had a baby seat in the car because she had a baby.

She patiently maneuvered the baby, wearing a pink, baggy jumpsuit into the back despite the fidgeting of chubby arms and legs and nonstop gibberish. "There you go. Now take this." She handed the baby a donut-shaped, rubber thingy. Chad counted all of four, widely spaced teeth as the baby opened her mouth and chomped down on the item.

Chad's gaze slid from mother to daughter, trying to get a handle on things and failing miserably.

Finally Hannah looked at him. Her soft blue eyes held a mixture of expectancy and... He couldn't quite read the other emotion. The only sounds he could hear were the gurgling of the baby in the back seat, and the slamming of his own heart against his rib cage.

It didn't take an MIT grad to do the math. There

wasn't a single, solitary doubt that the baby who even now regarded him with happy curiosity was his daughter.

His daughter.

Sweet Lord in heaven....

He cleared his throat. "Who—I mean, is that your..."

Finally he latched onto a curse and let it rip. Hope. He realized too late the other emotion in Hannah's eyes was hope. He knew this, even as he watched it crushed by gray disappointment. But what in the hell had she been hoping for? Hannah climbed into the passenger's seat, her stony silence more effective than any words could ever be. Chad blinked just to make sure he still could, and tried to shove his mind into working order. For a guy who prided himself on being quick on the uptake, who needed to think fast on his feet, he was lapsing at least two steps behind right now. And he had the sinking feeling he'd never completely catch up.

Like an echo from a lifetime ago, he remembered Hannah's words earlier, her explanation why they shouldn't work together, why they couldn't get intimately involved again. *Things have changed, Chad. Everything has changed.*

He absently started the car, with no idea where he was going, or a clue what he was going to do.

"Chad, meet my daughter, Bonny."

He stared again at the squirming baby in the back seat. The sparse-haired, drool-covered little imp stared back, chattering as if saying something directly to him, then holding out the toy she chomped on in his direction. He swallowed hard, his heart expanding, surging against the bands he'd wrapped around it so long ago. Her large eyes were open, so very trusting, her cheeks flushed, her entire face animated. She grunted. Chad blinked, then awkwardly moved to accept the offering, only it appeared she hadn't meant for him to take it, merely to feel it. When he released the slobbery rubber, she gave a peal of laughter, then stuck it back into her mouth.

A grin edged its way across his face and he swore he could feel one of the intangible bands in his chest snap and begin to unravel. A car passed on the street. With every ounce of concentration he still had left, he watched it, trying hard to pull himself together. His grin waned and he looked at Hannah, too wrapped up in his own thoughts to respond to her wary expression.

Things *have* changed....

The bottomless feeling in Hannah's stomach refused to budge, no matter how hard she tried to make it. She repeatedly clasped and unclasped her hands in her lap, not quite knowing what to do with them, and unable to do nothing at all.

Chad idled the Alfa Romeo across from PlayCo and she took in a shallow, uneven breath. He'd been conspicuously silent ever since they picked up Bonny, alternately staring at her, and her noisy eight-month-old daughter in the back seat, appearing so thoroughly dumbfounded Hannah felt the incredible urge to reach out and touch him. At one point she thought he'd murmured something like "things have changed," but she couldn't be sure, and couldn't bring herself to ask him what he'd said. In fact, she could focus on little more than the weightless, expectant sensation in her stomach.

She cleared her emotion-clogged throat. Often in the past eight months, usually after Bonny had finally fallen asleep against her chest and her own eyes were heavy, she indulged in images of Chad learning about his daughter. Saw him knocking softly on the door, stepping directly to the eight-month-old and sweeping her up in his arms. The fantasies had been harmless, she'd assured herself, because there was no reason Chad would be showing up on their doorstep any time soon.

Now that he had come back...

She bit down hard on the flesh of her bottom lip. Dreams were one thing. Reality something completely different.

What had she expected him to do? Hold out his hands to lovingly take a child he should have instinctively known was his?

No, she realized. In reality, she had expected him to leap from the car and bid her a final farewell. At least she thought that was what he would do—until she picked Bonny up and hope had blossomed in her stronger than she would have imagined. Who could deny this little girl? Surely her father would take one look at her and...

And what? Push aside the past? Declare his undying love for her and Bonny? Offer her happily-ever-after?

Stupid.

She chanced a glance at Chad, trying to read his thoughts as he watched Bonny. In the light from the street lamp she could see his face. His eyes were wide, as if someone had done a Three Stooges eye-poking number on him. He met her gaze and she quickly turned away.

"Um, you're going to have to go into PlayCo by yourself, for obvious reasons," she said quietly.

They sat parked in Manhattan's Lower East Side. A discreet white sign with blue lettering marked the ten-floor, foursquare building across the street as PlayCo Industries. Hannah eyed the watchman sitting in a lighted air-conditioned, multiwindowed guard shack next to the parking garage entrance.

"How old is she?"

Chad's question caught her unaware. Hannah forgot about not looking at him. For a brief moment, he appeared so incredibly...victimized in the stiff white shirt and conservative striped tie he had fished from his duffel and put on, she nearly reached out to smooth the confused creases from his forehead. She blamed the instinctive impulse on her new role as mother and locked her fingers together in her lap.

"She'll be eight months next week," she said to the windshield.

She waited for his next question, but it never came. Instead he followed her gaze to the watchful guard in the shack and lapsed back into silence.

"So," she began, injecting a businesslike tone into her wavering voice, "how are you going to get in there?"

He blindly moved his hand to reach into the front pocket of his shirt, missed by an inch, then looked down and took out a black leather bifold wallet. He absently held it in her direction and flipped it open. Hannah stared at an FBI identification that bore an appealing snapshot of Chad, and identified him as a Special Agent. The plastic was cloudy, the leather holder old and cracked.

"What did you learn in Florida?" she whispered. "You never impersonated a fed before. Or if you did, I never knew about it." He closed the ID then stuffed it back into his pocket. "Do you know you're committing a crime? This is fraud against the federal government. Do you have any idea what kind of penalty that carries?''

''Two to ten,'' he said, clearly distracted by a burst of mimicking sounds from Bonny in the back seat. ''But it doesn't matter because I don't intend to get caught.'' Chad stared at his watch, then shifted to fuss with his tie. Hannah noticed his movements were jerky, anxious, not the usual smooth, easy Chad moves. A couple of cars approached, apparently night-shift workers gaining access to the underground parking area.

''I thought you earned facts and clues the honest way,'' she said.

''For what it's worth, this is the first time I've impersonated a fed.''

Why didn't that make her feel any better?

''Trust me. Nothing's going to happen,'' he said in a preoccupied monotone. ''I'm going to take a look at Persky's and Furgeson's personnel files. The feds...'' he trailed off.

''The feds,'' Hannah prompted.

He glanced at her, apparently trying to recover his train of thought. ''The feds will never know.''

Hannah wasn't sure if her agitation sprang from his lack of work ethics, or from his obvious ignorance of his connection to Bonny, who rhythmically kicked her car seat with the back of her shoes.

''Do you have any better ideas?'' Chad asked and rubbed the back of his neck. ''Because if you do, I'm all ears.''

''Does it still hurt?'' she asked quietly.

He stared at her. ''Huh?''

''The bump you took at Persky's house.''

He dropped his hand back to his lap.

She resisted the urge to check the wound herself.

Touching Chad again would not be a smart move, no matter what the reason. "Anyway, I do have another idea. I say we get a move on to Atlantic City and see if that woman in the matchbook we found at Persky's exists."

"And what if she doesn't? What if it's like I said and she was a one-nighter, a nooner, a quickie whom Persky never saw again?"

Hannah decided she'd liked him better speechless. She grimaced and tucked her hair behind her ear. "I love your vocabulary, Hogan. Do you care to share any more of your colorful language with me and Bonny?"

"Forget my word choices for a minute here, Hannah, and give this some thought. Let's say we go to Atlantic City and turn up a big, fat zero? What then? Do we turn back to N.Y. and start from scratch?" His gaze lingered on Bonny and he slowly shook his head. "We don't have the time. I'm going in here, getting what I need, *then* we'll go to Atlantic City...."

His words trailed off. Hannah practically heard his unspoken question. Would the baby be going with them?

"I don't have anywhere to leave her," she blurted, disappointing herself. The last thing she wanted was to appear desperate. But desperate was exactly what she was, wasn't it? Her regular baby-sitter couldn't keep Bonny because she had plans for the weekend that couldn't be broken. And with no family to speak of, unless you counted Victor Marconi, and a distant aunt in Montana, she was in a jam.

"I didn't exactly expect to take this case, Chad. Don't worry, Bonny won't cause any trouble. And I certainly don't intend to put her in any danger. This is a routine case with an unusual time constraint, that's all. We're tracking white-collar criminals, not violent armed robbers.''

He touched her hand where it lay against her leg. An instant rush of awareness startled her at the feel of his warm fingers on her cold ones.

''Hannah, I didn't say anything about Bonny causing problems,'' he said softly.

She tugged her hand away from his and worried it in her lap with her other. ''No, you didn't. But I could always read your thoughts, Chad.''

His gaze was probing. ''Did you ever stop to think you couldn't read me as well as you thought you could?''

She stared at him wordlessly. Could he be right? Was she misjudging him? Had she misread him in the past?

She watched the guard wave another car into PlayCo's parking area.

''She's beautiful,'' he said so quietly she nearly didn't hear him.

The statement took her breath away. She searched for a response, but couldn't seem to match words to the emotions coursing through her. She almost said ''She looks like you,'' but caught herself.

She swallowed hard, relieved when he shifted the car into First. He pulled it around, heading straight for the guard still sitting in his shack next to the entrance to PlayCo Industries.

Chapter Four

Shell-shocked. That was the closest Chad could come to describing how he felt. No. That's exactly how he would describe it. Having served with the Marines in Kuwait, he knew what it was like to hear sniper fire and not know where it had come from. The strange thing was that in this situation no one else had noticed the shot. Around him life went on as normal.

In the personnel office of PlayCo Industries, the nondescript, white-collar-to-the-bone comptroller Robert Morgan hung up the telephone then began fingering through a filing cabinet to retrieve Persky's and Furgeson's employment records. Outside in the hall a couple of second shift workers laughed, presumably on their way back from break. In another room across the way, a telephone rang on, with no one around to pick it up.

Even as he registered every sound, placed every per-

son, he remained apart from them. The shot he'd taken
hadn't come from an unknown sniper's gun; it had
come from Hannah. Hannah and that precious baby girl
whose veins carried his blood.

Thrusting his fingers through his hair, he glanced
toward the open door, anxious to get out of there. To
get back to the car and start seeking some answers that
might help him make sense out of all this.

He'd never thought he'd be a father again. He'd
sworn another child wouldn't be born with the stigma
of his name attached. It seemed like another lifetime
since he'd even been around a baby. So long, he was
unprepared for the instinctive surge of parental protection, of unconditional love that overtook him the instant he understood Bonny was his.

Still, it was all so hard to believe....

Just last month marked the fourth anniversary since
the last moment he'd held his infant son, Joshua. Right
before Joshua had been taken from him.

Scenes twisted through his mind. Images of mis-
shapen metal, of an empty car seat lying in the middle
of the road. Of his wife's purse still sitting on the floor
of the front seat.

His family.

A highway patrolman had tried to pry him from the
scene when, at some point in the long nightmare, law
officials had been contacted. And Chad had hauled off
and slugged him, desperately needing to hold on to his
family, though they were already gone. Their faces
were burned forever into his memory, haunting him in
the dark hours of the morning, taunting him whenever
he experienced anything close to happiness...serving
as a constant, caustic reminder that he didn't deserve
to be happy.

A torrent of emotion ripped through Chad's gut. He focused on the back of Robert Morgan as he began copying the files he'd taken from the cabinet, but Chad really didn't see him.

They'd argued that day, him and Linda. He winced from the memory of her packed suitcases, Joshua's stuffed blue elephant hanging half out of a blue diaper bag, his son's lashes bearing remnants of tears. Linda had accused him of putting his career above his family, an argument she'd made often. But that night she'd had enough. She was leaving him. Going home to her parents in Pittsburgh, Pennsylvania. And there was nothing he could do to stop her.

Chad eyed the door, needing to escape. It was an accident, a voice in his head shouted. He resolutely refused to listen. It was no accident. He was to blame. He had killed his family as surely as if he'd driven them off that mountain road.

The experience had been more than Chad Hogan, Special Agent for the Federal Bureau of Investigations, had been able to handle. He'd quit the Bureau, and never told anyone about his work there, not even Hannah. Too many bad memories. It was better to let her think that ID he flashed was bought somewhere in Florida. After he quit, he'd taken odd jobs as a skip-tracer to cover the basic necessities, and resolved to serve out a life sentence in which he wasn't allowed to move past the guilt, the grief.

Then came Hannah.

The instant he met her, the shadows that dogged him began to recede. With all that curly red hair, those lively freckles and infectious laugh, she had loved life and lived to love. He'd been drawn to her like an addict was drawn to drugs. Okay, so maybe he hadn't deserved her. He'd known that, too. But he'd been helpless to stop himself.

She had my baby and I didn't even know it.

"I wish there was something I could do to help you."

Chad blinked away the images crowding his head and stared at Robert Morgan who held out two blue file folders in his direction. He took them and cleared his throat. "I understand. This is fine."

Morgan smiled and pushed up dark-rimmed glasses. "I have to admit, I still don't know what all this is about. Your associates told me it didn't concern PlayCo so I shouldn't worry, but I can't help it."

"They were right. You shouldn't worry, Mr. Morgan." He tucked the files under his arm and shook the other man's hand. "Thank you for your help, sir."

"My, but you're the independent one lately, aren't you? Want to test your boundaries, is that it?" Hannah gave in to Bonny's earnest attempts to escape her hold. She put her down in the driver's seat, disappointment niggling at her that Bonny didn't want to be held in the way Hannah needed to hold her after what had just happened—and didn't happen—between her and Chad. She glanced around the interior of the underground parking garage. Chad had gotten them this far with a flash of his fake ID and a capable disposition, but her apprehension wouldn't ease until they were out of the artificially bright parking area and well away from PlayCo Industries. And until he made it clear how he felt about having a daughter.

Bonny curled her stubby fingers around the door handle. Hannah realized her little girl wanted to follow Chad.

She reached into her purse and took out a bag of cheese crackers. Gaining her daughter's attention, she tried to feed her a cracker only to have Bonny balk and take the fish-shaped snack away so she could feed herself.

Hannah laid her cheek against the leather headrest. It wasn't too long ago when she had wanted to follow Chad, too. Everywhere. Anywhere. She smoothed back Bonny's tufts of red hair, reveling in the feel of the baby-soft strands against her skin.

"This whole situation is surreal somehow," she said quietly. "It's so outside the norm, isn't it, Munchkin?" Bonny just smiled and took another cracker. "Right about now Mommy would be feeding you dinner, wouldn't she? In our cozy little yellow kitchen with the sunflowers on the wallpaper." Right now their apartment in Little Italy couldn't have seemed farther away. Hannah vaguely noticed the mess her daughter was making and reached for a wet towel also stashed in her purse.

As she cleaned Bonny, she checked the rearview mirrors and saw nothing but rows of parked cars, not a person in sight.

"What else have you been up to in the past fifteen months, Chad?" she said, earning her Bonny's full attention. If she didn't know better, she'd think the eight-month-old already recognized her father's name.

Stuffing the towelette in a garbage bag on the door, she hoisted Chad's duffel bag from the floor of the back seat. Glancing at the lobby door he had disappeared through twenty minutes earlier, she loosened the pull string and coaxed open the leather mouth. Bonny grunted.

"What is it, Bon-Bon?" she asked. "Don't worry.

Mommy's just going to take a harmless look. There's nothing wrong with that, is there?''

The baby stared at her, her soft brows knitting together.

Hannah laughed shakily. "Good thing you can't talk yet, huh?'' She returned her attention to the bag. "You'd likely tell your—'' She caught herself, shocked she had nearly said "your daddy.''

Of course, if Chad caught her...

Her job included rummaging through other peoples' belongings in order to get a handle on their mindset, put together a profile of who they were and where they might be heading. Rifling through Chad's things, however, was something entirely different. She felt naughty at best, and traitorous at worst, neither emotion comfortable.

Still, her need to know outweighed her moral code.

Hesitantly pushing aside the T-shirt he had exchanged for the white shirt he now had on, packages of new socks and briefs, she sought the bottom where she hoped to find a clue to what he'd been doing since leaving her and New York. If she didn't immediately find something, she'd take it as a sign and stop. The back of her hand hit something solid. She curled her fingers around the smooth object and pulled out a half-full bottle of vodka. Her heartbeat slowed. Chad didn't drink. At least not that she ever knew. She briefly closed her eyes and pressed the bottle against her chest. What was Chad doing with a half-full liquor bottle in his duffel?

Making sure the cap was screwed on tight, she slipped the bottle back into the bag, then stuck her hand down further, until she hit the leather-covered bottom. Nothing. Okay, maybe she'd just allow a little sideways movement.... Her fingers at once found something flat and cool. Carefully fishing the item out, she stared at a professional studio picture of a woman and an infant she hadn't seen before. His wife? Stuck into the corner of the frame was a strip of photographs of Chad and her taken at one of those coin photo booths at Coney Island. She ran her fingertip over the grainy black-and-white, completely unflattering pictures. The photos easily could have been of another couple for all the connection she felt seeing them. If not for the love so obviously written on her face in the snapshots; a love she feared still resided in the secret recesses of her heart.

A clang echoed through the garage. Hannah put the photo back into the bag and thrust both onto the back seat floor. Where had the noise come from? She lifted Bonny and maneuvered over the emergency brake and stick shift to the driver's seat. Bonny protested as Hannah put her down in the passenger's seat.

The faint squeal of tires against concrete told her a car was coming. Instinctively she slid down in the seat, relieved Bonny was small enough not to be seen from the outside. She watched a blue four-door sedan pull in front of the door to the lobby of PlayCo two rows away. Four suited men exited the car in unison, the sound of closing doors feeding the acidlike dread in her stomach.

Bonny let out an excited squeal. Hannah prayed the men hadn't heard. She peered over the dashboard to see the door closing behind the men's backs. She sighed a breath of relief—relief that vanished as she realized who the men were.

"Oh God, Chad," she whispered, starting the car. The nondescript four-door sedan, the shrewd calculated silence of the men as they entered the building, their standard issue blue suits. All facts coalesced to tell her the *real* FBI had just entered PlayCo Industries.

Slipping the seat back, she plucked Bonny up and carefully leaned over to put her in her safety seat. She caught a glimpse of Chad darting out of the lobby, staring at the sedan as he passed.

In a tight voice Hannah said, "You do realize who—"

"Here…let me." He shifted her shaking hands aside and reached for Bonny's car seat belt. Hannah blinked at him, mesmerized as he made quick work of fastening the baby in properly, almost as if the move were a natural one for him, something he'd been doing routinely. Of course he had done it before. With his infant son. But seeing him do something so fatherlike now with their own daughter made her throat go dry. Finishing, he enveloped Bonny's small feet in his long, tanned fingers. The baby watched him in mute fascination then blurted, "Dah!"

Chad stared at Hannah, that thunderstruck expression back on his face. She feigned a cough and handed Bonny back her teething ring.

"'Dah' means dog. Her baby-sitter has one," she lied. Now was not the time to delve into a profound conversation about the past. No matter how much she wished it was.

He grimaced. "Dog."

"Uh-huh. But enough of that. I want to know if you realize who—"

"Yes, I realize who just went inside. I can even give you one of their names. Special Agent Randall McKay," Chad said, tugging his tie loose.

"What's the FBI doing here? And how did they get

here so quickly?'' Hannah asked, not about to believe their visit was coincidental. Not this late at night. Not a half hour after Chad had gone inside.

"I don't know, in answer to your first question. The second..." Chad tugged open the top buttons of his shirt. "Since the FBI is obviously involved in the case, they probably left a standing order that they be contacted if anyone showed up asking about Persky and Furgeson."

Hannah shifted the car into gear and backed out of the parking spot, heading toward the garage entrance. She spotted the guard stepping from his shack fifty feet away.

"Let's hope he lets us out as easily as he let us in," she whispered. "I swear, Chad, if anything happens, I'll..."

The rest of her sentence hung in the air as they pulled level with the guard shack. Her nerves fairly hummed with the tension gripping her. What was happening inside right now? Had the FBI discovered Chad had left? Hannah watched the guard move to Chad's side of the car.

"I trust your visit was satisfactory, sir?"

Chad slanted her a reassuring look. "Quite."

The guard peered at the baby in the back seat, then at Hannah. She stared straight ahead, hoping he wouldn't notice the anxiety she was sure showed on her face.

"Have a good—"

The ringing of the telephone interrupted him while the squeal of tires against concrete came from the depths of the garage. Hannah thought she'd have a coronary right then and there.

"Excuse me. I'll be right back," the guard said.

"Do you know who's on the phone, Chad?" Hannah said under her breath as the guard walked toward his shack. "Probably one of the FBI agents you were just impersonating." She looked at him. "You know, the ones who'll arrest us if they catch us?"

Chad seemed totally unaffected as he scanned her face. She had no doubt every freckle probably stood out as they always did when she was anxious.

"You know, Hannah, I think you're right," he said finally. "That's why I think you should put your pretty little foot on the gas pedal and go." He paused. "Now."

He said the words so softly that Hannah had to replay them in her mind before she understood. She flicked her gaze to where the guard stared at them, then he pushed a button, the telltale sound of an approaching car from the interior of the garage making her heart rate increase. A metal door began closing above the car.

"Oh God." With barely a moment's hesitation, Hannah shifted the car into First. The Alfa Romeo raced forward with the screech of rubber against concrete, dashing from the dim grayness of the garage into the street lamp-lighted night.

"Look out!" Chad shouted.

Hannah pulled the wheel sharply to the right, barely missing a car on the other side of the road. But her attention wasn't on the car they had just missed. It was on her rearview mirror and the guard who ran out onto the sidewalk, yelling after them while in the shack the telephone receiver swung back and forth from its black cord. Behind the closing metal security gate, the four-door sedan shrieked to a halt and the driver laid on the horn.

"Chad, we're supposed to be tracking fugitives, not becoming ones."

He turned to stuff his tie into his duffel bag. He looked at her. Hannah tensed, realizing she hadn't closed it.

"Hope you found something interesting," he said quietly.

She took a corner a little fast, earning a cry from Bonny.

"Slow down, Hannah. We don't want to scare the baby any more than we already have."

She eased her foot off the gas pedal, eyeing a squad car stopped at a red light on an adjacent street.

"Chad, I'm not even going to ask how you knew that agent's name." At a slower pace, she zigzagged through the Manhattan traffic, wishing she could camouflage her car in the sea of taxi yellow. Since PlayCo was on Manhattan's Lower East Side, Hannah headed west where she hoped to zip into the Lincoln Tunnel and on into Jersey.

In the back seat, Bonny began crying. "She's hungry," Hannah said.

"Hungry?" Chad repeated tightly, as if the concept was foreign to him.

"Yes, hungry. There's a bottle in the diaper bag—" She looked at him, realizing what she had almost asked him to do.

Instead she reached around her seat and groped around for the bag with little Sesame Street characters she had stowed on the floor there. Chad touched her arm, his fingers warm and firm.

"I can do it. You just concentrate on getting us out of New York safely, okay?"

Chad unfastened his seat belt and climbed into the

back seat. As he fished in the diaper bag for the bottle, he caressed the baby's downy hair and wiped the tears from her rosy cheeks. Hannah watched him, unsure what to make of his actions. She wanted to reach out to take Bonny, irrationally uneasy with the fact that her daughter had stopped crying and appeared happy.

She blinked, realizing she was looking at Chad through the rearview mirror and not the road.

Chad cleared his throat and began giving a now quiet Bonny her bottle.

Hannah wasn't sure, but among the confusing emotions filling her heart, one was fear. Not fear of the FBI and the deeper trouble Chad's little stunt had landed them in. No. The fear gripping her was even more acute. The fear that Chad might want to play a part in their daughter's life. A daughter he hadn't even admitted to yet. And what terrified Hannah most was she hoped he would.

Chad slipped the key into the lock of Room 116 and glanced over his shoulder at Hannah. She hiked a sleeping Bonny up a little higher on her hip. She avoided his gaze, much as she had throughout the entire drive through Jersey. He watched her kiss the top of the baby's head and felt a little nudge somewhere in the vicinity of his heart.

Following the incident with the FBI, they'd had little choice but to leave New York and quickly. He didn't doubt the agents or the guard had noted Hannah's plate number and had run a search. He turned the key in the lock. By now the FBI likely had her apartment under surveillance, as well as an APB out on her car. And since he'd used his real if old FBI ID, chances were pretty good they were on the lookout for him, as well.

He pulled the key out and grasped the door handle. "Here we are. Home—"

"Please," Hannah said. "Please don't say it, Chad. I couldn't bear it if you said 'Home, sweet home.'"

A muscle in his jaw twitched. "Sorry. Habit I guess." He pushed the door open. The darkness revealed nothing of the motel room they were to share until he reached in and flicked on the lights.

"Nice, if you've just had a fifth with the boys," Chad said wryly.

Hannah followed him into the room as he glanced at his watch.

"Three in the morning. I didn't realize it was so late." He tossed the key to a nearby dresser and tightened his grip on his duffel.

They'd made two stops before checking into the motel. The first was at a rest area in northern Jersey where Hannah had called a frantic Elliott Blackstone to let him know where they were heading. Afterward, they traded off on the driving so Hannah could feed and change Bonny, a normal, commonplace action for her, but he'd been unable to take his eyes off them while she did it. He didn't know why he hadn't seen it before, but Hannah had all the makings of a great mom. She was patient, attentive, knew exactly how to coax a smile from Bonny, and used the right amount of gravity in her voice for a reprimand. And there was no doubting she loved her daughter very much.

The second stop they made was in Atlantic City at the casino listed on the matchbook they found at Persky's house. Yes, the night shift bartender told them after Chad made him twenty dollars richer, the woman named Rita Minelli worked the morning shift as a waitress. Nothing they said or did after that, however, could

coax further information from the guy. They were
forced to wait until morning to talk to the waitress with
the unclear connection to Eric Persky.

Chad ran his fingers along his stubble-covered chin
as Hannah cuddled the baby closer then murmured
something into her tiny, pink ear.

It was hard to believe that only a few hours ago he'd
been hungry for her to answer a truckload of questions,
to tune him in on a situation that was too fuzzy. But
every time he'd gazed at Bonny, or saw the way Hannah nervously twisted her hands in her lap, he hadn't
dared ask a single one.

Admit it, Hogan, you're afraid of what she'll say.

"Which one do you want?" He shut the door then
yanked closed the curtains to the street-level room.

"What?" Hannah swiveled toward him a little too
quickly. If not for the baby in her arms, she would have
ended up flush against him. She drew in a quick breath.

Chad caught her so she wouldn't topple over. The
skin of her arms was remarkably warm under his fingers, her muscles tense. He gazed down at her, fascinated by the flashes of color on her cheeks, the movement of her tongue as she ran it over her lips. God,
what he wouldn't give to kiss her right now. An urge
that made absolutely no sense considering all that was
happening, yet somehow made perfect sense.

Was it unbearably hot in the room, or was it him?

He cleared his throat. "The beds…which do you
want?"

Hannah quickly turned away, disappointing him.
"Either is fine." She eyed the two full-size beds and
the narrow space separating them. She lay the baby on
one, propping pillows on either side of her before plac-

ing the diaper bag on a nearby bureau. She fished out
a bottle of juice and put it on the bedside table.

He still had trouble wrapping his mind around it. Not
only was Hannah a mother, but he was a father. A role
he never thought he'd play again. He watched her rub
the backs of her fingers against Bonny's cheek and
wished he could open his mouth to ask some of those
questions he needed answered. But the desire to cross
the room and feel the incredible softness of his daughter's skin drowned those questions out.

"I'm going to take a shower," Hannah said quietly.

Chad's gaze flicked from her to the sleeping baby.

"She should pretty much sleep through the night."
She looked decidedly anxious. "Don't worry. I won't
be long."

With that she darted into the bathroom and closed
the door behind herself.

Chad stood cemented to the middle of the floor.
Bonny's gentle breathing seemed to fill the room, emphasizing that they were alone together for the first
time.

Alone.

Slowly, as if afraid he'd awaken her, he moved
closer to the bed. Each step fed him another detail. Her
round cheeks were flushed from the heat. Her curly red
hair stuck up in some spots, and was plastered to her
head in others. Her tiny, perfect bow-shaped lips started
moving and he realized she was mimicking feeding
time, perhaps dreaming of it. Suddenly her face
scrunched up, much as it had when she'd protested
Hannah's trying to feed her pureed carrots at the rest
area, then she turned her head. A damp, pudgy thumb
seemed to seek her mouth on its own accord and the
sucking movements began anew.

Chad found himself grinning like a dumbfounded new father. Bonny might be eight months old but he'd just learned about her existence, so in effect that was what he was. A new dad. Without knowing he was going to do it, he reached out and ran a callused fingertip over the amazingly small knuckles of her hand, then gently tugged her thumb from her mouth. Her face scrunched up again, then just as quickly relaxed.

His mind filled with all the things he didn't know about her. When did she first smile? Sit up? Utter her first word? Did she have a full head of hair when she was born, or was she bald as a cue ball?

So many details he didn't know, both large and small.

He found himself smoothing her curly hair back, recognizing that there were some other, greater things he didn't have to know. He just felt them. Like the fact that he'd recognized straight off that she was his daughter. Not because of the math. Not because she looked like Joshua—she couldn't have differed more from his fair-haired son if she'd tried. No. He'd taken one look into her wide blue eyes and just knew.

He heard a soft sigh, then recognized it as his own. Those same blue eyes opened now. Not slowly or groggily. It seemed as if one moment she was deep asleep, the next she was gazing up at him, completely alert.

"Hi there, sweet pea," he murmured with a smile.

She didn't move, didn't make a sound, merely gazed at him in open curiosity. His heart gave a small lurch. She reached a hand up, index finger crookedly extended as if wanting to touch his face. He tunneled his own finger into her fist and she gripped it. The warmth that swept through his body was nearly overwhelming in its intensity as he sat down on the mattress next to her.

Immediately she began crying.

Panic waded in Chad's stomach. "What is it?" He grabbed for the bottle on the nightstand. "Are you thirsty?"

She turned her head away when he tried to coax the nipple into her mouth.

"Okay." He put the bottle back down.

What should he do? Joshua—

He rubbed his face. Joshua had been only two months old when he'd lost him. He could probably count on one hand the times he'd been left alone with him. And then the majority of those times was when he'd returned home late and had snuck in for a few minutes to watch his son sleep.

The differences in the situations struck him as ironic. He'd missed out on Joshua's future. He hadn't been involved in Bonny's past, as short as it was.

Wet. Maybe she was wet. That he knew how to check for.

"Do you need to be changed? Is that it?" Hesitantly he rested the back of his hand against her rounded belly then tucked his finger into the waist of her diaper. Dry as a bone.

"Okay, so you're not wet."

All at once he felt completely, utterly helpless.

Pick her up, a small voice in his mind told him.

He swallowed hard. It'd been a long time since he'd held a baby. A mixture of fear of not knowing the right thing to do and anxiety that he might somehow harm her combined to make him little more than a jumbled mess.

"Oh, for crying out loud, Hogan, you're a big bad

bounty hunter. How difficult can picking up a baby be?''

He reached out and tucked his fingers under her arms and gently lifted her until she sat in the cradle of his arms.

The sensation of her chubby baby body against his nearly knocked him over. She not only instantly stopped crying, she seemed intent on taking complete advantage of her new position and stuck her finger straight into his ear.

He chuckled and took her hand. ''Remind me to teach you the basics when it comes to manners, little one.''

The sentence was out before he could catch it. It seemed to convey that he would be around in the future, play a role in her life. He glanced toward the closed bathroom door. Until he and Hannah had a long talk, that future was foggy indeed.

A drool-covered finger poked at his eyeball. He groaned and caught her other hand. Bonny seemed to find this remarkably amusing and gave a baby giggle that made his smile widen.

''Let's see...what can I do to amuse you before you do something that leaves a mark?''

The thing was, he suspected she'd already made an indelible mark on his heart.

The sound of the shower reminded Hannah of the familiar hum of washers washing at Nash's Wet and Dry, Chad's uncle's Laundromat. Chad and she had lived in an apartment above that Laundromat for almost a year. She climbed into the tub and closed her eyes, giving herself over to the spray of water and the rush of images that crowded her mind.

It was all too easy to recall the old but clean speckled linoleum floor of the cleaners, the eclectic mix of customers who treated the place as a regular hangout. Then there was Chad's uncle Nash, a gregarious ex-Marine who wore white T-shirts and rolled-up jeans summer and winter, the tattoo of an anchor always visible on his right bicep. She smiled. To this day she didn't know if the big sweet bear of a man had really had trouble operating his old cash register or whether he just liked to keep her in the store for a few minutes before she headed upstairs. Not that she'd minded. After she lost her father and had a falling out with Victor Marconi, and before Bonny, Nash—and Chad—were the closest things to family she'd had.

The smile faded from her face. Oh, how she'd wanted to tell Nash about Bonny. She'd even tried calling once, only to hang up when the sound of his voice over the telephone line had reminded her too much of the time she'd spent with Chad.

Not that she never thought about Chad. It was just that the sound of Nash's voice had brought everything too close to home.

Oh, she had thought about Chad, all right. Beyond wondering what his response to learning about Bonny would be, she had replayed the night of their breakup so many times she swore the memory itself was frayed at the edges. She recalled all too clearly his words—remembered her own.

"Mmm, you taste good." Chad entered the apartment and crept up behind her, playfully nuzzling her neck.

Hannah leaned into his kiss, and felt the familiar shiver skitter across her skin. She didn't have to be

*reminded why she wanted to spend the rest of her life
with Chad Hogan. He was sexy, funny, mouthwater-
ingly gorgeous and made her feel whole whenever he
was around. For the first time in so very long, she felt
as if she belonged somewhere. With someone. With
Chad.*

*Then she shifted the bank statement she'd been hold-
ing so he could see it, trying to ignore the provocative
way he caressed her shoulders left bare by her tank
top. "Chad, where's the money from our savings account?"*

*Then her stomach did a funny little flip. Maybe he'd
bought her a ring! An engagement ring. Her heart
hammered hopefully against the wall of her chest.*

*"Why don't we forget about that for now," Chad
said and flashed that sexy, irresistible grin that had
endeared him to her from the beginning. "I've got
something else on my mind. More specifically,* someone
*else." He dangled a set of keys in front of her eyes.
"Happy birthday, Hannah."*

*She slid her gaze from his bedroom eyes and his
tousled golden-brown hair, to where his blue T-shirt
hugged his well-toned abdomen, then she focused on
the keys he held out. Since so many holidays had gone
by uncelebrated in the past, she'd nearly forgotten
about her birthday. Today she turned thirty.*

*Chad tugged on her waist. "Come here." He nudged
her toward the window, his breath teasing her ear, his
arms curving around her waist from behind. His body
pressed against hers, reminding her how perfectly they
fit together.*

*"Look down there," he said, pointing toward the
street.*

Right outside the Laundromat sat a cherry-red Alfa with a huge gold bow on the hood.

"It's an Alfa Romeo drop-top," Chad told her, blazing a trail down her arm with his fingertips, then pressing the keys into her hand. "And it's all yours."

Hannah stared at the car as if it were a red sun spot that would disappear if she blinked quickly enough. Or transform into an oversized mutant velvet box in which there would be a ring. But no matter how many times she closed her eyes, the car was still there when she opened them again.

Chad squeezed her hand and the keys bit into her palm.

"I don't know what to say...." she began in an unsteady voice.

"Come on. Let's take her for a spin."

She remained standing at the window, as if frozen in place.

"What's the matter?" Chad asked. "You don't like the color?"

"Color?" Her stomach suddenly pitched to her knees. He hadn't clue one why she was so upset. "No, I don't like the color, Chad. I want you to take it back." Her mind spun with all the plans she'd managed to spin in such a short time. A ring. Marriage to Chad. A family... "I want you to take it back and get me...oh, I don't know, a bracelet or something. Or maybe a ring."

The words had gushed out before she could blink.

Suddenly the room had seemed far too big. Only a few feet separated them, but it might as well have been miles.

"I—I can't believe you did this," she whispered. "You nearly emptied out our savings account to buy

an impulsive gift that will be more of a problem than a blessing in New York. That money was supposed to pay for Seekers...and maybe, um, a nice little, intimate wedding—''

''Whoa! Hold on a minute here. Ring? Wedding?'' Chad had broke in, strands of sandy-brown hair falling over his raised brow.

Hannah braced herself against the unpromising, painful shadow that crossed through his gray eyes.

''Yes, wedding. You know, the ceremony performed when two people get married? Make a lifetime commitment to each other? Certainly it's not the first time you've heard the word, Chad. After all, you were married before.''

He paced a little ways away. ''Yeah, and it's something I don't plan on doing again, so get over it.''

Hannah's heart gave an aching squeeze. ''Over it?'' she'd whispered. ''Over it? What do you think I have? The flu?''

''Something like that.'' Chad rubbed his hands down the length of his jeans. He looked suddenly untouchable, making her want to touch him all the more.

''But, Chad, I think we should talk about this.''

He'd turned back to her suddenly. ''No, Hannah. If you would stop talking long enough to listen to what I have to say, we wouldn't be having this argument right now. Look, the last thing I want to do is hurt you—''

''Hurt me?'' Yes, he had hurt her. ''You never had any intention of making a...making a commitment to me, did you, Chad?''

He held her gaze and said simply, ''No.''

Hannah stood under the cool shower spray, resisting the urge to nudge up the temperature to chase away the chill left by the memory of Chad's rejection. She only wished the water could wash away the confusing emotions clinging inside as easily as it cleansed her skin. What was she going to do now?

Only eight hours earlier she thought she'd never see Chad again. Now she was sharing a motel room with him. She caught her bottom lip between her teeth and thrust her head under the spray to ward off all the intimate thoughts that went along with their close proximity.

Before she and Chad split up fifteen months ago, their relationship had been basically carefree—until she found out she wanted the whole ball of wax. She wanted what she had never had—the until-death-do-you-part, happily-ever-after love, the white picket fence, 2.2 children, a husband who loved her... All of it. She'd wanted all of it.

But while her priorities had changed, Chad's hadn't.

Then she'd discovered she was pregnant.

When, two weeks after her and Chad's breakup, the doctor told her she was almost two months pregnant, she'd had no idea where to go, what to do. Should she tell Chad? Should she handle it herself? And what if she did tell Chad? Would he marry her for the baby's sake? Or would he turn his back on her? Neither prospect had emerged particularly inviting, so she had gone it alone. And had never experienced a moment of regret...until now.

No, that wasn't totally true. When she was six months pregnant, long after he'd left the city, she'd reasoned he at least had a right to know. She held no illusions that learning the truth would change his mind, bring him back. She simply thought he should know that in a few short months, he was going to be a father…again. Then a search for him turned up nothing. He'd essentially disappeared from the face of the earth. Not even his uncle Nash had known where he was.

It wasn't until Bonny was two months old that she'd learned Chad was in Florida, and Jack Stokes, of all people had supplied this bit of information. By then, Hannah figured she had pretty much set her own course and owed Chad little. Besides, he had made it perfectly clear he didn't want another family with both words and actions.

She rinsed the soap from her skin, remembering the day Bonny was born. Her daughter had given her what she hadn't had since her father died: family. Unconditional love, a connection to something much bigger than herself. Her entire take on life had shifted, revolving around the importance, the joy, of raising her daughter.

Chad's voice filtered through the door. Hannah quickly shut the water off. Was he talking to her? Bonny's playful squeal followed.

He's talking to the baby.

Hurrying back into her clothes, Hannah opened the door. Chad had his back to her, sitting on the bed feeding Bonny her bottle of juice with one hand, and holding up a newspaper in his other. Bonny's fascination was such that it stopped her from climbing from the bed and grabbing everything in sight to stick into her mouth. She was actually still. At least as still as Bonny ever got.

Hannah watched her daughter grunt and kick her pudgy legs.

"Another story? Demanding as your mom, aren't you?" Chad said and squeezed Bonny's foot. "Okay, then, let's take a look at this one…." He picked up the paper again. "In a stunning upset, the last-place Mets beat the top-ranked Braves after twelve grueling innings of play...."

Hannah's heart expanded at the way he made the sports piece sound like Cinderella. How many times had she awakened in the dead of night having dreamt of just such a scene? Longing for Chad to be a part of their lives? A part of Bonny's life?

She blinked, reminding herself that his presence now was only temporary. That he would end up hurting her again when he walked away at the end of their manhunt. But that didn't bother her half as much as the thought of what his leaving would mean to Bonny.

Hannah slid open a drawer then closed it, relieved when Chad stopped reading and jumped from the bed. Bonny cried out and she stepped forward to prop the juice bottle back up. She murmured reassurances to her daughter and smiled when she instantly settled back down.

Hannah stood...and found herself very nearly in Chad's arms when she turned. Her gaze slowly slid up to his face, the dark expression in his eyes making her shiver, even as her body tingled in overwhelming awareness. He looked confused, angry and restless...and about ready to kiss her.

Despite everything else going on around and inside her, Hannah wished he would. Wished he would just claim her mouth with his and ban every other thought and emotion from her mind. Her tongue darted out to moisten her lips. He watched the unconsciously evocative movement with rapt, hard attention...before turning away from her.

Hannah closed her eyes against the rejection.

"The clock's ticking," she said quietly, breaking the silence.

He folded the newspaper he still clutched then gestured toward a small round table and two chairs positioned in front of the silent air conditioner.

"After you." Was it her, or did his voice sound huskier than usual? "And don't bother with the air conditioner," he said. "It's broken. I already called the manager. There are no other rooms available."

Hannah rested her hand against the side of her damp neck. The last thing she needed was more heat. She leaned across the table and opened the window. Humid air arced inward, instantly filling the room. She tucked back the curtain. At least the air was moving.

A while later Hannah glanced to where Bonny had fallen back to sleep on the bed, a line of juice streaking her soft cheek. She closed the personnel file Chad had gotten from PlayCo.

"This isn't doing us any good."

She took a sip of iced tea she had gotten from a machine outside. The melting ice cubes clinked against the plastic cup as she poured more tea from the can.

Chad leaned back in his seat across from her. "Let's recap. What do we have so far?"

"Aside from a pounding headache?" Hannah plucked her vest from her sweat-covered skin, finding it difficult to believe she'd taken a shower only a short time ago. "We know two employees of PlayCo Industries, Eric Persky and Lisa Furgeson, were arrested for transporting stolen highly sensitive computer microprocessor chips, which doesn't tell us a lot about the chips except they're worth more than five hundred dollars and a hefty bond amount." She shrugged. "They were caught, let out on bail, which they promptly jumped.''

''Let's not forget that PlayCo is a toy manufacturer,'' Chad added. ''And that Lisa is—was Quality Control Manager. Eric was something or other in shipping. Which makes it plausible that they were using their positions in order to distribute the chips.''

Hannah watched his fingers squeeze the sides of his plastic cup. A shiver scampered over her hot skin. With vivid clarity, she recalled the feel of the rough, callus-covered pads of his thumbs against the sensitive skin of her neck. There had always been an urgent, almost obsessive air about the way Chad used to make love to her, seeming completely unaware of what he could do to her heart, yet increasingly mindful of, sometimes even fiendishly wicked with, his power over her body. He'd demanded primitive reactions from her no one else had made her feel before…or since.

It had been at times like these, when they were stuck in a motel room somewhere, forced to wait until they could continue their trace, when some of her most erotic memories were created. It was exactly at a time like this that they had created Bonny.

She wiped her damp palms against the gauzy material of her skirt. ''The personnel files say Lisa has a brother, but the sheet gives no first name or location, right? And the police information is so scanty it's pathetic.''

''It's my guess the FBI has been involved from the moment of arrest, which could explain why there's so little info.''

She stared at him, wondering why it sounded like he knew more than he was sharing.

Apparently unaware of her scrutiny, he stretched.

His jean-clad leg slid between hers under the sorry excuse for a table, rasping against her bare, suddenly oversensitive skin. She was instantly aware of every inch of male flesh a mere few feet away. When he didn't move, she assumed he didn't want to. Instead she shifted her legs away. She controlled the almost wild trembling of her fingers by flattening the faxed copy of the police file in front of her. It took her a moment, but she managed to compare the information with the little Elliott had given them.

She stared into Chad's eyes and recognized a familiar shadow of awareness in the smoky-gray depths. *He knows exactly what he's doing to me.*

The room was unbearably quiet. The only sounds those of ice cubes clinking in plastic glasses, the curtains stirring from the hot air drifting in through the window, and the low, even breathing of Bonny sleeping on the bed a few feet away.

Hannah lifted her hair from the back of her neck. "It's hot in here."

Chad watched her over the rim of his cup. "Yes, it is." He appeared suddenly agitated, abruptly running his fingers through his sandy-brown hair. "Anyway, I think we're looking at this thing from the wrong angle. What does what they stole have anything to do with how we find them?"

"Well, it would probably give us a better idea of exactly how much trouble they're in. Not just with the law, but with the others who obviously want these chips. Namely the two thugs in Persky's house."

Chad's gaze was on Bonny where she slept on the bed. Hannah shifted and he turned to stare at her for a

long, quiet moment. She began to wonder if he'd heard
her. Tucking her hair behind her ear, she thought about
repeating herself when he said, "Why in the hell didn't
you tell me, Hannah?"

Chapter Five

Hannah felt as if every last molecule of air had been sucked out of the room.

"Why in the hell didn't you tell me, Hannah?" Chad had said the words so softly she almost hadn't heard them. But she had. Her heart constricted in her chest. There it was. One of the questions she had been expecting and dreading. The first had never come. *He already knows Bonny's his.*

Chad leaned forward, his every muscle bunched. "Don't you think I had a right to know you'd had my baby?"

On the bed, Bonny twitched involuntarily. Hannah somehow managed to speak past the lump in her throat and asked him to lower his voice. The request caused Chad's jaw to flex and she feared he might talk louder.

"Why didn't I tell you?" she repeated, her voice quavering despite the calm she tried to infuse herself with. How could she be calm when he looked a word away from hating her? "I didn't tell you, Chad, be-cause…because you didn't want to know."

His gaze nailed her to the opposite wall.

"Hannah, if you say again that you can read my thoughts…"

"This has nothing to do with reading you, Chad," she said hesitantly, trying to fill in the gap his sudden silence created. "Please understand, I did think you had a right to know. I even tried tracking you down so I could tell you. But when I couldn't find you, I had to accept you didn't want to know anything about me…or Bonny."

He slowly sat back in his chair, giving her some breathing space. The distrustful expression on his face scared her more than any anger-filled stare. She'd hurt him. She was sorry for that. "You're one of the best, Hannah. You want me to believe you couldn't find me? Admit it, you didn't want to, because…"

He drifted off, leaving his words to ring in her head. "Because what, Chad? Because you might not have wanted me to keep her?" All sympathy for him dis-appeared, and the self-reliance that had seen her through fifteen long, lonely months resurfaced, thrum-ming through her body like an electrical charge. "Be-lieve me, that didn't have a thing to do with it. No matter what you might have said, I would have kept Bonny. She's *my* daughter." She sucked in a deep breath, but it only served to give her time to find fault. "And as to my not being able to find you…I might be one of the best, but so are you. You hid yourself better than any professional con because you knew exactly what not to do. Admit it, Chad. You didn't want to be found."

He got up from his chair and pulled back the curtain, his solid chest rapidly rising and falling. He stood there for a long time, saying nothing, saying everything. Hannah stared at the way his brown hair curled slightly against his neck, the soft material of his blue T-shirt and jeans as they clung to his slender, corded frame. She tried to imagine what it would feel like to be in his shoes. To learn that somewhere out there her baby had been born without her knowing. A second child, because the first had been ripped from her life. To discover someone she had shared her life with had kept something so vitally important from her.

Her anger slowly ebbed away.

"Damn it, Hannah, how could this have happened?"

She blinked at him and he turned and grasped his plastic cup.

"You're right. I didn't want to be found," he said. "I—I needed time to think after our breakup. Time to work everything out." He sought her gaze, looking as if he needed to convince her of something. "You have to believe me, if I had known—"

"Chad, I—"

Abruptly he turned away. She swallowed her words and swiped at a lone tear that plopped down her cheek and onto the table.

"Tell me one thing, Hannah."

She shifted her gaze to his back.

"Did you know you were pregnant when you asked me...what you did?"

Hannah's tongue felt like a wad of cotton in her mouth; her heart throbbed an erratic rhythm in her chest.

"Forget it. It doesn't matter," he said roughly. "It's all over." As if seeking reassurance in the commonplace, he took a long sip of his iced tea. "I need something stronger than this." He started for the door. "You want anything?"

The door slammed behind him before she could answer and she winced. He strode stiffly past the window in the direction of the minimart on the other side of the motel parking lot. The bright beam of a car's headlights stabbed her eyes and she leaned back, away from the invasive rays.

Hannah kneaded her forehead, denying the seductive urge to give in to the hot tears pressing against the backs of her eyes. Her and Chad's words fifteen months ago had been so very, very final. But time and circumstance somehow had dulled their significance, taking away their bite, making Hannah question if she had either heard or said them at all. But if there was one thing she knew, nothing, nothing would dull the memory of what had just happened.

Chad had said he'd needed time to work everything out. She pressed shaking fingertips against her closed eyelids. Time was something she had never had.

Trembling from head to toe, she slid her chair back from the table, urgently seeking the rock inside that had supported her so steadfastly before Chad had come back. Why did his reaction to not having been told about Bonny hurt her so much? Fifteen months had passed since their breakup. Fifteen months in which she had endured her pregnancy...alone. Gone through labor...alone. Learned to raise her child...alone. She had grown accustomed to being alone during those times when Bonny napped or slept, wrapping herself in the love she felt for her daughter even when she wasn't with her. She didn't need anything more than that. Did she?

Hannah pulled the file on the table closer to her, not really seeing it through a sheet of irrepressible tears.

"It's late," Chad said quietly.

She turned to find him leaning against the open door frame. She drew in a deep, unsteady breath at the sight of him tugging at his T-shirt. She scrubbed her cheeks with her fingertips and watched him take the shirt off, then mop his neck with it, the tanned, firm waves of his abdomen rippling as he moved.

She noticed he didn't have the "something stronger" he had gone after. Glancing at his duffel lying at the foot of the free bed, she remembered the vodka bottle she'd found inside earlier. He'd said he'd needed time to sort things out after their breakup. Had that bottle, and others like it, helped him do that? And had their conversation pushed him to seek comfort in liquor again?

Hating the bleak silence weighing down the already heavy air, Hannah motioned toward the table, grasping for something to ease her pain...their pain. And, strangely, above everything swirling between them hovered a stronger attraction, a need for him that hadn't been there before. She had always wanted Chad. But she had never needed him.

"Chad?"

He didn't acknowledge her query.

"Why did you come back?"

She wasn't aware she was holding her breath until she was forced to draw a fresh one. She wasn't sure how she knew, but she was pretty sure that he hadn't returned to New York solely because Elliott had called him. If that were the case, he would have gone on the trace on his own and not insisted to go with her.

He shifted his head to meet her gaze. "I came back

to apologize to you, Hannah.'' She saw the truth in his eyes. The sincerity. Also the pain. He again turned his back to her. ''I returned to tell you I was sorry. Only it looks like I have a whole lot more to be sorry for, doesn't it?''

Absently she watched him move around the room, taking things from his duffel, pulling the cover from the other bed, his words penetrating the batting her head seemed to be stuffed with. She didn't know quite what to say. She didn't know what she'd expected him to say, but what he had wouldn't even have made it in the top one hundred.

She stared at the papers in front of her on the table.

''Don't you...don't you think we should put the personal stuff aside?'' Her words sounded so far away, as if another person said them. ''We need to talk about the possibility that Persky and Furgeson were working with someone else. If they were, and we can uncover that person, he or she can probably lead us straight to them—''

''It's late, Hannah. I'm tired. You're tired. Everybody's tired.'' He stepped toward her and closed both files, but there was no anger in the move, only calm determination. ''Like they say, time flies when you're having fun.''

She slowly rose, her legs threatening to give way. She reached to close the curtains, the sound of a dull clatter near the open window halting her hands. Fear laced through her bloodstream, making her dizzy with the sudden shift. Chad instantly shut off the lights.

''What was that?'' he asked, standing close behind her. Too close.

''I don't know.'' She vaguely remembered the headlights that had pierced her eyes a few minutes earlier, when Chad had left. She swiveled to face him, finding herself in the cradle of his arms.

"What did you buy?" she whispered.

She sensed rather than saw him in the darkness. "Nothing."

"Did anyone follow you?"

"No."

Hannah reached for the can of pepper spray fastened to her concealed waist belt, trying to summon the strength she had lost during their encounter. Shifting to the other side of the window, she peeked through the crack between the curtain and the wall. A shadowy figure hurried down the darkened sidewalk, away from their room.

Chad opened the door. He bent and picked something up off the walkway. Hannah turned the lights back on.

"He's gone," she said quietly.

"Looks like our nighttime visitor is into playing kick the can." He held up a crushed soda can, then bent to put it back outside the door.

She shivered despite the heat. "I didn't see anyone pass the window."

"Neither did I. And an innocent passerby doesn't normally run in the other direction when you hear them."

Hannah rubbed her arms, unsure if she could handle this one more thing heaped on top of everything else. "Looks like we're being followed."

Chad eyed her, his gray eyes filled with an emotion she couldn't immediately identify. Concern? Fear? "That it does."

She stepped back to the window and peered out at the eerily quiet parking area and walkway. She recalled the two thugs at Eric Persky's house. Could their prowler have been one of them?

"Are you okay?" Chad asked.

Foolishly, Hannah wished he would put his arms around her, if only for a minute. If only to calm the demons haunting her from within...and to show her in a definitive way that he didn't hate her.

"I'm fine," she said, looking over her shoulder at Bonny sleeping soundly in the middle of the bed. "Maybe we're overreacting. Maybe the guy is a motel guest out for a stroll. Who else could it possibly be?"

"Not the FBI, that's for sure," Chad said quietly. "They would have barreled in here by now."

"Thanks for reminding me."

"Look, standing here all night waiting for the guy to return isn't going to accomplish anything. He won't be coming back. Let's say we get some sleep. We're going to need it."

She nodded numbly. "Sleep, yeah."

She carefully pulled back the covers next to Bonny, and slid under the sheet. Chad stood watching her and she rolled to put her back to him.

"Could you turn the lights out, please?" she whispered.

He flicked the switch. Darkness claimed the room, the outside streetlights backlighting the curtains. Hannah awkwardly tugged her skirt and bra off, laying them both next to the bed where she could put them back on at a moment's notice. She stared at the ceiling, listening to Chad rustle around, then she closed her eyes. How could she possibly sleep with her heart thudding, and every muscle aching with the restraint she used to keep herself from climbing into the other bed next to Chad?

"Hannah?"

His ragged voice reached out for her in the darkness.
"Yes?"

"She—Bonny, I mean—she looks just like you."

Hannah burrowed her face in her pillow and gave
herself over to the sadness clutching her heart.

The following morning Hannah shaded her eyes
against the overly bright sun rising up over the endless
gray of the Atlantic. She followed Chad up the walkway toward the casino, hiking an agitated Bonny up a
little higher on her hip, earning a grunt of protest in
response. At quarter after five, her daughter had awakened with a vengeance, filling the motel room with her
inconsolable wails and refusing to take her cereal or
even the strained peaches that had always been her favorite. Chad had paced the room restlessly, giving Hannah gazes she didn't know what to do with. From confusion and helplessness, to uneasiness, his expressions
ran the gamut. At least until he murmured something
and left the room, leaving Hannah to deal with the
crying baby alone.

Disentangling Bonny's chubby, curious fingers from
where they tugged mercilessly on her hair, Hannah
pressed her lips against her daughter's temple.

"You have another tooth coming in, don't you,
Munchkin?" she said quietly.

Bonny robustly delivered her response, her soft
mouth pinched. Despite the heat, Hannah hugged her
a little closer. She knew exactly how her daughter felt.
Being with Chad again after everything that had happened, and suffering his rejection in new and different
ways, she'd welcome the pain of an emerging tooth.
At least that pain would eventually go away. But his

acting like he didn't know what to do with her or Bonny...well, she feared that pain would stick around far longer.

She tugged her gaze away from where he walked next to her.

"Are you ready?" he asked.

Hannah hesitated, not fond of the idea of handing her daughter over to him. But they both knew she was the better person for the job of finding out who Rita Minelli was. A woman asking questions about another woman was almost always easier, while a man could be suspected of being a spurned boyfriend. Reluctantly she kissed Bonny and tried to pry the baby's hands from her hair.

"Now, you're going to have to hold on to her. When she decides she wants to go, she goes, and her lunges can be pretty hard to handle. And since she's teething, anything she gets her mouth on, she chews—"

"I'm familiar with taking care of babies, Hannah," Chad said quietly.

She gently bit her tongue, feeling stupid and inconsiderate. She supposed her overlooking that he'd not only had a child before, but a wife as well, was a subconscious protective measure. No, right now she didn't need the reminder that he'd already had a wife and child. A wife and child he had loved, been part of a family with...and tragically lost. She didn't want to think about his inability to love her in the same way. His reluctance to bond with their daughter the way he'd bonded with his lost son.

The picture that sat at the bottom of his duffel was reminder enough.

Bonny easily went to him. Too easily. Her daughter's mood lightened the instant Chad put his arms around her, no matter how awkwardly he did so.

"I—I shouldn't be long," she said haltingly, battling the urge to take her daughter with her.

Bonny tried to stuff her fingers into Chad's mouth and he caught them gently in his. "Take your time."

Hannah started to walk away, then stopped, hesitant to leave her child with a man who didn't care so much that she was his daughter, but was more concerned with the fact that he hadn't been told. She hastened her steps toward the casino entrance. She intended to do this as quickly as possible.

Chad watched as Hannah rushed to the casino entrance as if the devil had a death grip on her ankles. He knew she was nervous about leaving the baby with him. He stared at the flyaway tufts of dark red hair peppering the girl's head, not sure who was more worried about his being left alone with Bonny: Hannah or him.

He crossed the street, moving toward a park bench set up beneath a shady oak. He sat down and clumsily positioned Bonny on his lap, finding a sharp contrast between his tanned, corded forearm and her pale, chubby legs. The comparison struck him solidly in the solar plexus. He represented a bitter past with little hope for the future, while Bonny had a clean slate on which to write anything and everything she chose.

"Dah!"

Chad grimaced, torn between wanting to keep a safe distance between himself and the baby, and needing to crowd her closer. Inhale her sweet baby smell. Marvel in the feel of her tiny, soft body weighing in his arms.

What did he know about being a father? His own

father had been little more than a "maybe later" kind of dad who was rarely around, had never come to any of his baseball games, missed his two graduations, and hadn't bothered to come to the airport when he'd returned from serving in the Gulf War. The military had supplied Chad Hogan, Sr. with all he'd ever needed in a family. And when his mother died ten years ago the rift between him and his father had gaped even wider. The last time Chad had spoken to his father he'd been stationed at Twenty-nine Pines, California. Was he still there? Chad couldn't say. Not that he'd been exactly accessible himself for the past fifteen months.

No, his father hadn't given him a good example of paternal behavior. And Chad had gone on to make the same mistakes with his own wife and son.

Chad repositioned Bonny on his lap, realizing he'd never at any time in his life said, "I want to have a child." When Linda got pregnant with Joshua…well, that was just the way things went, wasn't it? You graduated from college, did your tour in the military—at least, according to the way he'd been raised—got married and had kids. He'd never made a conscious decision to take that path. That was what everyone did and he'd done it, too. Then he'd lost his wife and son and he'd realized that having families *was* a choice. A choice a man should give thorough thought to.

Of course all that didn't matter now. He *was* a father. And he needed to consider everything attached to that role in a way he hadn't before, had to stare all his faults in the face. Problem was, he didn't like what he saw.

A burst of pain shot up his right arm. A pain he quickly recognized was the result of Bonny chomping down on his forearm.

"Hey there, short stuff," he said gruffly. He pulled

the eight-month-old and her four teeth away from his flesh. "Do I look like a teething ring to you?"

Her answering giggle and the bright twinkle in her wide blue eyes as she looked at him were enough to knock the breath right out of him.

And enough to tell him that he didn't dare grow any more attached to the child in his arms than he already had. If it wasn't too late already.

"You don't want me as a father, Bonny," he said roughly. He used the towel Hannah had left with him to wipe at the slobber on her chin. "I can't be the type of dad you need. I'm afraid I'll never be able to look at you without thinking of…him. I'm terrified that I'll only end up disappointing you."

She jabbered, a frown marring her soft, feathery brow.

"Trust me, my staying out of your life just may be the best for you. For all of us."

He jerked his gaze away from her open curiosity, new emotions meshing with the others already crowding his chest. Feelings of regret. Bitterness that Hannah had never told him about her birth. And finally fear that he should not play a role in Bonny's life.

He imagined not seeing the little imp on his lap grow into a young woman, and a pain he'd never known seized his chest.

Bonny launched a fresh attack on his arm, thankfully giving him a pain of a whole other ilk to think about. Chad rose from the bench and swept her up into the air above him, gazing at the only solid proof that he existed in this world. "We need to get you a stroller, sweet pea."

He spotted a shop nearby and started in that direction.

Twenty minutes later he returned to the bench, Bonny strapped into a brand-new stroller the salesclerk had assured him was top of the line. She squinted at him against the sun. Opening one of the two bags he held, he took out a floppy pink hat and carefully put it on her head.

"You went shopping." Hannah's voice sounded odd as she came to stand behind him.

Chad turned to face her. "Uh, yeah." He held out the other bag. "I picked up something for you, too. You know, in case you felt left out."

She appeared not to know what to do.

"Take it, Hannah."

She did, but she didn't look inside at the form-fitting T-shirt he'd picked out.

Chad corralled the emotions connected to the decision he had yet to make, then took the photo she offered. He watched as she took Bonny from the stroller and propped her against her hip.

She said, "Our Rita Minelli is in there enjoying her morning coffee before punching in. Last stool at the far end of the bar. Looks just like her picture so maybe it wasn't taken so long ago."

Chad wondered at the relief that eased Hannah's tense features as she looked over the baby.

"Guess it's time for the phone call then, huh?" He frowned at the way she fussed over Bonny. What did she think? That he'd brainwashed their child during the fifteen minutes she'd been inside?

"Bonny and I will go get the car. Wait out front here when you're done."

He squinted against the sunlight as she hurried away. She hadn't looked at him directly since coming out of the casino.

Ever since seeing her with the baby the day before and realizing Bonny was his, he'd felt an odd sense of disorientation. He told himself it was because a man didn't find out every day that he had fathered a daughter that was now eight months old. And it wasn't every day that the child's mother looked as if she wanted nothing from him. Lord, she looked like she would be happier if he'd just up and disappear from the face of the earth.

He rubbed the back of his neck. Then why had she agreed to their partnership, however temporary? Sure, she had put up a fight initially, but it had been no more than a token protest. Even he knew that. And there was nothing keeping her here now. Unless...

Unless she needed the money.

Clenching his jaw, he turned toward the casino. Why hadn't that occurred to him before? In all the thinking he'd done on the situation, he'd never once stopped to consider how all this had impacted Hannah. Life as a single parent, much less a single mother in a career where you couldn't exactly take your baby to work if you couldn't find a sitter, had to be challenging at best. If for support reasons alone, she should have sought him out more diligently, sent child support agents, or whatever they were called, after him. Bonny was also his daughter, after all. His responsibility.

Chad slowed his step as he entered the casino. He realized then that Hannah, herself, had never made any mention of his financial responsibilities. And she probably wouldn't, either. Not the Hannah McGee he knew. No. One of the many characteristics he'd always admired about her was her strength. Her courage. It probably never even occurred to her to ask him for money. To ask anyone for help, for that matter. He figured her disposition likely stemmed from having limited family to rely on while growing up. Her mother had died during childbirth. Her father had been a cop and probably spent more hours on the job than off, then even he was taken from her while she was still a teen. Those two events alone were enough to majorly screw anyone up. It didn't take a psychologist to figure that out. But not Hannah. Instead she'd become a better, stronger person as a result of them.

God, he felt lower than the patterned pile carpeting he stood on. He also admired her more than he ever had.

Suddenly the sounds of the casino penetrated his thoughts and he remembered why he was there and what he had to do. Despite the early hour, the place bustled with activity. From the shining chandeliers in the lobby to the rows of one-armed bandits and gaming tables just visible through large archways, there was an aura of excitement, promise and a taste of anticipation. And a timelessness no watch could defeat.

And Chad wanted nothing to do with any of it.

He immediately spotted a pretty brunette sipping coffee and talking to the tender at the far end of the bar. He knew instantly it was Rita Minelli.

Striding toward two pay phones he had noted the night before, he took an Out Of Order sign from his pocket and taped it to one of them, then picked up the receiver of the other. Smoothing out the yellow page he had torn from the motel's phone book that morning, he inserted the coins and dialed. By now Hannah was out front with the car. The line rang and he shifted slightly, watching the bartender leave Rita and move to the other end of the bar.

"I have a message for Rita Minelli," Chad said the

instant the bartender picked up. "Tell her it's urgent that she come home immediately."

The bartender started to say something, but Chad pulled the receiver from his ear and hung it up. He slanted a gaze toward the bar. Come on, tell her.

One thing he had learned, the quicker the phone answerer relayed the message, the more urgency he conveyed, and the more likely it was the receiver of the message wouldn't check before following through on it. Especially in cases where illegal activity was involved. Chad clenched and unclenched his fists, watching the bartender poke at the body of the phone. Finally hanging up, the guy looked at Minelli and stepped in her direction.

"Here we go," Chad said, watching Minelli take her purse from where the bartender handed it to her from behind the bar.

The brunette hurried toward the door, not even giving the pay phones a second glance. Chad left the Out Of Order sign on the other phone and followed her out at a discreet distance.

"That must be it. The brownstone," Hannah said.

Chad slowed the Alfa a block away from the building Rita stopped her scratched and dented Chevy in front of. It was indeed a brownstone, but not in the same sense as those found in The Village or Upper West End of Manhattan. Instead, the building's first floor served as a secondhand furniture store, while the upper two floors were apparently divided into apartments. The label "brownstone" came from cheap brown shingles covering the outer walls of the building. Hannah's gaze drifted to the upper floors. Which one held Eric Persky, if indeed Persky was the one Minelli was hurrying home to?

A rusted Monte Carlo momentarily blocked her view and she frowned. The car looked familiar. She considered the darkly tinted windows, then remembered that a similar vehicle had nearly run her over in Queens yesterday. The Monte Carlo turned a corner, taking her thoughts with it.

Hannah reached for her door handle. Chad grasped her arm, sending an unwelcome warmth surging through her. A warmth that had nothing to do with the already stifling heat of the day, and everything to do with Chad.

"I'm going in. Alone." His stare dared her to object.

Hannah uneasily shrugged his hand off, for the first time in a very long time not knowing what to say. There was no mistaking the protective shadow in his eyes as he looked at her, then at Bonny in her car seat.

"You never offered to shoulder my share of the load before, Chad. Why now?"

He opened his mouth apparently to answer, then closed it again.

Hannah sighed. "Oh, I get it. Now I'm a mother and I'm incapable of bringing in even a white-collar criminal." She took a deep breath. "Having a baby doesn't incapacitate a person, Chad. I can get this guy just as easily as you can."

"Did I say you couldn't?" he said, his gaze shifting to Minelli, who had parked her car in front of the brownstone.

"You might as well have."

He opened the driver's door. "This has nothing to do with your being a mother, Hannah." His guilty expression seemed to indicate otherwise. "If it makes you feel any better, you can get the next one, okay?"

Hannah opened her mouth to protest further, to tell him she'd done just fine on her own up until now, thank you very much, when he curved the fingers of his right hand over her jaw and slid them back toward her ear. He gently pressed the callused pad of his thumb against her lips to prevent her from saying anything.

Her breath caught in her lungs.

His gaze meandered over her hair and he seemed to lose his train of thought. "I'd forgotten how soft your hair is," he murmured.

Even she heard her thick swallow. He smiled and she felt her cheeks go hot.

"Please, Hannah, don't argue with me on this one. We'll talk about the how, when and why later, okay?"

The pressure of his thumb and his fingers was suddenly gone and so was he as he climbed from the car. Hannah stifled a needy whimper.

It had been so long since she'd felt exclusively like a woman. A young, desirable woman who wanted to give as much as receive pleasure. So very long since she'd been kissed silly, made love to. Somewhere down the line she'd convinced herself her happiness could come solely from being a good mother to Bonny. The signals her body sent her told her how very wrong she'd been.

Mystified, she sank back into the seat, watching him sprint after the brunette who had disappeared into the building's apartment entrance. She caught herself appreciating the solid curve of his rear beneath his faded jeans and purposely turned her head. Beyond her confusing sexual feelings toward Chad, she didn't quite know what to make of his behavior this morning. Last night he was so upset with her. Today... Today it seemed he was going out of his way to make the situation easier for her. The leap only added to her baffled state.

Chad disappeared into the building and Bonny started crying in the back seat. Hannah started to turn toward her when something caught her eye. More specifically, someone. From the doorway Chad had entered, a dark-haired man stepped outside. Then from the shadows nearby, another joined him and both crossed the street, meeting a third man with balding hair and glasses. The three spoke for a moment, then they strode down the street away from her and the car, their gait easy. Too easy.

The smell of dust and heat assaulted Chad as he shadowed Rita Minelli. Sounds drifted down the stairs. Morning cartoons...someone doing dishes...the smell of something cooking. All distinct, ordinary sounds.

As he neared the second floor, he heard the squeaking of a door being opened. He ducked off to the side of the stairwell.

"Why, Miss Minelli," an elderly woman said, stepping into the hall and smoothing down the material of her plain, flower-print dress. "This *is* a surprise. Aren't you supposed to be working this morning?"

Rita Minelli didn't look too pleased by the woman's greeting, but she stopped to address her neighbor just the same. "Yes, Mrs. Gardner, I am. But something came up. If you'll excuse me..."

She hadn't moved two feet before the old woman said, "Then you must not have been home when I heard that noise."

Rita froze as did Chad where he hid.

"Noise?" Rita asked.

The old woman smiled. "Normally I'm not one to pry in others' affairs, but this noise was a bit difficult to ignore. Interrupted my breakfast, it did. Sounded like someone moving furniture around. But that couldn't be, I told myself. You had already left for work. And it was only eight o'clock in the morning."

Chad wiped his forehead with the back of his hand, his jacket not helping the heat but necessary to hide the 9 mm revolver he carried.

"I'm sure you're mistaken, Mrs. Gardner. It was probably something outside," Rita said.

The old woman was unconvinced.

"I'm rarely mistaken, Miss Minelli. Especially when two men came from the apartment right afterward, and neither of them was your gentleman friend. One went out that way." She motioned toward the back hall. "The other went out the front."

Rita hurried toward the door to the next apartment, her hands obviously shaking as she fumbled with her keys. She began to slide her key into the lock, but the pressure caused the door to open instead. Chad cursed. Despite how secure Eric—and he was sure Eric was the elusive "gentleman friend"—felt in his girlfriend's place, he doubted the bail-jumper would leave the door unlocked.

Chad bolted into the hall and shifted the brunette away from the front of the door.

"Step aside, Miss Minelli." He motioned for Rita to get behind him. "Stay here. It may not be safe."

Rita was visibly shaken. "Safe? What do you mean? Why wouldn't it be safe? Who are you?"

"FBI," Chad said, blocking the woman's words out

and concentrating instead on the sounds—or lack of them—inside the apartment. He wasn't taking any chances. Sliding his hand under his jacket, he withdrew his revolver.

Rita gasped, then clamped her hand over her mouth.

''Maybe you should go have a cup of tea with Mrs. Gardner,'' he said, nudging Rita to where her neighbor still stood in the hall watching them.

Chad slowly pushed the door open, squinting into the murky darkness. Nothing but silence. Thick curtains were drawn against the morning sun, and very likely against the heat. Not that it helped. The small apartment was as hot as an overcrowded jail cell. He stepped warily inside, scanning the dim interior. The living room was off to his right, threadbare furniture and scarred wood tables the decorator's choice, while off to his left was a small dining room. He leaned in that direction, earning a clean view into the empty kitchen, the muzzle of his gun pointed toward the ceiling, but ready to fire at the first sign of threat.

Everything appeared normal enough. In fact, too normal. And too quiet.

On the far wall were two closed doors. The bedroom and the bathroom were his guess. He silently crossed the room and flanked the door to the bedroom. He smoothly and quickly opened it, his pistol following his gaze as he visually searched the interior. Nothing. No Persky. Only a pair of slacks draped across the made bed gave any indication that a man had been there. And very recently at that. He opened and closed the closet door, then backtracked to stand outside the bathroom.

Unlike the bedroom door, which had been slightly ajar, the bathroom door was solidly shut. Chad stood flush against the wall next to it and slightly moved his head closer to the wood, listening for any sounds. No water splashed in the sink. No toilet refilling. No rustling of clothing that would accompany someone's movements.

Slowly reaching out, he gripped the tarnished doorknob. The old woman next door said she hadn't seen Persky leave. That meant he had to be in the apartment somewhere.

"You put your career before everything and everyone." His wife Linda's voice chose that moment to haunt him. *"Even before Joshua and me."*

"I'm doing this for you," was his forever ready response.

But it wasn't Linda's face he saw now; it was Hannah's. In her arms she held a crying Bonny, much as she had at the motel that morning when she'd tried to comfort the teething baby. And he'd walked out.

A rivulet of sweat trickled down over his brow, but he ignored it and threw the door open, this time staying right where he was with his gun at the ready rather than filling the open doorway.

Nothing.

He cautiously moved to peer into the small bathroom and immediately spotted Persky. Only he had nothing to fear from the man. No one would have anything to fear from Eric Persky ever again.

Chapter Six

Hannah carefully held the bathroom door to look inside. The man who had to be Persky was sprawled in the old claw-foot tub, naked and very obviously dead. The sound of Rita Minelli crying in the nearby kitchen completed the grim picture.

Shuddering, Hannah closed the door then met Chad in the hall. Bonnie squealed and leaned in her direction. She took her from Chad.

Chad shrugged out of his jacket, his gun and holster plainly visible. "Let's see if Miss Minelli knows where Furgeson is."

"Do you think Lisa Furgeson could be behind this?"

"Hell, I don't know, Hannah. Money has a strange effect on people." He studied her face. "If she didn't do it, she may be next on the killer's hit list."

For the second time that day, Chad did something she would have never expected. Slowly, as if weighing the wisdom of such a move, he brushed a strand of damp hair from her cheek, then rested his hand on her shoulder. She stared at him, spellbound. The curious expression in his eyes battled with something else, causing her heart to skip a beat.

"Are you okay?" he asked.

She stared at him, unable to breathe.

"I'm fine," she forced out, avoiding his gaze by concentrating on the stubble marring his strong chin.

Apparently not pleased that she'd been forgotten, Bonny squealed willfully. Hannah smoothed her hair back, then looked at Chad, her heart contracting. This wasn't turning out to be a routine case at all. The way it was going, this skip-trace was their most dangerous to date. She shuddered, trying to tell herself everything would be okay, but she wasn't buying it.

"Come on, let's go see what Minelli's got to say," Chad said.

In the cramped, fried fish-smelling confines of the kitchen, Chad held out a box of tissues. Rita Minelli grabbed a handful. Angling the baby away from the buttons of the wall-mounted telephone, Hannah punched out Elliott Blackstone's number in New York. She didn't even want to speculate on how Chad had introduced himself to Minelli.

"Rita, there are a few questions we have to ask you."

Red-rimmed eyes lifted. "Who would do this?" she whispered. "He never hurt anyone. Who would want to hurt him?"

Hannah frowned at the restless baby in her arms, waiting for the line to ring.

"Rita, what did Eric tell you about his situation? Did

he share anything with you about his personal finances, partnerships?'' Chad asked.

''I'm not sure what you mean.'' She rolled her eyes to stare at the ceiling. ''The only thing I know about his personal finances is that he said his aunt died. A distant one, I guess, who left him a large inheritance.'' Tears burst from her eyes anew. ''We had plans. Once his attorney cut through the red tape we were going on a long trip.''

Hannah shifted the receiver slightly so the baby could hear the ringing. Bonny instantly quieted.

Chad crouched down so he was at eye level with Rita, but there was no gentleness in the action. ''Did Eric ever mention a woman named Lisa Furgeson to you?''

The line rang once, then Blackstone barked a hello into the receiver. Hannah pressed it tightly against her ear, ignoring Bonny's vocal protests.

''Elliott?''

''Hannah! My God, I've been going crazy here waiting for you to call. Where in the hell are you? What is going on? Did you find Persky and Furgeson—''

''Slow down,'' Hannah said. ''One question at a time, El.''

She could practically see the bail bondsman trying to control himself and distantly wondered what color silk-blend suit he wore today. Probably the green, since he'd worn the blue yesterday.

''All right, all right.'' He enunciated the words carefully. ''Tell me, what's going on? Is Hogan with you?''

''Yes, Hogan is with me.'' She paused. ''Has anyone been asking about us?''

''Anyone?'' he repeated loudly. ''Try the FBI, for

God's sake. Some guy named McKay who wants you two—badly."

"Great." Hannah clutched the receiver. Chad had been right in not returning to her apartment before leaving New York. Obviously the agents *had* gotten her plate number. That they had already talked to Blackstone meant McKay was a fast worker.

Hannah heard a female voice on Elliott's side of the line, then he said, "Look, Hannah, I got an important call I've got to take. Hold on a minute, okay?"

She opened her mouth to object, then sighed, the sound of Muzak filling her ear. Rocking Bonny back and forth to quiet her, she looked to where Chad still knelt in front of Rita Minelli.

"Think, Miss Minelli. Lisa Furgeson. Does it ring any bells?" Chad asked the shaken woman.

"I don't know about the first name," she said. "But Eric's attorney's last name was Furgeson."

Chad met Hannah's gaze. "When was the last time Eric talked to...his attorney, Miss Minelli?"

"I don't know. I can't think! Yesterday, maybe." She rubbed her nose with the tissue. "Yes, definitely yesterday."

"Eric made the call from here? To this Furgeson?"

Rita mopped her cheeks with a wad of tissue. "Yes."

"What time?" Chad pressed.

Shrugging, Rita obviously tried to recall. "About four, I guess. Maybe four-thirty."

Blackstone's voice came back on the line. Hannah stretched the twisted phone cord to give her enough length to step into the living room.

"Elliott, I have some good news and some bad

news," she said quietly, so Rita Minelli wouldn't overhear. "It's Persky."

"What is it? Did you find him?"

"Yes, we found him, all right." She lowered her voice further. "We found him in his girlfriend's bathroom—dead."

Silence drifted across the line and Hannah made no attempt to break it. Finally he said, "What's the bad news?"

This wasn't the first time a target had showed up dead. Though the other two times it had happened to Hannah, the deaths had come about as a result of natural causes. Neither occasion had been anything to celebrate, but she had gotten her bounty nonetheless.

A black-and-white poster from the old Western era filled her mind. Dead Or Alive, the signs always read above simple sketches of the person in question. The same rules applied today, even though they weren't advertised.

She cuddled Bonny closer. "The bad news is that Furgeson wasn't with Persky and we haven't a clue where she is—"

The line suddenly went dead. Hannah peered around the kitchen doorway to find Chad pressing down the cut-off button and holding out his hand for the receiver. Bonny giggled and reached for his hand.

"I can't believe you just did that," Hannah said.

"I need the phone." He took the receiver from her when she didn't offer it. He glanced at her and the baby. The gray of his eyes had changed again to warm mercury. "What did Elliott have to say? He was pretty relieved, I bet."

"*Relieved* isn't the word," she said. "What are you doing?"

"I'm going on the assumption the call Persky made from here yesterday was long-distance. If that's the case, Minelli's carrier will have a record of it." He paused. "If I can access the records, bingo. We'll have Furgeson."

Chad asked Rita for her phone number and verified who her carrier was. She answered both and he turned toward the olive-green telephone.

Rita loudly blew her nose. "But Eric never charged his calls to me."

"Do you mean he used a phone card whenever he called anyone?" Hannah asked.

Rita nodded. "He always kept it in his wallet. Said he didn't want to make me pay any large telephone bills."

Rita Minelli burst into a fresh bout of tears at the reminder of her lover's thoughtfulness. Hannah squeezed her shoulder, the baby following her lead by laying her chubby hand on top of Rita's head.

A few hours later, the Alfa Romeo safely stored in long-term parking at the Atlantic City International Airport, Chad sat back in the coach seat and adjusted his awkward hold on Bonny when the plane hit a pocket of turbulence and lurched forward. The phone number Persky had called yesterday was tucked safely in his wallet. With a little charm, a lot of cajoling and a hard luck story about an ill mother, he'd gotten the long-distance service rep to give him the number with a Houston, Texas, area code. It was the only number Persky had called, and he'd called it twice before he met the bullet with his name on it. Chad absently rubbed his forehead. He only hoped Furgeson was still at the number and hadn't moved on already.

Next to him, Hannah dozed. Chad lay his head against the seat and watched her. Repressing the urge to push back a red curl that lay against her cheek, he thought she looked exhausted. As well she should, since she hadn't gotten much sleep the night before. Hell, he hadn't gotten much sleep, either. He'd spent most of the night alternately listening to Hannah restlessly toss and turn and Bonny make soft sucking noises and occasional cooing sounds. Both unfamiliar sounds to him. Somewhere near five in the morning he'd finally drifted off, only to be awakened with a start to Bonny's crying and, for a weighty moment, he'd been flung back in time when it hadn't been Bonny's cries that filled his ears, but his son, Joshua's. Chad closed his eyes against the reminder.

Concentrate on the case, Hogan. The rest will work itself out. He tightened his hold on his slippery daughter who didn't appear interested in sleeping and hoped he was right.

They'd get to Houston, find Lisa Furgeson, and then contact Randy McKay at the FBI before McKay found them by tracing the tickets he'd put in his name. Then he'd barter for the slate to be wiped clean so he and Hannah would have some sort of lives to return to when all this was over. Bonny squealed and he loosened his hold, allowing her to bounce around on his lap and entwine her wet fist in his T-shirt. Of course, in order to get McKay to agree to anything, Chad needed something to barter with. Something more than his past connection to the FBI agent. The way this trace was going, he was sure he'd come up with something. He had to.

It was a dumb move to have got Hannah in trouble with the FBI. Looking at Bonny, he guessed it was pretty dumb he'd gotten himself in trouble, as well. Even if his identification wasn't totally fraudulent. He just hadn't touched it in four years. Not until he needed it again. And need it he did. He intended to use every fraction of power he had to end this trace so that his daughter was no longer in danger.

Chad watched the baby toss her teething ring to the airplane floor. He closed his eyes and sighed. He only hoped the person Persky had called in Houston had indeed been Lisa Furgeson.

The soft, feathery feel of something against his cheek brought his eyes back open and he stared at the eight-month-old girl in his lap. She made her favorite "Dah" sound. Chad reminded himself that "Dah" meant dog. Not anywhere close to Daddy. Though he wondered if there was much of a difference in Hannah's eyes. He'd acted like a rangy mutt when she'd asked him to marry her. His need to set things straight between them was what brought him back. Only he'd discovered he was an even meaner dog than he could have ever imagined.

Bonny studied him intently, her blue eyes wide with curiosity as she patted her stubby, damp fingers against his stubbled chin. He caught her wrist and spontaneously brought her fingertips to his mouth and nibbled on them, eliciting an excited squeal. Despite the pang of doubt at having given himself over to the playful gesture, he smiled. Really smiled. For the first time in, it seemed, forever.

In that instant, he knew that despite all his posturing, all his vows not to bond with her, the little girl had stolen her way into his heart. He released her hand, suspecting Bonny had found a permanent home in his heart the moment he first laid eyes on her, even before he realized she was his daughter.

"You're going to be a little beauty, just like your mom," he said soberly. Bonny continued to probe his face, almost as if learning him, familiarizing herself with him. She tweaked his nose and he frowned, trying to pry her fingers from his face. He succeeded, but she gave a shrill shriek of annoyance. He chuckled. "Obviously you're going to be just as ornery as Mom is, too."

He tried to distract her by offering her the barf bag sticking out of the chair pocket in front of him. What would have happened had Hannah told him she was pregnant fifteen months ago? He didn't dare prod too hard, afraid what he might find if he rummaged through the past too diligently. Hannah had come into his life at a time when he hadn't cared much about anything. He had been wandering from job to job, not throwing himself into much of anything until he discovered bounty hunting. It wasn't until much later that he figured out his fascination with the profession had more to do with the hope that a crazed skip-tracer could do what he couldn't—namely, end his suffering in a permanent way—than any real need to prove anything.

Then came Hannah.

Bonny smiled at him, and Chad grinned back. He plucked a bottle of juice from the bag on the floor and offered it up. The baby took it, jabbering on about something or other as she put it into her mouth.

Chad remembered that Blackstone had sent him and Hannah out on the same trace. Upon meeting her, he had been immediately drawn to her colorful spirit, her fresh, direct personality, her slender, tempting body. She was so full of life that whenever he was around her, he couldn't help but feel her incredible vitality seep into him, warm him, make him feel something other than the numbness he had been living with. And it had been her directness that convinced him that perhaps they could forge something workable together. When she'd moved in with him, he'd told her straight out that they'd never marry. That he could never marry again. That he didn't have anything left to bring to a marriage. He had guessed that telling her once would be enough. Obviously he guessed wrong. Because marriage was the one thing she wanted from him that he could never give.

He watched Bonny's eyes droop closed, then she swayed toward his chest. She caught herself and jerked upright, only to sway in his direction again a few seconds later. Finally she gave in to her tired body and snuggled against his chest, the bottle dropping from her mouth to join the teething ring on the floor.

The seat belt light dinged on. Chad glanced at Hannah. Even asleep, she exuded that same vitality that had drawn him to her three years ago. He supposed it could be her bright, wild red hair that gave that impression, but knew it was much, much more than that. Hannah was a fighter. A passionate lover of life. And most of all, she was a survivor. That much was evident from the sleeping baby in his arms.

Still, since seeing her again in Elliott's office the day before, he was coming to realize that she was right in saying that things had changed. But he suspected their take on the changes were different. Several times since yesterday he'd witnessed a vulnerability in her that had never been a part of her makeup. A fear that had caused her to call to him at Persky's house. A hesitation that made her involvement in the present situation all the more dangerous.

This new side to Hannah made him feel that much worse for having hurt her before. And made him hate himself for knowing he'd have to hurt her again.

"What are you thinking?"

Chad's gaze flicked to Hannah's eyes to find them open. Seemed Bonny's uncanny ability to move from sleep to wakefulness was an inherited skill. The only evidence that she'd been asleep at all was the huskiness of her voice. He cleared his own throat. "Just wondering if it's Furgeson we're going to find at the end of this flight."

She turned her head and tried to work the tangles out of her curly hair with her fingers. An impossible task he longed to do himself.

"Did you have a difficult pregnancy?" he found himself asking.

She looked at him for a long moment, apparently trying to decipher if she'd heard him right. "I, um, wouldn't say it was difficult, exactly." She lay her hand against one of Bonny's plump legs, then covered her with an airplane blanket. "*Challenging* is more the word I would use." She smiled. "Much like Bonny herself."

"Did you have morning sickness?"

"Oh, yes. The beginning of my second trimester, especially, was intolerable. My OB-GYN wanted to submit my name as the master of projectile vomiting."

Chad chuckled, thinking of a scene he could only imagine.

She shook her head. "Not a pretty picture."

Bonny moved in her sleep. Chad tried to reposition her.

"Here, why don't you let me take her."

Chad reluctantly removed his hands so Hannah could scoop Bonny from his chest and cuddle her against her own. Bonny gave a brief, baffled look around, then settled immediately back to sleep. Chad put the blanket over both of them and caught himself smoothing the blue flannel over Hannah's leg. He glanced up into her face to find her watching him curiously, heat evident in her eyes.

He coughed and sat back. "Tell me more."

He felt her gaze on his profile. "Are you sure you want to hear it?"

"Yes," he murmured.

"Okay...." She was silent for a long moment. "Since this was my first pregnancy, the doctor said chances were I'd be in labor for what seemed like forever— But you, well, you probably already know that."

Why would he...? Then he realized she was talking about Linda. "No, actually, I didn't." He didn't explain that when his son was born, he was too busy with yet another high-priority case to know what was happening. Instead he met her gaze. "So did you? Have a long labor?"

Hannah's sudden smile was contagious. "As luck would have it, our little girl was nearly born in a cab. She was in a hurry to get out and greet the world, and nothing or no one was going to stop her."

Chad grew more and more aware that he loved to hear her talk. "Sounds like somebody else I know."

He watched the smile slowly fade from her face. She seemed to put extra concentration into finger-combing Bonny's red hair. "Was your son—I mean, was he a lot like Bonny?"

"Joshua?" For the first time he shared his name with

her, and he wasn't sure who was more surprised. He wasn't so much surprised by the fact that he'd said it, but that he hadn't choked up while doing so. He suspected he hadn't said his son's name aloud since losing him. "No. Joshua was quiet. Too quiet, it seemed. He was happy, smiled a lot. But quiet."

He felt Hannah's hand on his before he even realized she'd moved. He welcomed the warm feel of her fingers against his as she leaned her head against his shoulder. "Seeing Bonny must bring back a lot of painful memories of Joshua."

He ran his other hand over hers. "Hannah, when we get to Houston, I want you and Bonny to turn back for New York."

Her hand in his went still, then she slowly withdrew it. "I can't do that, Chad."

"If it's the money, don't worry about it. I'll still give you half the bounty on both traces." He looked at her. "Then there's the matter of the back support I owe you—"

Hannah sat up so quickly, Bonny was startled awake. "I don't want any money from you." He watched her throat convulse around a swallow. "Is that why you think I told you about Bonny? Because I wanted money from you?"

Chad briefly closed his eyes, wondering if she could have misinterpreted his words more. "No, Hannah, that's not—"

"I don't, you know. Want money from you. I'm perfectly capable of looking after all of Bonny's needs on my own."

He groaned. "I know you are—"

"So you can just forget about my going back to New York, because it's not going to happen."

He stared at her for a long moment. At the heightened color in her cheeks. The challenging flash in her eyes. The protective way she cradled Bonny who was also watching him, her thumb in her mouth.

"Okay," he said, a smile tugging at his mouth.

Hannah's eyebrows lifted a fraction of an inch. He could virtually see the wind leaving her sails. She sat back again and tucked her hair behind her ear. "Okay."

"On the going back to New York part, I mean," he added. "The rest... Well, the rest we can talk about when we get home."

Home.

Hannah appeared as surprised by his use of the word as he did. But neither of them had a chance to comment as the pilot announced their descent into Houston.

"We probably could have driven here quicker." Hannah rolled her shoulders, attempting to loosen the kinks, though it wasn't her muscles she was concerned about. It was the funny tickle in her stomach caused by Chad's genuine interest in the details of her pregnancy. The niggle of confusion edging her thoughts as the result of his request that she and Bonny go back to New York.

She slid a gaze to where Chad walked beside her holding Bonny, even though he also rolled the folded stroller. His expression as he looked at their daughter was more relaxed than she'd seen it recently. She forced the thought away, not ready to consider the changes he was going through when she was going through so many of her own.

She patted her concealed stun gun, making certain it was stable after claiming it from security, having checked it in with Chad's gun and his duffel in Atlantic City.

Bonny lunged for her and Hannah hoisted her into her arms. She led them to a row of chairs, then fumbled through the diaper bag for a handy wipe. "Tell me, Chad, what do we do if the person at the other end of this leg doesn't turn out to be Furgeson?" She hated to ask the question, but time was ticking by. The four days they were given was now down to two. It wasn't so much the money involved that concerned her, though she certainly needed it. She didn't like not knowing what Chad would do when the manhunt was over.

He watched her clean the juice smears off Bonny's cheek. "I guess we'll have to cross that bridge when we come to it."

Bonny leaned away from her and started crying. Hannah threw the wipe into a nearby garbage bin.

Chad studied the crowded lobby. "All I know is that we'd better find Furgeson ASAP. The others looking for her are definitely not afraid of guns or using them."

Hannah shivered. Whoever killed Eric Persky would probably not hesitate to do the same to Furgeson. Unless Furgeson was the power behind the trigger.

She blinked when Chad stared at her. She fought the urge to swipe at her own face, afraid she had a peanut crumb or salt stuck to her upper lip, compliments of the plane ride. "What? Why are you looking at me that way?"

His expression was unreadable. "What way, Hannah?"

The low, husky sound of his voice made her realize his probing gaze had nothing to do with peanuts. She tried to concentrate on straightening the top of Bonny's yellow jumper.

"You know what way." Why was it, even when discussing the most innocuous subject, one well-directed look from Chad could make her feel incredibly...unmotherlike?

"No, Hannah, I don't know." He crossed his arms over his chest.

Her gaze locked with his across the open air. That maddening expression was back. The one that said so much, though he said nothing. Like how much he'd like to touch her. The unspoken promise that if she succumbed, she wouldn't regret it. At least not until after he was gone.

"Come on," he said, tugging his gaze away from hers, and taking the suggestion with it. "I say we find a motel and get some rest before we begin our search for the elusive Lisa Furgeson."

Hannah tried to strengthen her watery knees. "Okay. But first I think it would be a good idea to get a newspaper and a map."

Gathering her wits about her, she headed for a newsstand and bought both items. Meeting Chad back in the wide concourse, she attempted to figure out exactly what his attention meant. If it indeed meant anything at all beyond "I'm a man, you're a woman, and it's been a long time since we've been intimate."

He touched her arm and halted midstep, staring at something across the way.

"What is it?" she asked.

He began walking again. "Don't look now, but see those two men over by the doors? They may be FBI."

Hannah ignored his suggestion not to look. Through the windows, solid sheets of rain slid down the glass.

Just inside stood the men Chad was talking about. "Oh God, I think those are the guys I saw outside Rita's apartment in Atlantic City. Right before you went in and found Persky."

Chad glanced back to the doors where the two men in identical dark blue suits stood like stiff sentinels. Hannah crowded Bonny closer, earning a wet, indignant squeal.

Digging coins from his pocket, Chad slipped them into one of the middle telephone slots. "They're making their way toward us. Act natural."

She watched him punch out a series of numbers. "Natural? I'm not sure what that is anymore." She tried not to glance in the men's direction. "Who are you calling?"

"No one." He held the receiver to the side of his face, grasping Bonny's hand when she reached for the instrument. "I'm stalling until we can figure out what to do."

"Do you really think they're FBI?" She recalled the conversation between the two men at Persky's house in New York. *They* definitely hadn't been law enforcement agents. But these ones looked exactly like them. She rubbed her forehead, trying to piece everything together. First Persky's house in New York...then Minelli's place in Atlantic City...now here. Could they be the same men? If so, how did they fit in to all this?

"I don't know, Hannah, but if they are FBI, we're in a bit of a jam." Chad's mouth tightened around his smile.

"Great." She shifted her weight from one foot to the other. "What do we do now?"

"We wait to see what they're going to do. It might not even be us they're after."

"Right, somewhere in the airport are probably fifty other people on their short list."

Chad's smile turned genuine for a moment. "I always did love your sense of humor."

He did? Hannah felt suddenly warm, inside and out. "Just stop with the jokes, all right? We could be in serious trouble." The men stopped. "Jeez, they look like something out of a Bond film."

"Yeah, all one of them needs is a mouthful of metal." Chad grinned at her grimace. "Okay." He turned away for a moment, feigning conversation with the person he pretended to call. "They're standing guard at the doors. That means leaving the airport is out of the question for now."

Hannah nodded. "So we should try to lose them inside the building."

"A building we've never been in before," Chad said half to himself, considering the foot traffic.

"Yes, but if luck is with us, our two friends don't know their surroundings, either."

"That would make our job a little easier," he agreed.

"Are you ready?"

"No."

Hannah stared at him. With a low chuckle, he replaced the telephone receiver in its cradle, ignoring the clink of his coins as the machine returned them. The baby reached for him and Hannah shifted her away.

"What's the plan?" she asked.

"I don't know yet, but we'll figure something out. Whatever you do, you can't use your weapons. It would only complicate matters if they are FBI."

As if she would with the baby around. Hannah watched him open the stroller then allowed him to take

Bonny so he could fasten her in. The vocal eight-month-old wasn't pleased with the new seating arrangements and gave an indignant wail. Chad leaned over and put on the funny little hat he'd bought for her, instantly placating her. Hannah tucked her arm into Chad's as he steered them back into the terminal area, away from the outer doors and the two men guarding them.

Her heart beat a steady, loud cadence in her chest as she glanced around, pretending their walk was a leisurely stroll. She ignored the fear that swept up from her stomach. If the two men were FBI, they presumably wouldn't be alone. Somewhere in the building at least another couple of them would be waiting and watching as well. She swallowed. What would that mean for her and Chad if they were caught and charged with fraud? She gazed anxiously at Bonny. What would it mean for her? Hannah's throat grew dry. They had to find a way out of this mess.

They moved fifty feet.

"All right, they're following us," Chad said.

Hannah fought the urge to turn around. "Now what? We have no chance of losing them if they shadow our every move."

"Hannah, Hannah, Hannah," Chad spoke quietly. "You should know by now chance plays no role in our lives. Skill does."

"Sometimes you can be such a braggart, Chad."

"If it gets us out of here alive and free, does it matter?"

Hannah swung her gaze to him. Alive? Did he believe their lives were in jeopardy? The baby made a "hah" sound and Hannah stared at her, realizing Bonny was trying to say her name.

"Oh, no, it's Mommy to you, Munchkin," she said firmly.

Chad's fingers curled around her upper arm. An immediate jolt of awareness swept over her skin. "What does that make me?" he asked.

Hannah's cheeks blazed under his scrutiny. Despite the possibility for chaos swirling around them, the two men who even now shadowed them, Hannah couldn't have felt more aware of Chad. More conscious of their tentative personal situation than if they had been completely, utterly alone, away from the rest of the world.

"I guess that's up to you, Chad." She met his gaze meaningfully, trying to read him, hoping for some sort of response, positive or otherwise, to let her know where things stood between them after all that had happened in the past two days.

Her hopes were quickly dashed as Chad turned his head, leaving her to wonder if he'd even asked the startling question, or if she had answered it.

She averted his gaze, trying to calm the rapid beating of her heart. She reminded herself that they didn't have time for this. Didn't have time to probe past hurts, to talk about a future that at best was immediately in danger.

She jerked her gaze back to his face, having found the weapons she needed to crowd Chad from her mind, and her heart—however temporarily.

"I've got it," she said suddenly.

She ignored Chad's skeptical expression and motioned for him to resume walking.

"You have to go to the bathroom," she told him.

The rest was a blurry sketch with too many variables. She took the stroller from him and moved it away from a shelf of stuffed animals Bonny was eyeing a little too keenly. For her sake, they had to make this work.

"After that?" Chad asked.

Ahead, signs pointed to the rest rooms. Hannah noted them and the shops surrounding the entrance hall. Her gaze settled on a shop selling postcards near the corridor that led to the bathrooms.

"Bonny and I are going to give you enough time to reach the men's room, keeping the guys out here with us."

Chad grimaced, obviously not enthralled with her plans. They'd stopped just outside the hallway.

"I'll give you three minutes," she said. "Then I'm gonna get the urge to go to the ladies' room. That's when you'll jump out from the men's room across the hall and tackle one of them while I go after the other. Now go."

He disappeared down the long hall, shaking his head as he went.

Hannah stared after Chad for a long moment, then moved down the hall. "Now, you don't suppose they have a book here detailing the best way to disarm an FBI agent, do you, Bonny?"

Her daughter giggled as if understanding the question and amused by its ridiculousness.

Hannah feigned interest in the postcards, casting a cautious glance in the direction of the two men watching her as she did so. Neither followed Chad to the rest rooms. With her standing outside waiting for him, it was a pretty safe bet he would return.

Abandoning the postcard rack, she pointed the stroller toward the rest rooms.

"Come on, guys," she whispered, the men following quickly behind her. "Don't get too close or you'll screw up my plan."

The hallway was long and hollow. The sound of her footsteps and the men's mingled, sounding strangely out of tune as theirs sped up. Risking a glance behind her, Hannah increased her pace, earning an excited cry from Bonny.

"Okay, Chad," Hannah whispered, eyeing the closed door to the men's room a few feet away. "You can jump out any time now."

The echo of the footsteps behind her changed drastically. Hannah turned to find the two men had broken into a run. Her pulse jumped. Oh, no! That they were no longer concerned about their presence being known sent off an alarm. Hannah sprang into motion and sprinted toward the door to the ladies' room, fear for Bonny thickening her blood. Where was Chad?

Finally the door was within her grasp. She pushed the stroller into the ladies' room then turned to force the door shut. But her pursuers didn't care whose privacy they invaded, or about the child with her. Through the crack that remained, Hannah watched one of the men break from the other, dashing across to the men's room. He was going after Chad!

Her grip on the door slipped, and Bonny's happy squeal confused her. Trying three times, Hannah finally slid her pepper spray from her concealed belt and held down the button, covering the guy's face with red powder. She stared into his reflective sunglasses, her efforts earning nothing more than a short sneeze. The glasses had protected his eyes.

"All right, you asked for it," he spat out.

Hannah drew in a deep breath, then yelled, "Fire!"

The guy who had gone in search of Chad suddenly appeared in the hall. The men stared at each other.

"He's not there," one said.

The interaction gave Hannah the opportunity to finally slam the door shut. She searched frantically for something with which to bar it closed. She turned, then froze solid. Chad was crouched a few feet away, entertaining Bonny with a set of keys. He met her gaze, then stood and pushed the stroller toward the back of the room and into an empty stall. "Look, sweet pea, toilet paper. Knock yourself out."

"Fire?" he asked, coming toward Hannah. He shifted her away from the door then jammed his foot against it.

"Nobody pays attention to 'rape.'" she explained. "Have you been here the entire time?" She already knew the answer.

The door he held shut jerked violently inward.

Hannah noticed he held a two-foot-long length of pipe in his right hand and guessed he must have dislodged it from one of the stalls.

"You see, Hannah," he said, "I improved on your plan. Then again, how were you to know you weren't supposed to fight them, but to walk in here and let them follow you?"

"What?"

"Get with the program, McGee, and move out of the way. The sooner we get this over with, the sooner our daughter is out of danger."

Our daughter? Hannah hurried toward the wide throughway separating two rows of stalls, protecting the route to Bonny. She reached for her stun gun. "You realize we'll be in a lot of trouble if they are FBI."

"A decided understatement." Chad moved his foot

from the bottom of the door. The two suited men spilled into the room in a sudden flurry of activity. Chad hit the first across the shoulders, sending him sprawling to the floor, where he hit his head. The other reached for his gun. Instantly Chad brought the pipe down hard on the man's head, sending his gun flying into a full-length mirror and shattering it. He joined his partner on the floor.

Hannah carefully made her way over the broken glass. Their reflection in the shattered mirror made her and Chad look like twenty instead of the meager two they were.

"That's all I need. Seven more years of bad luck," Chad commented.

Hannah bent down to pry the gun from the unconscious man's hand. "Is a silencer standard FBI issue?" she asked as she noted the two-inch attachment meant to muffle the sound of a bullet.

Chad searched the men's pockets, coming up with little more than money from each. No identification. No credit cards. Nothing that could give them a clue to their identity.

"They're not FBI," Hannah said with a little relief.

The worried lines on Chad's face told her he didn't share her relief. "Do you really think that's better?"

Hannah bit down on her bottom lip and decided it wasn't. She hurried back to the stall where Chad had put Bonny and found the baby wreathed in lengths of toilet paper and unraveling even more, completely unaware of what had gone on outside. Hannah said a silent prayer and lifted her daughter out of the stroller, cuddling her close to her chest, toilet paper and all.

When she came out still holding Bonny and dragging the stroller, she found Chad locking his hands under the gunman's arms and pulling him toward an empty stall.

After he positioned the two men, Hannah tore two of Bonny's blankets into long strips. Chad took them, cutting them to fashion a makeshift rope and gags. It didn't take long to make certain the men wouldn't get out of the ladies' room without assistance.

"Come on." Chad grasped Hannah's arm and ushered her and the baby toward the door. "Let's get out of here."

As Hannah followed him out into the concourse, she couldn't resist pressing a lingering kiss to Bonny's forehead, ignoring her daughter's soggy protests.

"I'm sorry, Hannah," Chad said quietly, his voice sounding notably somber in the din of conversations in the lobby.

"What are you sorry for?"

"For getting you and Bonny into this mess."

"You're not to blame," she disagreed.

His eyes were warm silver as he gazed at her. "I'm to blame for much more than this, Hannah. A lot more than this."

His expression was solemn as he gently grasped the baby's foot and put his arm around Hannah's shoulders. She didn't protest. This time she merely absorbed the warmth the simple gesture conveyed, her mind too jumbled to try to make sense out of his words.

Chapter Seven

Hannah sat up on a rumpled motel bed and budged her dusty shoes aside where she'd tossed them to the floor two hours earlier. For long minutes, she listened to the sound of Chad taking a shower, then stared at where Bonny slept quietly next to her. Despite the exhaustion that had claimed her on the plane, she hadn't been able to sleep a wink, her body and mind thrumming with an unsettled awareness she swore at times she could actually hear.

Her gaze rested on Bonny's sweet face. She gently caressed her daughter's silky cheek with the backs of her fingers. So delicate. So defenseless. Hannah never knew being responsible for another life would carry such worry, concern…and such an incredible sensation of pride and contentment. For the past eight months she alone had been responsible for feeding, bathing, changing and attending to her baby's needs, including providing a sense of security that allowed her to sleep as peacefully as she was now. Hannah tugged a toy away from where Bonny had been gnawing on it, thinking her daughter's smiles, her nonstop gibberish, her robust protests for freedom were all part of what made her special. Yes, this child was a talker. She was also the sweetest thing that had ever touched Hannah's heart.

Afraid she might wake her, and squashing the desire to do just that, she stared at the closed door to the bathroom. There was one other person who had touched her life and heart so completely. Chad.

Her heart gave an involuntary squeeze and she forced her gaze away from the bathroom door...and Chad.

Working her way around her restless emotions, Hannah tried to concentrate on the case. She lined up one by one the unusual events over the past two days. First, there was the Monte Carlo that had tried to run her down in New York, then had driven by Minelli's place in Atlantic City. Second, there was Persky's hitlike murder moments before she and Chad had arrived at his apartment. She swallowed against the image. Third, the appearance of the goons at the airport where she and Chad had ceased being the couple paralleling the steps of the others involved and instead became a target themselves.

Hannah fitfully worried her hands in her lap, then shoved her tangled hair back from her face again. An undeniable measure of wistful longing and guilt twisted inside her as her gaze again fastened on the closed bathroom door. What was it Chad had said when they were leaving the airport? He was to blame for more

than their current predicament? Her empty stomach felt
suddenly wooden.

Not once had she stopped to consider that Chad had
as much at stake as she did. Or reflected on how an
arrest might affect him. She sank back against the pillow. She guessed her one-sided attitude came from the
need to block out bail-jumpers' claims to innocence
whenever she caught up with them and hauled them
back to jail. If she had stopped to listen to their claims,
she might have let half of them go. Then where would
she be?

Nowhere.

Still, it didn't excuse her unforgivable behavior
when dealing with people who weren't suspected criminals. People she loved.

Loved.

Had loved. She had loved Chad. But something new,
something frightening and more powerful was beginning to push through the cold ashes of her former love
for him. It both scared and excited her.

Scooting herself to a sitting position, she stared at
the bed across from hers, trying to concentrate on anything other than how cool she'd been to Chad the past
two days. Judging from the messiness of the other bed,
he must have tossed and turned as much as she had.
In fact, she knew he had, because she had counted the
times he'd rolled over, shared in his restlessness even
as she pretended to be asleep.

She shifted her gaze to where his duffel bag sat open
at the foot of his bed. Unlike her, he already had been
packed when they met up at Blackstone's. She rubbed
her leg through the gauzy fabric of her skirt, reminding
herself he had a bag because he had just flown in from

Florida. A place he would return to when their assignment was finished.

Trying to ignore the tightening of her throat, Hannah fingered the T-shirt he'd bought for her in Atlantic City. If she hadn't been so preoccupied with his showering uncertain attention on Bonny, she might have thought of buying a few necessities for herself. Conscious of the continued sound of running water, she slowly rummaged through the duffel bag a second time. She pulled out an extra large T-shirt, then fingered a pair of new low-cut briefs before taking them out as well. Tugging the plastic wrapping apart, she held the crisp white cotton briefs up to her hips. Eyeing the closed bathroom door, she peeled off her clothes.

The spray of the shower stopped. Her heart skipping a beat, Hannah quickly tugged the T-shirt over her head and balled the briefs, hiding them under her arm as Chad opened the door.

"Good, you're finished," she said anxiously, hurrying past him into the bathroom.

"McGee, isn't that my T-shirt you're wearing?"

She froze at the rough sound of his voice. Slowly, she turned toward him. His gaze, steely hot, roamed over her, from where she feared he could see the pounding of her pulse in the hollow of her neck, down to where the white cotton draped over her taut, bare breasts, to the hem of the shirt where it grazed her thighs. She stood spellbound, expectant, incapable of movement, unable to do more than watch the darkening of his gray eyes, the tightening of his muscles. His throat contracted as he swallowed, the sound unusually loud in the quiet room.

Hannah forced her gaze away and rushed into the

bathroom, closing and locking the door against him and her own confused feelings.

I'm to blame for much more...

The strong spray of hot water chased away the chill of the air conditioning as Hannah stepped into the shower, but the echo of Chad's words drowned out the sound of the water hitting the fiberglass tub. For the second time, she wondered what, exactly, he had meant by his being to blame. He said he hadn't been referring to just their current situation, so did the statement cover the length of their relationship?

You're making too much out of this, Hannah, an inner voice intoned. *You always analyze everything to the extreme.* A habit that was a good quality as a cop and a skip-tracer, but a drawback when it came to personal ties. Chad was talking about now. Why would he want to bring up anything from the past?

Still, her gut instinct told her differently. He had been talking about her...about them.

Did she blame Chad for everything that had happened between them? For their fights, their breakup, for his leaving...for Bonny?

Her skin grew hot, but it had little to do with the steam surrounding her. For the first time, she recognized she did—and had—blamed Chad for everything that had ever gone wrong.

Why?

And did he believe everything had been his fault?

With jerky movements, she turned off the water and opened the shower curtain. She didn't like the guilt coating her like the water, though she knew she needed to face it or the uneasy emotion was going to surface again. This new truth about her treatment of Chad during their relationship...well, it changed everything, didn't it? Or at least some things. If she had made Chad feel at fault for every move he made while they were together, then it was possible she was to blame for his walking away, not him.

Ridiculous, her mind told her resolutely.

The truth, her heart said, giving a little squeeze for effect.

Hannah grabbed a towel and roughly mopped her skin, reminding herself that it didn't matter now.

Besides, Chad had no place in her and Bonny's lives, however much she might be starting to long differently. That was what she believed before yesterday, and what she fought hard to make reality now. It was difficult because she'd seen the flashes of pain in his eyes when he looked at Bonny. Saw the way his touch turned gentle in those moments when he'd thought she wasn't looking. And in those few moments, Hannah's heart had learned how to hope again.

Despite the aching loneliness, the pain of her pregnancy, the exhausting midnight feedings, Hannah found the memories of those hard times fading fast, being quickly replaced with the secret hope she had always harbored in her heart. The hope that the three of them would one day be a family.

A knock on the outer door of the motel room halted her movements. Ignoring her hair, Hannah pulled the T-shirt and briefs on and picked up her stun gun from where she had placed it on the basin.

She leaned against the wall next to the door, holding the stun gun at the ready. Her heart beating anxiously, she waited for the visitor to say to Chad, "FBI."

"That'll be twelve dollars and sixteen cents."

Hannah dropped the hand holding her stun gun to her side, wondering what she would have done with the thing anyway. Unlocking the door and pulling it open a few inches, she watched Chad hand money to the woman they'd seen in the motel office upon check-in. She held a baby not much older than Bonny on her hip, and two older boys raced around her, one running into the room, both holding what looked like two-way radios.

"Come on, Ray and Tom, stop it now and get back to the office," the woman said with a refreshing accent, handing Chad a bag and a couple of fresh towels. "How's the little one doing?"

Chad looked over his shoulder, meeting Hannah's gaze briefly as he handed over the money asked for. "Bonny's sleeping."

"Probably plum tuckered out after your trip," the woman nodded. "Look, if you need a baby-sitter or anything, I'm here. I didn't introduce myself properly earlier. I'm the owner, Betty Browning. And as you can see, I've got plenty of experience with kids."

"Thanks," Chad said. "We appreciate the offer."

He slowly closed the door after her.

"I ordered in some Chinese," he said, glancing to where Hannah still stood in the bathroom doorway. He noticed the stun gun in her hand. "Don't tell me you're going to zap me for it."

Chad's hair and T-shirt were clean, but his grin was filthy as he looked her over from head to toe.

"The shirt looks better on you, Hannah. Keep it."

She felt every inch of revealed skin tingle under his heated gaze. She put the stun gun back in the bathroom and carefully sat down on the bed where Bonny still slept. The chicken Chad held out to her smelled inviting. She took it, along with a pair of chopsticks.

"What are you looking at, Chad?" She self-consciously slid a bit of food into her mouth and returned his stare.

"Nothing. I was just remembering sweet and sour anything was always your favorite. It's nice to see some things don't change."

She chewed the food slowly. What did he mean by that? She took another bite but found swallowing the food difficult. "Chad, I was wondering about something."

She liked his growing beard, she realized, following his rugged, tanned cheeks up to his eyes. And she had always loved his eyes. It was more than just their silvery gray color; it was the intensity they always held. Even when staring at her, his eyes betrayed a deeper emotion.

"Anyway," she said, pushing around the food with her chopsticks, her cheeks flaming. "Something you said has been bothering me and I was wondering…was I, you know, so awful to you? I mean before…when we lived together…did I make you feel that you were to blame for everything that happened?"

She chanced a glance in his direction.

"Only for the bad things," he said quietly.

Hannah placed her food carton on the night table and pulled the blanket across her lap. "Come on, Chad, I'm serious. Can you let your guard down for two minutes and talk to me? I mean really talk to me?"

"We talk constantly, Hannah. That's one thing we've never had a problem with. That and—" He stopped suddenly then stuck his chopsticks in his carton so they stood upright. "What is this? Twenty questions?"

"I don't know. God, I hate feeling this way." Hannah puckered the blanket with her hands, then smoothed the material out.

"Feeling what way?"

She met his gaze solidly. "Like there are still so many unresolved issues between us. Too many things that have gone unsaid." *Too many new things that were happening now.*

His gaze was strangely thorough. "And you want to say them now?"

She nodded. "I think I'd like to try. If for no other reason than to achieve some sort of...closure."

He grimaced.

"Oh, just forget it, okay? It was a stupid idea anyway."

"No, Hannah. I've never seen you this way before."

"Yeah, well, maybe I should have been this way a long time ago," she murmured, staring at the slumbering baby next to her.

"What was that you said?"

"Nothing," she said quickly, surprised to find tears gathering at the corners of her eyes. She cleared her throat, meeting his gaze, then retreating. It was hard enough trying to stare her own faults in the face. Staring into the handsome planes of Chad's face as well made it all the more difficult. "Let me just say this, okay, then I can get dressed and we can get out of here." She was having a tough time, but she was going to say it if it killed her. "I know what you said earlier—about how I held you responsible for the bad things that happened between us—might have been a throwaway comment, but I suspect it's the way you really feel. I just want you to know, even if it seemed like I blamed you for everything that went wrong— something I'm not entirely sure of yet—that you were also responsible for the happiest times of my life.'' She swallowed hard against the emotion that nearly choked her. "I'm sorry I never made that clear.'' A lone tear scalded her cheek and she swiped at it in exasperation.

Pushing off the bed, she hurried for the bathroom, dismayed with herself for being incapable of saying something so simple. Why was it easy for her to point out the negatives and so difficult for her to say anything positive? Maybe Chad was right. She *had* shoved the lion's share of the responsibility for their breakup onto him. Still, that didn't answer the question of why he had accepted it. Why he hadn't told her before how unfair she'd been. And what she could do to make all that go away now.

Chad caught her before she could disappear into the bathroom and lock the door. His hand felt like a gentle handcuff around her wrist. She tried to shrug him off.

"Hannah, look at me.''

"I can't.''

Warm fingers gripped her chin and tugged her face toward his. The raw emotion mirrored in his eyes stopped her breath. It was that look. The tender, solemn expression she'd seen on his face a million times before but had never been able to explain.

"I really hate you sometimes, you know, Chad?''

He slowly shook his head. "It's taken me a long time, Hannah, but I think I've finally learned to translate your words. For as long as I've known you, I've taken everything you've said at face value. I was so very wrong.''

She buried her face in his clean-smelling neck, inhaling the thick, male scent below the soap that was wholly male and all his. A smell she had missed during their long months apart. She pressed her lips against his neck, then dragged her wet eyelashes against his skin.

All at once, Chad's hands pressed against her back. He flattened her against him, forcing the breath from her, while his lips sought the top of her wet, tangled hair.

"I've missed you, Hannah. You'll never know how much."

His soft confession sent shock waves of warmth flowing over her. He threaded his fingers through her damp hair, his potent gaze searing her face. Then a new, more urgent heat rushed through her, moving along with his longing look, traveling down the length of her torso. She pressed her palms against the flat, solid muscles of his back. She had forgotten how good it was to be held by him, truly held. A familiar swell of yearning surged through her, empowering her, yet making her inexplicably vulnerable as his mouth slowly moved to the sensitive skin behind her ear.

He traced a maddening line from the base of her jaw to her collarbone, leaving not a millimeter of clean flesh left untouched by the rough, exciting feel of his lips, his stubble. His breathing grew ragged, uneven. Hannah tensed, arching her back, seeking closer contact, impatiently tugging at the back of his shirt. She pulled it out of his jeans, seeking the hot, velvety skin of his back. Her breath caught as the familiar planes tightened beneath her fingertips.

Chad's lips finally sought hers. She responded wholeheartedly, languishing in the moistness of his mouth as it bespoke his feelings—his true feelings. It was not the skilled, calculated kiss of a seducer, but the unadulterated, uninhibited action of a man who had waited too long. His hands fumbled with the T-shirt she wore. She in turn opened the button on his jeans and tugged the denim down his slender hips, running her fingers along his muscled thighs before seeking his embrace again. His kiss deepened, coaxing her out by inches. Then he abandoned her mouth and knelt, pressing his lips against the taut, trembling muscles of her stomach. It was then Hannah remembered she wore his white briefs.

She dragged in a deep breath and watched for his reaction even as she held his gaze. His hands moved slowly, intuitively down her body until they met the thick elastic band. He hesitated, dropping his gaze and eyeing the white cotton, then laying his head against her lower stomach. Hannah felt him smile. She crowded her fingers into his hair, reveling in the thick, soft mass.

"It seems you not only look better in my T-shirt, but my underwear too," he said gruffly.

He rose, leaving the briefs in place, and shifted her not to the comfort of the bed, but to the bathroom and the waist-high basin. He lifted her to sit on top of the cool tile. She drew in a sharp breath, her arms never allowing him to move more than a centimeter away as she wound her legs around his waist, pulling him closer.

He closed the door behind them, then reclaimed her body, moving his hands along the smooth line of her back, then around to her sides where he skimmed the outer curve of her breasts. Hannah gasped. He grazed her nipples with the pad of his thumbs, enticing them to taut, aching peaks, then covered them completely with the fiery inner circles of his palms.

A sense of urgency seized her. She urged her hands down past Chad's shoulders, then parted them at his waist, one continuing down to his firm, muscled rear, the other urgently seeking the ridge of his erection where it pressed earnestly against her stomach.

"I hate you, Chad Hogan," she whispered, pushing aside the cotton of the too big briefs and guiding him to press against the place she wanted him most. "I...hate...you..."

Chad invaded her with an uncontrolled thrust, catapulting her irreversibly into the dark, deep tunnel of sensation she so desperately sought. She closed her eyes and her hands ceased their restless movements. The only thing she was aware of was the thick, overwhelming throb of her pulse.

Then Chad moved. Gently, slowly, as if he intended to savor her, to prolong these few minutes for as long as he could. But the fine reserve Hannah built up in the fifteen months they were apart cracked—the same reserve that had tried to convince her she didn't need Chad, didn't need him physically, didn't need him emotionally.

Suddenly that control was gone. As the steady pressure within her belly built into a dizzying, overpowering urgency, she found herself incapable of thought, incapable of conscious movement. Her body took over, screaming the feelings her mouth was unable to communicate, and listened to Chad's body, interpreting his wordless responses. His almost reverent attention and gentle thrusts spoke of the changes in him, in them both. He hadn't forgotten her needs, her favorite places to be touched. But somehow his touch was different. She sensed now, when she hadn't been trying to sway him to her wants, that she'd somehow managed to reach a part of him that was shut off from her before.

The realization was dizzying and she slumped back, breathless.

It was this new sensation that made being with him now special, unforgettable. On this unexplored plane she forgot their past and enjoyed the simple, primeval pleasure of the present.

And yes, Hannah realized breathlessly, resting her hands against his chest and wondering at the beat of his heart beneath his sweat-slick skin. This wasn't just sex—this *was* making love.

Chad buried his hands deep in her hair, his thrusts growing more urgent, more demanding. As his passion built, he gently pulled the locks, gaining access to her neck. His wet kisses ceased, the hot breath against her skin stopped, and Hannah felt the unmistakable quake travel from his body to hers. It grew to uncontrollable proportions, gripping, grabbing every ounce of energy she had, making any movement impossible, almost physically painful. At that moment, she let go, locking her legs tightly around his hips, rocking with the sheer emotion filling her, consuming her, linking her together with this man she had once loved—and feared was coming to love again. In a whole new, frightening way.

She tugged hungrily on his mouth, a whimper vibrating her throat.

"You are still the most incredible woman I've ever known," Chad said roughly, almost as if to himself.

In one motion he tilted her hips closer to his and lifted her from the cool basin. Opening the door, he carried her to his bed and stripped back the covers, before laying her down. Slowly he dragged his fingers down the length of her bare torso, then scraped his fingertips against the aching tips of her breasts before traveling on until he reached the men's briefs she wore.

Leaning over her, he slowly tugged the cotton down, baring her dusky triangle of hair. He groaned. Tossing the briefs aside, he pressed his palm against her, finding her tender bud with his callused fingertips. Hannah strained upward, seeking closer contact. She shuddered when he moved a finger along her swollen, slick entrance.

"Please," she pleaded, trying to pull him up. She writhed insistently, her legs moving restlessly, her body pulsing with sensation.

He slid over her, dragging a russet-colored nipple into his mouth, laving the aching tip with his tongue. Hannah whimpered, thrusting her fingers into his hair, thrusting her hips against where he rested between her thighs.

Finally he drew back, holding her gaze as he fit himself into her a second time. He moved slowly, torturously, then languorously shifted his gaze to where their bodies were joined. She followed his lead, marveling at the sight of his strength melding into her softness, and retreating, then melding again. All at once, she came apart, a fireball exploding in her belly, consuming her with liquid fire. She mindlessly sought his mouth, tangling her tongue with his, lifting her legs to allow him deeper access. He rocked into her, obviously battling to hold on to the controlled, leisurely pace he had set, then giving himself over to the need to drive into her, to possess her, pinning her legs higher, molding her soft flesh to his. Hannah felt her climax gather, then erupt in a kaleidoscope of heat.

Chad groaned and tumbled after her.

For long moments he lay quietly on top of her. She reveled in the feel of him cradled between her thighs, the rasp of his stubble against her sensitive neck. She smiled, tasting the salty skin of his forehead, her heart thudding erratically against the wall of his chest.

He didn't move. In fact, he had yet to look at her at all since they blew apart in each other's arms. She drew her head slightly away and tried to meet his gaze. Had he fallen asleep?

"Chad?" she said quietly.

From the bed next to them, Hannah heard movement. She glanced over to find Bonny awakening. The baby took three deep breaths then started crying.

Chad got up so quickly Hannah felt as if a blanket had been stripped from her body in the dead of winter.

Still, he refused to meet her gaze.

"Chad?" she said again, this time more urgently. Certainly he didn't feel guilty because they had made love with the baby in the room? With growing dread, she watched him snatch up his T-shirt and yank it on, along with his jeans. Dressed, he picked up his duffel then stalked toward the door.

"Chad!" she called over Bonny's cries.

Finally he met her gaze. The regret in his gray eyes, the confusion, made her wish he hadn't.

"I'm sorry, Hannah," he said, then left the room, closing the door after himself.

Chapter Eight

The hazy, midafternoon sunlight slanted through the windows, signaling the rain had ended, and making the wheezing air conditioner work twice as hard to keep the searing Texas summer heat from taking over the cool motel room. Hannah lay listlessly next to Bonny on the double bed. The bed that didn't remind her of what she and Chad had just shared. She tried to entertain her daughter with a doll. Bonny slapped her arm and let loose a cry. It seemed she was incapable of even the simple task of entertaining her daughter. Her throat tightening, Hannah sat up. Bonny scooted to the edge of the mattress, and Hannah helped lower her to a blanket on the floor, making sure there was nothing in the room her curious daughter could break, eat, or otherwise damage or hurt herself with.

"Come on, Chad, where are you?" she whispered. She looked at her watch, then stared at the closed door.

After the way he had left her, she wasn't sure which scared her more: his leaving for good...or his coming back.

Bonny pulled at the bedspread and tensed her pudgy little body. "Dah...dah...dah."

Hannah blinked. "No, honey, there's no doggy here." She grabbed a hold of the bedspread before it slipped to the floor. Watching her daughter's expressive face, she supposed now that she wouldn't be going out on any more road trips seeking bail-jumpers, maybe she would get Bonny a dog.

"Dah!"

Hannah frowned and stuffed the doll back into the nearby diaper bag. "No, it's more like duh," she mimicked. That word about summed up what a fool she had made of herself.

What had she been thinking when she gave in to the emotions she had for Chad? Emotions it had taken her over a lonely, long year to master, to suppress? Her heart mocked her by giving a painful squeeze. Obviously she *hadn't* been thinking. If she had, she would never have taken this assignment. Would never have given herself the rope she had just used to hang herself.

Chad would never change. Perhaps he was even incapable of changing given the pain that lay in his past. She had deluded herself by reading more into his expressions than had been there, by hoping he could somehow love her the same way he loved his wife. She had opened herself up again, allowed herself to start to fall in love with him again—only to have her new feelings unreturned.

She absently traced the quilted material of the bedspread with her finger over and over again. Despite all that, she knew that Chad had changed. Then again, maybe it wasn't Chad who had changed, but the addition of Bonny to the picture that made him more accessible somehow.

Rising restlessly from the bed, Hannah stepped to the window and stared out at the parking area. The rental car wasn't there and neither was Chad. She followed where the sun refracted through the windowpane and drowned Bonny in a yellow pool of light, then glanced down at her watch again. If Chad didn't return, she'd have to decide where she went from here.

And where could she go? Home? It seemed the only logical answer. Go home. Forget Chad. Forget this assignment that had turned more dangerous than she'd anticipated. Get Seekers off the ground. And create a happy environment for Bonny to grow up in. An environment that had seemed so stable, so satisfying, but after only two days of Chad Hogan, had been severely undermined.

A cold blast from the air conditioner in front of her legs made her shiver. But what about the two men at the airport? The FBI agents in New York?

Biting on her bottom lip, Hannah stepped between the beds and reached for the telephone on the bedside table. She called the motel office.

"Hi, Mrs. Browning—"

"Please, it's Betty," the nicely accented voice of the owner said.

"Okay." She moved the receiver to her other ear. "Um, could you tell me if there are any messages for Room 112, Betty?"

"No, honey, I'm sorry, but your husband hasn't called in yet."

Hannah winced. It was natural for Betty to assume she and Chad were married. But if it was one thing she and Chad would never be, it was married. He'd made sure of that.

"Thank you." Hannah blindly replaced the receiver in its cradle.

A dull rattle sounded over the hiss of the air conditioner. Hannah stared at the door, then dropped her gaze to where the round brass handle jiggled. Her heart pounded hopefully in her chest. Plucking Bonny away from the front of the door, she opened it. Only it wasn't Chad she stood face-to-face with.

She backed away, staring at the last person she expected to see. "What are you doing here?"

Chad hung up the phone, then tore a page from the phone book. He folded the tissue-thin piece of paper in half, then half again, until he distantly realized he'd nearly folded it into oblivion. Grimacing at the mess he'd made, he shoved it into his front jeans' pocket, picked up his duffel and stepped away from the telephone booth. He hadn't exactly intended to do any work when he left the motel room and Hannah two hours earlier, but when he saw the telephone book hanging from its steel cord in the mini mall, he'd found the perfect excuse to get his mind off what he had just done. More specifically, to stop the incessant sound of Hannah saying his name from echoing in his head, and his own curses at himself that followed.

Why did I make love to her?

Damn, stupid fool question. He knew exactly why he'd made love to her. Ever since seeing her again he had longed to hold her once more. To mold her body to his. To hear her soft cries when he touched her in the most intimate of places. He rubbed his fingers against his mouth, swearing he could still taste her on his tongue. Still feel her hot breath on his skin.

But that wasn't what he'd come back for. He'd returned to set things straight between them. To apologize for starting something he knew he would never finish. To ask for her forgiveness. Then he saw Bonny and understood that just because he'd stayed the same the past fifteen months didn't mean she had. And that a lot had happened between then and now. All his previous arguments against marrying again, the pain of losing his wife and son...well, they didn't seem to make much sense when he held his daughter.

Still, he owed it to Hannah to figure everything out before he was intimate with her. But he'd underestimated what had begun happening between them these past two days. This time their lovemaking wasn't just about satisfying a physical hunger. He thrust his fingers through his hair, realizing their lovemaking had never really been about that, though that was what he'd told himself. But this time that something he suspected had always lurked in his heart for Hannah had refused his arguments, ignored his attempts to block it, and seeped out, possessing him with an intensity he had never felt before. And it was that same intensity that made him feel confused, troubled...and like the biggest jerk on earth for the way he had treated her.

She deserved so much more than him and his inability to escape from the cloud of confusion forever following him around.

He readjusted his hold on his duffel bag, then remembered exactly why it was so heavy. Before leaving Florida, he had stashed his last bottle of vodka inside, a bitter reminder of exactly how he had spent the months away from Hannah. Shoving his hand into the bag, Chad yanked the half-full bottle out and stared at it, weighing it in his hand. His mouth watered, and he recognized the longing that urged him to take a sip even now. In the middle of a mall.

Letting the bottle slip down so he clutched the neck, he walked to a trash bin and tossed it inside without slowing his stride.

Florida was behind him now, pushed there the instant Blackstone had called him with the chance to make amends with at least one person he had hurt. Unfortunately he could never gain forgiveness from Linda and Joshua.

He dragged in a deep breath and stopped in front of a flower shop. His gaze caught on a square, ceramic plant holder shaped like a toy block intended as a gift for a new baby. He knew it would play a lullaby when wound up. He stared at it, wishing he could have bought one of those for Bonny, after her birth. He shoved his hand into his back pocket and pulled out the cash there. It was only as an afterthought that he realized he'd gotten a flower pot just like this one for little Joshua when he and Linda brought him home from the hospital.

He stood still for long moments, waiting for the anguish to seize him. For the guilt for having thought of someone else before Joshua to claim him. He stood up a little straighter. The paralyzing emotions he constantly lived in fear of never came. Instead, he experienced a manageable sorrow, a mix of joy that he had known his son if only for a few precious months, and grief that he had lost him.

He shifted his gaze to two dozen yellow roses. On one of the long stems, a card read, How Do I Love Thee? Let Me Count The Ways.

It was then he realized that in all the time he had known Hannah, after all the sizzling hours of love-making, of talking, of laughing with her, of pretending to like her cooking, and holding her when the world got to be a little too much to bear, he'd never once told Hannah he loved her.

And now it was too late.

"What are you doing here?" Hannah tried to look formidable, but the appearance of Jack Stokes on the other side of the motel room door threw her for a loop. She automatically reached for her stun gun, then remembered she'd left it in the bathroom after her shower. She backed into the motel room.

The Australian took advantage of her surprise and followed, closing the door after himself.

"I thought it was for the same reason you were here, luv," he said, mimicking the words he had used when they met up at The Bar two days ago, both of them seeking the same bail-jumper, Eddie "The Snake" Fowler. What had he said after she snatched Eddie out from under his nose? I'm going to get you for this?

Jack Stokes pushed his leather cowboy hat back on his dark head and shifted his gaze to the disheveled bed behind her. "At least I thought I was here for the same reason. I'm beginning to wonder if that's the case."

Hannah crossed her arms over her chest. "Get your mind out of the gutter, Stokes."

"My, aren't we the touchy one this afternoon."

She glanced to where Bonny played on the other side of the bed, out of sight. "How did you find us?"

"It was quite easy, actually. You would be surprised

how willing a few females are when asked by a man such as myself for a little information.''

Hannah grimaced. ''An investigation like that would take days. You had to find out from someone else.''

She thought about what she was saying—and it hit her. No. It couldn't be true.

''I can't believe it.'' Hannah stalked to the phone and snatched the receiver from its cradle. She quickly punched out a number she knew by heart.

''Hannah, luv, let's not go and get hasty now,'' Jack said, taking a step toward her.

She stared at him and listened to the line ring once before it was picked up. ''Blackstone, you better have a good explanation for sending Jack Stokes out on this trace—''

''Hannah! Where are you?'' Elliott cut her off. ''I've been going out of my mind here. I thought I told you—''

''Just answer my question, El.''

Jack stepped a little closer to her.

''I wouldn't if I were you, Stokes.'' Her voice was deep and forbidding.

The Aussie held up his hands.

''Stokes is there?'' Blackstone's voice wavered across the line. ''What is he doing with you?''

Hannah frowned. ''You mean you didn't send him here?''

''Of course, I didn't send him! How could I send him there if I don't even know where 'there' is?''

The response didn't make any sense. If Elliott hadn't sent Stokes after Persky and Furgeson, what was the Aussie doing there?

''Hannah, where are you?'' Elliott asked.

Satisfied that Elliott hadn't sent Stokes, she depressed the hang-up button, cutting off Blackstone's rapid-fire questions. Then she rushed toward her baby, whom Stokes had just picked up.

"Don't worry, luv," he said quietly. "I won't hurt her." He bounced Bonny up and down and smiled. The softening of his rugged features, the gentle way he held Bonny, surprised Hannah. "You know, I wondered why you disappeared there for a while." He glanced at her. "Guess this explains it, huh?" He tickled Bonny's terry-covered belly and she gave a delighted squeal. "Our mate Hogan knows about her, I take it?"

Hannah moved toward the window. "Yeah." Several yards away she noticed an older model Monte Carlo sitting in a parking spot. The car jiggled something loose in her memory.

She faced Jack and crossed her arms over her chest. "You were the one in the Monte Carlo, weren't you? Outside Blackstone's, then again in Atlantic City at Minelli's and outside our motel room." Perhaps Blackstone had been telling the truth. Jack wasn't working for him. He was out on his own and had followed them the entire way.

She could tell by Stokes's agitated expression that the Monte Carlo was indeed his.

"I need the cash, Hannah. I gotta get out of here. The States, I mean. A man such as myself can only spend so much time up over before he needs to go back down under, you know?"

Bonny reached out to grab the rim of Jack's hat and he leaned back. He used the vantage point to take a more thorough look at the eight-month-old. "Well, I know where she gets her beauty, and it sure as hell ain't from Hogan."

Hannah cracked a nervous smile, unsure how to react to this kinder, gentler Jack Stokes.

Bonny tugged on his dark blond hair and he winced.

"Here, you better let me take her," Hannah said.

She slipped her hands under Bonny's arms and started lifting her when she heard the knob of the door being turned. A split second later, Chad filled the open doorway. Hannah's heart leapt into her throat.

Chad had undergone a series of physical changes in the time he'd been gone. His rich light brown hair, though still somewhat long in the back, had been trimmed. The forever-present stubble that had made her tender skin raw was gone.

"I'd better be going." Stokes plopped his hat back onto his head and waited for Chad to move from the door. For a moment, Hannah was afraid he wouldn't. Then he stepped aside and the Aussie quickly moved through the opening. "Congratulations on the new addition to the fam, mate."

Chad glared after him then closed the door.

Hannah cuddled an overactive Bonny closer to her chest as every minute of the past two hours Chad had been gone, every pang of punishing pain she'd felt, flooded back with vivid clarity. She started to head for the bathroom when Chad's voice stopped her.

"Hannah, I…"

She waited with her back turned to him. But he didn't continue. So she spoke instead. "Don't worry, Chad, I didn't say anything to Jack to make him think anything has changed between us. And I don't expect anything to change just because you now know you happened to have fathered a child or because…we had sex." She patted Bonny's back, disappointed to find her hand shaking. But the outer display was nothing compared to the ache ripping through her insides. Her throat pinched so tightly closed she couldn't swallow. She walked to the bed and searched through Bonny's diaper bag. "Let me just change Bonny and we can go. The sooner this case is over, the better for all of us."

She chanced a glance at him, noticing for the first time that he held something in his hands. Her stomach did a crazy little flip-flop. Flowers. He'd brought flowers. And he stared at them now as if even he didn't know how they'd gotten there.

She straightened, uncertain what to say, unsure if she should say anything at all.

Then Chad tossed the brilliant bouquet of yellow roses across the bed they'd shared together mere hours before then opened the door.

Hannah's heart skipped a beat.

"I'll wait outside in the car," he said without looking at her.

The click of the door closing sounded louder than if he had slammed it.

Chapter Nine

Hannah glanced to where Chad tightened his grip on the steering wheel of the rental car. To say the ride to the outskirts of Houston had been tense would be a major understatement. And without Bonny there to concentrate on, she felt strangely out of sorts. Reluctantly she had arranged to have Betty Browning, the motel manager, baby-sit, only leaving her daughter in the other woman's care when she saw how well she interacted with her own three children. Besides, Hannah had only to remember what happened to Persky in Atlantic City, and the two armed men at the Houston airport, to know that it was unsafe to keep Bonny with her.

"Hannah...I want to apologize," Chad said quietly.

She stared intently out of the window. "Apologize? Apologize for what?"

Chad pressed the button to roll down his window

though the heat outside was unbearable. "Never mind. Forget it."

Hannah wished she were anywhere but there in the car with him. She felt dangerously near tears. "No, I didn't mean you didn't have anything to apologize for. I just want to get it straight up-front which one of your sins you think deserves forgiveness." She switched the air conditioner to high.

"I said forget it."

She nodded slowly, her stomach pitching to her feet. Forget it. "That's what I thought." She avoided his gaze, her voice dropping to nearly a whisper. "Look, maybe we should just admit to ourselves that we made a mistake. Today, and three years ago." She swallowed hard, forcing the words past her throat. "You were right. You know, when you said we should keep this temporary partnership professional, and forget the rest."

She forced herself to glance at him. His jaw muscles flexed and he looked at a complete loss as to what to say.

"From here on we stick to the original plan, okay? No more personal involvement." She shook her head and stared in the rearview mirror, glancing at the empty residential street behind them.

He sighed, running a restless hand through his newly trimmed, sandy brown hair. Impulsively, Hannah longed to reach out and touch his clean-shaven cheek. She took a deep breath, saddened by her weakness where Chad Hogan was concerned.

She rubbed her damp palms one by one on her skirt. "Where are we going anyway? Do you know where Lisa Furgeson is?"

He made a turn, then looked at her. His gaze was strangely penetrating and she looked away.

"After I left the room earlier, I did some checking to see how many Furgesons were in the area. There happens to be a Jeff and Jolene Furgeson with the same number Persky called."

"Lisa Furgeson's brother?"

"Looks that way." He turned again, then slowed the car to read the numbers of the houses they passed. He parked near the next corner.

It bothered Hannah that he could put everything that had happened between them aside so easily. Bonny. Their lovemaking. Her cheeks burned and she reminded herself that was exactly what she wanted, wasn't it? They weren't any good for each other. She demanded from him what he could not give; he took what he did not want.

If only she could put things aside as easily as Chad had, things would be so much easier.

"The house is the brick one on the opposite side of the street," he said.

Hannah eyed the modest, two-story structure in the sprawling suburban development. It seemed the least likely place for a criminal to hide. Which meant it was probably the most likely. Chad switched off the engine, then pulled on the release to lower the back of his seat. He looked like he was resting, ready to be there for a while.

Sitting back, Hannah crossed her arms over her chest. She tried not to worry about Bonny, and battled back the urge to ask Chad why he'd brought her flowers.

She hadn't dared touch them before leaving the room, no matter how much her heart longed to. Didn't trust herself to read the card dangling from the long, leafy stems.

Now she wished she'd had the courage to do both.

At any rate, whoever cleaned the room—she suspected Betty performed that duty as well—was in for a pleasant surprise.

Ask him, a tiny voice nudged her.

She closed her eyes, hating that she hurt so much, yet hating the silence in the car more.

"Chad, I—" She cleared her throat.

He shifted in his seat, then looked at her.

"Never mind." She stared resolutely at the house across the street.

Chad said softly, "I thought that was my line."

Her gaze flicked to his and held. What a pair they made, she thought, sitting there, neither of them willing or able to break the tension between them.

His lips upturned in the smallest of smiles. She returned it, unfamiliar with the emotions tumbling inside her chest.

Then they both shifted their attention back to the house.

Hannah rubbed a cramp from her right calf and stared at her watch.

"I think we're wasting our time," she murmured. Her gaze drifted from the house to the empty disposable coffee cup on the dash. The caffeine had not helped her anxiety any. The last two hours closed in the car with Chad had taken their toll. She was little more than a series of thinly stretched nerves, beneath which lay a vulnerability she didn't want to face. She cleared her throat. "Aside from the girl we saw go inside a while ago, there's no sign anybody's home."

About an hour before, a swarm of children had descended upon the neighborhood, signaling that some sort of summer school or summer program had let out. Nearly every house was invaded by one or two kids, including the Furgeson household. A brown-haired girl had hastened up the walkway, picking at a sprawling rosebush before letting herself into the house with her own key.

"I don't think we're wasting our time," Chad said quietly. Too quietly. "What did you expect? That Furgeson would come out with her hands up because a strange car is parked on the street outside?"

Hannah frowned. "I wonder what it feels like to have a family member with a price on their head."

"Who says her brother and his family know about her jumping bail? Sure, they may know Lisa is in trouble, but do they know what kind of trouble? Then there's Furgeson herself. After what happened to Persky, does she know there's more than a dollar sign hovering above her head?"

He shifted in his seat, bringing his seat back up. His shoulder came in contact with hers. Hannah leaned against the passenger side door, as far away from him as possible, and jerkily opened a Twinkie he had offered her from a little bag of goodies a while ago.

Chad looked at her. "Of course, that's leaving out that *she* could have been the one who finished off Persky."

Hannah chased the bite of cream-filled cake with bitter coffee and almost choked.

"The house," she managed to say between coughs.

Chad's lips pulled into a thin line.

"Look at it. It's modest, well tended, in a neighborhood with good schools. How old did the girl who went inside look to you? Seven? Eight? Would a mother keep her seven-year-old daughter around if she knew her life was in jeopardy?''

Chad sank lower in the seat.

Twinkie crumbs fell to her skirt and she brushed them away. ''Is that your way of saying I'm way out in left field?''

''No,'' Chad said. ''I just think you should stop second-guessing everyone. It would make things a whole helluva lot easier.''

''Oh?'' Hannah hesitantly stuffed the last of the Twinkie into her mouth. She swallowed. Was he talking about her second-guessing of Furgeson's mind-set? Or of his actions and motivations? ''So you're telling me Lisa Furgeson has flown the coop?''

''If that's what I'm saying, then I think she's just flown back in.''

Hannah turned toward the house to find a late model black Buick pulling into the driveway. They sat silently watching as the brake lights went out. A brunette climbed out and hurried to the door, casting nervous glances about as she did so.

''Interesting,'' Hannah said.

''Is that Furgeson?''

''I don't know. The fact sheets list her as blond, but five bucks and a half hour could change that.''

The woman disappeared into the house, closing the door quickly after herself.

''You're a lot of help,'' Chad said.

She stared at him. ''We're a little far away to make a composite sketch.''

A few minutes later, the woman left the house with the little girl who had gone in earlier. Within moments both were in the Buick and backing out of the drive-way.

"Looks like the action's picking up. Maybe they spotted us," Hannah said, removing her seat belt. She emptied the remainder of her coffee out the window, then tossed the empty cup into the back seat. Snatching up her purse, she climbed out of the car.

She slammed the door, tossing Chad one of a pair of two-way radios. "Take this. I borrowed them from Betty's boys. They probably don't have very good range, but they're something."

Chad took it. Hannah tried not to remember the way those long, tanned fingers had touched her only a short time ago. Awakened a part of herself long asleep. Coaxed out emotions she had never felt.

Hannah watched the Buick speed down the opposite side of the street. "Keep in contact. I'll be listening with the one I have in my purse."

He turned the ignition key. "I don't like this," Chad said, staring at her through the open window. "Get back in the car, Hannah. We're sticking together on this."

She stared at him, her heart thudding in her chest, time curiously at a standstill. In that one moment, she pushed aside the past few hours and the pain he had caused her, and gave in to a sudden swell of fear.

Fear had never played a part in their professional partnership before. They had always been equals on a level playing field, she never asking for help she didn't need, Chad never trying to dominate the relationship as most men would.

Now? Well, now she wasn't that fearless Hannah McGee, ex-police officer unafraid of taking anyone on. She was a mother with a tiny human being to think of before herself. And she sensed Chad was no longer the live-and-let-die man she had once thought him, because he was a father.

A father.

This was the second time he had tried to protect her. And despite a tiny spark of indignation, she found herself dangerously close to liking his concern for her safety.

Her gaze drifted down to the clean line of his jaw, then slowly up to his strong, inviting mouth, her heart beating a potent rhythm in her chest. She found her own mouth watering, longing to feel again Chad's lips on hers. She blinked and looked into his eyes, the melting metal in them reaching inside and grasping something elemental within her. Holding his gaze, she began to lean in, to tell him without words how much it meant to her that he cared, no matter how much he tried to hide it. To cling to his mouth for a brief second, to remind herself how wonderfully vital she felt when she touched him.

She caught herself. Her throat tightened as she pulled away.

She needed more than a kiss. She needed a man who wasn't afraid to admit his feelings for her. Who was strong enough to overcome his past and not only profess his love for her, but shout it from the rooftops. A man who could be a good, solid, stick-around father figure for her daughter. Not someone who ran for the door every time he was confused.

"Be careful," she whispered thickly.

He grasped her wrist when she would have turned away.

Hannah pooled every last instinct for self-survival she still had and tugged her wrist away from his velvety grasp. "What are you waiting for, Hogan? Christmas?" Her words were rough, but she couldn't bring herself to look at him, to back up her words with a stern look. She was too afraid she would fall apart. She swallowed hard. "Get a move on."

Chad stared at her intensely as she stepped away from the car. Then he bit off a curse and shoved the gearshift into Drive, speeding after the Buick and the woman in it.

"Chad?"

Chad turned the steering wheel to the left and merged with the traffic of the six-lane highway, trying to follow the Buick without being detected. He stared at the squawking two-way radio on the passenger's seat next to him.

"Chad, are you there?"

He groped blindly around the seat until he felt the smooth plastic of the radio. He picked it up.

"What is it, Hannah?" he asked.

Despite his slightly abrupt response, he realized he liked the fact that she was worried about him. Maybe because it meant that not all had gone bad between them. Perhaps because he needed her to.

Moreover, he wanted to worry about her. What seemed like a long, long time ago, Hannah had never given him an opportunity to protect her. But her new vulnerability touched off something inside him he couldn't quite control. A need to wrap his arms around her in a way that had nothing to do with sex, hold her head to his chest, and fight off the world and everybody in it in order to keep her and their daughter safe. To protect them in the way he hadn't been able to protect Linda and Joshua.

The Buick turned a hundred yards ahead of him. He pulled his own rental around the corner after her.

"Chad? Do you still have the car in sight?" Hannah's voice floated through the small box again.

Chad pulled the radio to his mouth. "Has no one ever taught you the art of patience, Hannah?"

"You don't have to yell. I just thought you might want to take a look in your rearview mirror."

Putting the radio down, he adjusted the mirror, then reached for the radio again. "Help me out here. What am I looking for?"

"A silver older Cadillac and a black late-model Lincoln."

He searched the road behind him and saw neither vehicle in the thick stream of rush hour traffic.

"Anything going on there?" he asked.

"Not yet." There was a brief silence. "What I do here depends on what you turn up."

"Right." He didn't like this. He didn't like this at all.

"Have you spotted the Caddy or the Lincoln?" she asked.

"No. Why?"

"When you pulled away, both were on your tail. I think I saw Stokes in one of them. Must be a cheap rental."

"Let me guess, the beat-up Caddy?"

Hannah's silence told him he was right. He tossed the two-way onto the passenger's seat and shook his head. His attention strayed to the rearview mirror again. Nothing. Until the shift of a car behind him revealed the silver Caddy two lengths back. His knuckles began to itch. It was their good old friend Jack Stokes, all right. A dead giveaway with his leather-rimmed hat, despite the fact that they were in Texas in summer.

"Hannah?"

Silence greeted him as he shifted his gaze between the car behind him and on the Buick ahead. There was the sound of static, then Hannah's voice. "The transmission is beginning to fade."

Chad looked around, searching for something, anything he might recognize. He realized the road was one of the few he'd seen during their brief stay in Houston.

"Hannah, I think the Buick is leading me to the airport." He released the button and shoved his hair back where it rested against his temple. "I've spotted Stokes. What was the other car?"

Static crackled over the receiver as he waited for her response. He swerved quickly to the left, nearly tearing a door from a car a woman climbed out of near the curb. He laid on the horn, and chanced another glance behind him. A black Lincoln. That's what she said the other car was. And there it was. Three car lengths behind the Caddy, mimicking his move by changing lanes.

"Chad," Hannah's voice floated over the radio. "We'll have to break this transmission soon."

There was a long silence. He began to think he had reached the limits of the transmission radius entirely. He tossed the radio onto the seat, blindly searching for the button to cease the incessant static when her voice sounded again.

"Chad...be careful."

The click as Hannah turned her radio off sounded and Chad switched off his as well. He was on his own now. Something that had always been the case.

Except when he was with Hannah.

But her absence now was more than just the empty seat next to him. Somehow when they were together, either working or...otherwise, he felt...complete. As if everything would be okay; it couldn't help but not be. He remembered what happened earlier back at the motel and tightened his fingers around the steering wheel. At least sometimes he felt everything would come out okay. Now he wasn't so sure.

Maneuvering himself so he could gain access to his pocket, he tugged out the small velvet pouch there. He fingered the soft material, then wound the cord around the rearview mirror where he could see it. A reminder of what he had almost done. A reminder of what he had yet to do.

He ran his hand over his face. It was obvious she hadn't read the card attached to the flowers. If she had, then they might still be back at the motel instead of tailing cars and communicating via two-way radios.

Then again maybe she had read the card, compared his words to his actions, and questioned his sincerity.

Oh, he was sincere, all right. Confused as hell. Uncertain. But sincere. It was what he should have done two days ago when he discovered Hannah had had his baby. Only he'd been too wrapped up in his own shock to respond to much of anything.

Now it might be too late.

With a mental shove, Chad pressed all emotion from his mind. This was not the time to deliberate his future with Hannah. If there even was one in her book—something he doubted despite her almost kissing him before he left her on the street outside Furgeson's brother's house. Looking past the Buick, he spotted the airport in the distance. Soon his ride would be over. The knowledge roused impatience and a sense of danger. The danger entered when the rearview mirror told him the Caddy and the Lincoln were still there. Stokes he could understand. But who was in the other car?

Dusk blanketed Houston in a blue haze, making it impossible to see the driver of the Lincoln. He thought about the two guys he had tied to the toilets at the airport. Could it be them? If it was, then they probably weren't very happy with him right now. He returned his gaze to the sleek black Buick in front of him. It didn't surprise him when the blinker switched on at the airport turnoff.

"Where are you going?" he said aloud, following the Buick's lead. "Are you Lisa Furgeson hoping to hop a plane for anywhere? Or are you her sister-in-law leading me on a wild-goose chase?"

The congested causeway found Chad with two cars between him and the Buick in front of him and one between him and the shadow of the Caddy behind him. He couldn't see the Lincoln, but had no doubt it was there somewhere. Briefly, he wondered what Hannah was doing. The woman was a puzzle with a lot of pieces that didn't fit. She'd always been a hotly passionate woman who could melt with one touch of his hand, yet make a decision in the face of danger without hesitation. But now, he supposed Bonny might be the new factor that had changed Hannah. Made her more vulnerable. Easier to hurt.

The Buick pulled into the fire lane in front of the airport terminal. Flicking a glance at the Caddy behind him, Chad drew in a deep breath, then spotted the Lincoln growing closer. Without moving his head, he watched the woman and the little girl leave the Buick and dash for the airport doors.

With vivid clarity, he remembered Persky in Rita

Minelli's bathroom. An image of Bonny, chattering and slobbering on everything in sight, immediately followed it.

"Damn." Chad yanked the steering wheel to the left, away from the fire lane. Immediately he spotted a similar model Buick ahead of him and sped after it, making it look as though it was the car he'd been following all along, leading his tails away from the woman and the child heading into the airport terminal. With relief, he noticed the Caddy and the Lincoln followed him.

He swallowed the risk that he had just lost Lisa Furgeson and the large sum attached to her. When it came down to it, he was incapable of taking the chance that he was leading what could be two killers in the Lincoln to the woman and the child.

Hannah squeezed the useless two-way radio in her hand, then shoved it into her purse. Twenty minutes had passed since Chad's last transmission. She wondered distractedly if he'd ever spotted the Lincoln, or if the fact that the vehicle had followed Stokes's likely rented Cadillac could have been nothing but sheer coincidence, a local resident seeking an evening out. Rubbing the heel of her palm against her temple, she thought it bad enough Stokes had followed them. But with an unknown element thrown in...

She puffed out a long breath. What was going on with this case? What had appeared to be a routine skip-trace had turned into a race against time. Not just for the money. But a race to stop anyone else from losing their lives. She rested her hand against her throat. Including hers and Chad's. Especially hers and Chad's.

She turned toward the Furgeson house across the

street. Light flickered in the front window. Flickered. Hannah narrowed her eyes. Lights didn't flicker. They burned or glowed. That meant it wasn't a light at all. It was a television set. Which meant...

Looking up and down the street, Hannah crossed it. Someone was in the house. Subconsciously she knew she should wait until Chad contacted her. Should wait for word of his results. But she had no idea how long that would take. Climbing the front steps, Hannah curled her fingers around the doorknob. It refused to budge. She lifted her gaze to the small fan window cut at the top of the wood. Through it she could see the light from the television drifting into what was probably the entry hall.

Then she heard it. The sound of the TV. She listened to the viewer change channel after channel, apparently looking for news flashes. The fact that the station kept being turned back to CNN confirmed that.

She thought of Chad. No. Now was definitely the wrong time to start falling back on him. Not when he wouldn't be around tomorrow to rely on. Besides, she wasn't sure the woman he was following was Lisa Furgeson, so there was no sense waiting to hear what she already suspected. She hesitated, but only briefly. If it was Lisa inside, how much trouble could a five-foot-six Quality Control Manager cause?

Silently she skirted the house and peered into the front window. But the shades that had been half-open earlier were now effectively closed, allowing her not even a glimpse at the interior, much less the person sitting in front of the television.

Hannah gave a quiet yelp. A thorny rosebush had attached itself to her calf. She tried to yank her leg out of the tangled mess, immediately regretting it when the long thorns tore at her flesh through her skirt.

"Just peachy," she muttered, bending to untangle herself. She was midway through when she noticed something had changed. It was the television. She no longer heard the sound. The dark window told her it had been turned off.

Had the person heard her outside? Grown aware of her presence? If she had, that meant...

Cringing, Hannah pulled her leg out of the bush, the tearing of her skirt meaning little compared to the frustrated scream threatening to spill out of her mouth. She bounded toward the door, stun gun in hand.

"Open up!" she called, banging on the wooden barrier with the butt of her stun gun. "It's the police!" A lie, to be sure, but considering her status with the FBI, this was small time.

From inside she heard the shuffling of feet and her heart beat a hopeful rhythm. Moments later, the television was turned on twice as loud as it had been before.

Hannah flanked the side of the door, ready to pounce if it opened. She didn't like this. A door slammed somewhere in the house. Switching her stun gun to safety so she wouldn't accidentally zap herself, Hannah sprinted around the side of the house toward the back. She only hoped she could beat the person inside. Which seemed impossible since her opponent had the straightest and shortest route while Hannah hurdled a girl's bike, a terra-cotta flowerpot, and a half dozen other obstacles.

Finally she emerged from the side of the house, stopping dead in her tracks. The back door was firmly closed, with no sign a person had just escaped through it. Hannah took one step toward it, keeping well to the shadows. It could be a trap, she told herself. There was no sense being an easy target if it was.

She flanked the side of the back door, becoming one with the outer wall, and stared at the immobile door handle. For long, quiet moments she stood watching it, hoping, daring it to move.

Then it did. Adrenaline pumped into Hannah's bloodstream as she watched the brass handle turn ever so slightly. The door opened—and Hannah jumped from the shadows.

"That's far enough, Lisa."

Hannah had no doubt that was who the woman was. She had memorized her PlayCo Industries security photo.

"I haven't done anything!" the woman responded in a high, strained voice. "You won't take me back. I'll do anything to stop you." Lisa sounded surprisingly convinced.

A small amount of admiration pricked Hannah's cool exterior. The woman had guts.

"I hate to tell you this, Lisa, but I'm taking you back and there's nothing you can do to stop me." She slipped her stun gun into the waist of her skirt and reached for her handcuffs. In the millisecond, Lisa took off in a mad dash across the grassy backyard.

Hannah groaned, watching her run away. She wasn't much in the mood for a foot chase. Gripping the cool metal of the handcuffs with her fingers, she bolted toward the retreating figure.

The distance between them quickly disappeared. Hannah lunged for Lisa, grabbing her around her legs. They both fell to the damp, hard ground.

"You didn't think it would be that easy, did you?"

Hannah reached for the woman's hand, only to find her opponent had not given up. Furgeson used her balled fists to fight her off. It was all Hannah could do to keep the hard blows from hitting her in the face.

"Would you cut it out?" she shouted, trying to restrain the woman's damaging arms. "This isn't going to get you anywhere."

"Leave me alone! Let me go!"

Hannah finally grasped the flailing arms, her body effectively blocking any movement the woman's legs might make.

"I can't let you go, Furgeson. Not if I hope to get you back to New York—alive—in time for your hearing the day after tomorrow."

The clank of the metal handcuffs as Hannah locked them around Lisa's wrists placed an exclamation point at the end of her statement.

"You're not a cop?" Lisa asked with a trembling voice.

Hannah shook her head. "No, Furgeson. I'm a bounty hunter."

Then it occurred to her that she couldn't say that. Not anymore. With the capture of Lisa Furgeson her career as a skip-tracer was essentially over. She swallowed hard, realizing it marked the end of many other things, as well. Namely the reason for her and Chad being together.

Chapter Ten

Chad pulled the car to a screeching halt in exactly the same spot it was parked before he went off on his fruitless chase. He had shaken off both the Caddy and the Lincoln miles on the other side of the airport before he hooked a U-turn and headed back to the Furgeson house. For long moments he sat there, waiting for Hannah to approach, but she didn't. He stared at the two-way radio. Nothing but static. He picked it up.

"Hannah?" he called again as he depressed the Talk button.

He gave her a moment to respond then spoke into the radio again. Nothing. Where was she? He tossed the radio on the passenger's seat, a cold fear sweeping over him. He shifted his gaze to the dark house up the block.

A wave of fear washed over him at the next thought. No.

Surely she didn't go in by herself? She would have waited for him, right? Wrong.

"Damn."

Chad yanked open the car door, his hand reaching automatically for the 9 mm he'd stuffed into the waist of his jeans. He broke into a run, slowing only when he reached the front door of the house. The prospect sent another surge of fear through his taut, restless muscles. He couldn't lose her, too. Not like his wife and son...

Under the cover of night, he took his lock-picking kit from his pocket and went to work. Within moments the lock gave and he slipped inside. Quick, cautious footsteps took him to the living room where the television blared out a cosmetics commercial. Nothing. No sign of Hannah. He backtracked to the hallway. Where was she?

"Hannah?" Chad yelled over the sound of the television.

Holding his gun steady, he clung to the shadows. Slow, careful footsteps carried him down the passageway while he strained to pick up any sound other than that of the TV. She had to be there.

Up ahead he saw a shaft of light. He approached the partially open door to what he believed to be the kitchen and flanked the right side. Problem was, he didn't know if the person on the other side was Hannah or Lisa Furgeson. Since he hadn't been able to identify the woman in the Buick, it was possible she had been Lisa's sister-in-law, and that Lisa herself had stayed behind in the house. He would have to play his cards carefully, for if Lisa Furgeson had managed to take Hannah McGee hostage, she had to be one hell of an adversary.

"Freeze!"

Chad stormed the kitchen, holding the gun out in front of him.

"What took you so long, Hogan?"

Relief flooded Chad's twitching muscles. Hannah wasn't tied up. She wasn't lying unconscious on the floor. To the contrary, she was the prettiest piece of work he had ever seen, healthy and unpredictable with her face nearly the color of her gorgeous red hair. She stood staring at him as if he'd gone mad. He dropped his gun hand to his side. The smudges on her cheek told him she hadn't won without a struggle.

"What is this?" he asked, stepping closer to touch the swelling near her right eye.

Hannah flinched. "Lisa Furgeson may have worked for a toy company, but she has one of the meanest right hooks I've ever played punching bag to."

She motioned toward the corner. Chad spotted a just-as-scuffed Furgeson handcuffed to the metal handle of the refrigerator. The blonde looked exactly like her photo in the file. "Gave you a run for your money, did she?"

"Where were you anyway? I expected you back a half hour ago."

"The airport isn't exactly close. Especially when you have two tails that refuse to be shaken off. And just what in the hell did you think you were doing facing off with Furgeson without backup? You—"

"What were you doing at the airport?"

In the corner, Lisa Furgeson snapped to attention.

Hannah looked in the woman's direction, then turned back to him and continued. "And what did you want me to do? Sit here on my hands waiting for you to come back?"

"Yes." He wasn't sure he liked what he saw in Hannah's eyes. There was a shadow that seemed to say that she wouldn't be waiting for him again.

Lisa yanked on her handcuffs. "You followed Jolene there, didn't you?"

Chad shoved his hands into the pockets of his jeans. "Yes, I did. Only I was under the impression that your sister-in-law wasn't your sister-in-law. That, in fact, she was you."

"Are you saying you followed Jolene to the airport on the assumption she was me?" Lisa asked.

Chad grimaced at the woman. "Yes. And I'd like to point out that if I couldn't be sure she wasn't you, there could be others out there who could make the same mistake."

"Are they...are they okay? My sister-in-law...and the girl?" Lisa whispered.

"They're fine. When they ran into the terminal, I let them go." He met Hannah's gaze and noticed the curiosity in her eyes. She didn't have to ask. They both knew what he'd done—and why. He'd sacrificed what could have been a healthy bounty in order to keep the woman and the girl safe from whoever was tailing them. From the same fate that had caught up with Eric Persky.

He cleared his throat and went on. "Forget about Stokes, though. He wasn't the one I was concerned about anyway. But I couldn't get a handle on who was in the other car."

"The Lincoln," Hannah said.

"Yeah."

Chad searched Hannah's smudged face, suddenly realizing their apprehension of Lisa also meant the end of the assignment. As soon as they got her back to New

York, gone would be the reason for their partnership. Gone would be Hannah—and Bonny—from his life.

That is if he couldn't do something to stop it beforehand....

"We don't have much time," Hannah interrupted his thoughts. "You may have lost Stokes and the Lincoln, but it won't be long before they find their way back here."

The legs of Lisa's chair screeched against the tile floor, the metal handcuffs clanking as she yanked on the door handle.

"What are you doing, Furgeson?" Chad asked.

"Someone's out there." Lisa indicated the door leading to the hall.

Chad tried to pick up any proof of movement. The only sound he could hear was the television. He wished he'd turned it off before.

"This isn't a ploy," Lisa whispered fiercely. "There *is* someone out there!"

"Suppose she's right?" Hannah asked. "I don't know about you, but I'm in no hurry to meet up with our two friends from the airport again."

Chad gripped his gun. "Stay here. I'll go check it out."

Hannah anxiously watched the door close behind Chad, suppressing the urge to call out to him, demand they leave the house. Now. They could slip through the back and leave whoever had made the sound in the living room to fend for themselves. To search through the empty house and find them long gone.

"What if someone *is* out there?" Lisa asked.

"Then we get out of here as fast as we can."

Lisa offered her handcuffed hands, metal clanking against metal as she did so.

Hannah started for the kitchen door, then paced back to the middle of the kitchen. Why didn't Chad turn the television off so she could hear?

"All right, I'll free you from the refrigerator." She neared Lisa with the keys. "But the cuffs stay."

Once liberated from the appliance, Lisa stood up, starting for the doorway Chad had disappeared through.

"What are you doing?" Hannah hurried after her. The sound of a loud crash from the front of the house sent her pulse into overdrive.

"Oh God." Hannah pushed the kitchen door open, rushing into the outside hall with her stun gun drawn and charged. Darkness greeted her, and her eyesight was slow to adjust to the sudden change in lighting.

Hannah led a slow march down the hall to the living room. The only sounds were those of a sitcom on television. The periods of laughter following a joke were unsettling, echoing through the deceptively empty house.

She debated whether she should call out to Chad. After all, he could be waiting around the corner, gun drawn, thinking her the intruder. Her breath snagged in her throat. She remembered the last time she had called out for him and earned him a whack in the head.

She decided to be quiet.

"Get back in the kitchen!" Chad's harsh whisper sounded from her left in the main hall.

"Hey, Hannah, luv. Bet you didn't expect to see me so soon." The familiar voice reached out for her in the darkness from her right, startling her. But not as much as the arms that snaked around her waist.

"Stokes? What in the hell are you doing—"

A light switch clicked and Hannah found her guess correct. Jack Stokes knocked he. stun gun from her hand, then strengthened his hold around her waist. "Told you I'd get you back for taking Eddie the Snake out from under my nose, McGee."

Regaining her breath, Hannah said, "If it helps any, El hasn't even paid me for the privilege."

A broken hall lamp lay in pieces on the floor. Her gaze darted to Chad, but he looked none the worse for wear. Stokes must have been the one who had taken the hit.

Chad stood a few feet away in a shooter's stance, his legs spread shoulder length apart, his arms stretched out in front of him as he aimed his gun straight at Stokes's chest. Hannah swallowed. The only problem was the bullet would have to go through her before it could rip through its target.

From the entrance of the kitchen, Lisa Furgeson moved, seizing their attention.

Jack eyed her.

"Don't give it a second thought, Stokes." Chad stepped closer, playing a dangerous game of chicken as he continued to aim his gun at Jack's forehead. "She's ours."

"Now, now, you wouldn't shoot me, would you, Hogan? Not your ole pal Jack Stokes? Especially after all the trouble I've gone to."

Chad stepped ever slowly closer. He shifted the safety off his gun in support of his willingness to use it. Hannah felt panic begin to swell in her stomach.

Jack clucked his tongue. "I daresay you would do it, wouldn't you?"

"You're damn right I would." Chad waved the gun

toward the door. "Now why don't you just turn around and leave the way you came in?"

Jack clucked his tongue. "Can't do that." He motioned his head toward Furgeson. "Not without her."

"The way I see it, Jack, you don't have much choice in the matter."

His deep-throated laugh filled the room. "Come on, Chad. Put that thing away before somebody gets hurt."

Chad took another cautionary step forward. Hannah drew a deep, steadying breath—until she felt cold, unyielding metal encircle her right wrist, then ratchet close. She tried to jerk her hand free, but it was securely bound. Stokes yanked her arm behind her back, searching for her other wrist. She refused to give it to him.

"Do it!" he snarled into her ear, cocking his own weapon where it poked against her ribs.

Hannah immediately put her other hand behind her back.

"You don't know how much I've wanted to do this, Hannah, luv," Jack whispered into her ear. None too gently he fastened the other cuff to her free wrist. "You messed me around one time too many when you handcuffed me to that bar back in Queens."

Lisa Furgeson started backing farther into the kitchen.

"Oh, no, you don't, lady." Before Hannah knew what was happening, Stokes pushed her aside. She stumbled to her knees, losing her balance without the assistance of her arms. In two strides, he grabbed a handful of Lisa's shirt, yanking her back into the main hall. "You are not going anywhere until I tell you to."

Hannah jerked her head up to see Chad coming after

her, concern marring his handsome face. Behind him, Stokes shoved a still-bound Lisa into the closet, then started after Chad.

"No!"

Hannah flashed on the scene at Persky's house, when her scream had distracted Chad. But this time it served its purpose as a warning. Chad swung on Stokes before the Aussie could hit him with the butt of his gun. The two men faced off, both holding their firearms on the other.

Hannah struggled to a sitting position, yanking on the cuffs binding her.

"Drop the gun, Stokes," Chad ordered.

"Not on your life, mate."

Hannah was too far away to be of much help in the situation, but suspected Chad didn't need her help anyway. In fact, her mind fastened on the way he had stood before, and the way he stood now, in a traditional shooter's stance. She'd been taught the position at the academy. Feet shoulders length apart. Arms outstretched with one hand on the gun, the other underneath, supporting the weight for a cleaner shot. Chad had probably learned the technique in the Marines.

Jack Stokes, on the other hand, showed no technique whatsoever. Too cocky, he stood relaxed and held the gun with one hand, the weight of the revolver causing his wrist to turn a little so he almost held the gun horizontally. With his other hand, he wiped sweat from his forehead.

"There ain't no way in hell I'm gonna let you two take this one, so just sod off, Hogan," Jack said, and shrugged. "Your call. Either you let me take her the easy way…or the hard."

''And the hard way would entail exactly what?''
Chad asked.

''Well, I'll just have to shoot you, won't I?''

Hannah leaned against the wall and used it to support
herself as she struggled to her feet.

By inches, Chad closed the distance separating him
from Stokes, his revolver almost muzzle to muzzle with
Jack's. Hannah stopped her movements, watching as
Chad used his support hand to slap Stokes's revolver,
forcing his aim at the opposite wall. The report of a
round ripped through the house, drowning out even the
sound of the TV. Stokes cursed, and Chad was all over
him in a matter of seconds, pushing first one gun, then
the other, away from the fray. Hannah lifted herself to
a full standing position and kicked both guns even farther away.

''God rot you, Hogan!'' Stokes said after taking a
particularly nasty-looking fist to the nose. The two men
tumbled into the living room, half falling onto the steps
leading to the second floor.

Hannah pulled on the cuffs biting into her wrists,
even though she knew better.

The sound of metal teeth grinding against each other
seized her attention. But it wasn't her cuffs that had
made the sound. She rushed into the living room to
find Chad cursing ripely and pulling against a pair of
handcuffs secured to the spindle of the stair railing.

''Damn you, Stokes, unlock these blasted things!''
he spat out.

The Aussie stood back, rubbing a scrape on his chin.
''Not if you got down on your hands and knees and
begged me, mate.'' He chuckled. ''Got you there,
didn't I? A man with a plan, I am.''

He spotted Hannah where she stood in the doorway. "You," he said, "get over here."

When she didn't budge, he shot to her side and dragged her to the stairs. She had a choice between falling to the floor or doing what he said. She did what he said, and was ready when he opened one of the cuffs. Swinging her leg around, she tried to kick him to force him off balance. Stokes effectively caught the limb and yanked it, forcing her to the floor. She struggled to sit up and Stokes threaded the cuffs through the spindles near the foot of the stairs and re-trapped her free hand. She gave the metal shackles a violent jerk, but the wood was solid.

"I got Hogan's cuffs." He smiled, clearly impressed by his clever work. "Where's the key to your cuffs, Hannah?" He felt in her skirt pocket. "Got it." He held it up for her to inspect, then disappeared into the hall. Moments later he stood in the entryway, Lisa Furgeson's bound arm in his. He plopped his battered cowboy hat back on his head, a grin greeting Hannah from underneath the rim.

"G'day, McGee. Give my regards to that beauty of a daughter of yours. And, oh, no hard feelings, huh?"

Chapter Eleven

Hannah gave her handcuffs a final yank, then sank back in defeat to the floor next to Chad. The thick wooden spindles were solidly attached to the railing. No amount of wrenching or off balance kicking had succeeded in budging the one to which she was shackled. She sighed, wishing the television remote were nearby so she could at least turn the blaring thing off.

"There's nothing more humiliating than being bound by your own cuffs," Chad said.

She blew her hair from her face. "Technically these aren't mine." She smiled. "Furgeson has that honor. These must be Stokes's."

Lying beside her, Chad grimaced. "I should have shot him when I had the chance."

Hannah skimmed his disheveled tangle of light brown hair to where the telltale stubble was beginning to show again on his strong jaw. It was unfair for him to look so good after what he'd gone through. Even with his hands bound above his head, he tempted her touch. She swallowed. *Especially* with his hands bound above his head.

Frowning, she tugged her gaze away from him. The only way she would survive Chad Hogan was if she stayed as far away from him as possible. A dubious task, given their present predicament.

She closed her eyes tightly. Why were things always so complicated? What logical explanation could there be for the feelings roaring within her? One moment she wanted nothing better than to see Chad walk off into the sunset—alone. The next she wanted to hold him and feel his skillful hands exploring every part of her body. To watch him bond with Bonny in the way all fathers bonded with their children.

"Tell me, Chad, how did we ever get into this?"

"It all began when Lisa heard a noise," he said wryly.

She jabbed her knee into his. "That's not what I meant."

Ten feet away the television blared a preview of what was coming up on the late evening news. Hannah ignored it and looked at him.

"If I could take everything back, do it all over again…" She pulled in a long breath then blew it out soundlessly.

"You would do everything exactly the same way." Chad tapped his boot against her shoe. "We both would." He fell silent. "No matter what happened, what we had was special." His voice lowered. "I realize that now."

An ache took up residence in Hannah's heart. There was a sincerity in his gray eyes she'd never witnessed before. A hum of regret in his voice that made his words nearly inaudible. She only wished his realization had come a year and a half earlier. Even a few hours ago. Now...

Well, now she had experienced too much pain, endured too many lonely nights, had her hopes dashed one too many times, to allow herself to trust him again. At least not with her heart.

"What's that?" Chad eyed a six-inch plastic tube that must have fallen to the floor during Hannah's struggle with Stokes. Inside were square, green objects less than a half inch in diameter.

"Microprocessor chips."

He frowned at her. "Where did you get them?"

"Lisa gave them to me earlier."

"Let me guess. Persky and Furgeson were distributing these through PlayCo."

"In one of PlayCo's toy telephone models to be more precise," Hannah said. "And it was just Persky."

He stared at her. "What do you mean just Persky? Both Persky and Furgeson were arrested, Hannah."

She shrugged. "Well, you could say Lisa and I had an interesting conversation. A very interesting conversation." She swallowed. "It was about men."

Chad raised his brows. "Men?"

"Yes, men." She moved the plastic tube with her shoe. "Namely the ones who made her look responsible for smuggling these through PlayCo. Well, not just these. From what I understand there are two boxes full of them still in toy telephones in a storage locker across town. A locker Lisa was only too happy to give me the key to. From what she told me, an eight-by-ten-inch sheet of these chips are worth—"

"I know what they're worth, McGee. Suffice it to

say we're talking big money.'' Chad's gaze moved
from her bare ankle to her face. ''How did you get
Furgeson to give them to you?''

''It was easy, really. Lisa wasn't involved in any of
it. The smuggling, I mean. She stumbled across the ring
when she worked the third shift one night to get a rush
order out. She took two of three boxes, trying to figure
out what she should do, then she and Persky were arrested.''

''You bought that?''

Hannah stiffened and shifted the cuffs around her
wrists. ''Yes, I bought it. And for a very good reason.
The girl we saw earlier, the one you let go at the airport
with Lisa's sister-in-law? That's Lisa's daughter, not
her niece.''

''Oh.''

''Oh'' about summed up her reaction to the news as
well.

For long moments neither of them said anything
more. Then the sound of Chad shifting captured her
attention. She watched him test the limits of his movements then aim the toe of his right boot at an end table
seven feet away. The dark lamp fell to the carpet along
with a vase filled with dried flowers and the remote.
The remote!

''Nudge it over this way,'' she said when he couldn't
quite get a toehold on it.

He did and together they brought the remote control
to knee level. Eyeing what seemed like a hundred buttons, Hannah watched as Chad jabbed his knee near
the top. He missed the power switch, but managed to
hit Mute. The house was suddenly, blessedly silent.

Hannah sighed, relieved that she didn't have to com-
pete with the television. ''So what do we do now?''

She felt Chad's gaze on her, but refused to look at him. Instead she feigned interest in the voiceless images flickering across the television screen.

"Any chance Stokes will have an attack of conscience and come back?" Chad asked.

She forgot not to look at him and smiled. "Oh, I'd say zero to nil."

His gray eyes twinkled at her as he shrugged. "Then I guess we wait until someone stumbles across us."

Hannah began calculating the likelihood of that, then swept the thought from her mind. She'd only work herself up into a panic at the thought of being out of contact with Bonny...and spending so much uninterrupted time with Chad.

She looked at him. Then again, with no bail-jumpers to stake out, and with him unable to run for any doors, maybe now was the time to clear the air between them. Ask those questions she may not have dared before.

He looked at her, questions of his own filling his eyes, and she turned her head away. Coward.

She cleared her throat and said instead, "I wonder what chaos Bonny's wreaking on poor Betty right now." She thought of the detailed instructions and food she'd left behind, hoping her daughter wasn't too miserable in the unfamiliar surroundings.

"I'm sure she's fine, Hannah," Chad said quietly.

Her cuffs clanked as she shifted.

"Betty's kids seemed intrigued by the addition of another hell-raiser. Bonny herself didn't even seem that interested in our leaving by the time she got an eyeful of the toys she'd get to mangle."

He was right, of course. Her daughter seemed overjoyed at the prospect of exploring her new environs, and Betty's apartment behind the office emerged a virtual child's paradise, what with three children of her own. Relief suffused her muscles and she lay back a little easier.

"You're a great mother, you know?"

Hannah looked at Chad, her heart dipping low in her chest at his words. She felt her cheeks heat and smiled. "Thanks." She didn't know why his compliment should please her so, but it did. "I used to worry a lot, you know, when I first brought her home." She briefly caught her bottom lip between her teeth. "There I was, this new mother, with this new baby, and all I could think of is how much I wished an operating manual was sent home with Bonny. It took me a good week before her crying didn't threaten to send me into an anxiety attack. To get comfortable with my ability to feed her—was it enough, too much—then there was changing her diapers. Which was the right brand? Should I be using natural cotton instead of disposable? Oh, and forget the first time she got a cold." She could laugh now, but it hadn't been very funny then. "I rushed her to the emergency room, convinced she had contracted some life-threatening illness. Ended up spending the night there. By the time we finally got home, I was as sick as she was."

Chad was quiet. She looked at him, wondering if she had rambled on too long. Recently she'd noticed that if anyone asked the simplest question about her daughter, she'd launch into a long answer that would leave her wondering if she hadn't shared too much. It made her worry that she was turning into one of those obsessed mothers whose conversations never wandered far from their children.

Then again, she was an obsessed mother—and proud of it.

"I never thought I'd be a father again," he finally said.

"I don't know, I guess I always knew I wanted to be a mother. I just didn't think it would happen so soon. Not that I regret having Bonny. I don't. Not for a minute." She gave a long sigh. "I couldn't imagine my life without her in it anymore, you know?"

There was a long silence, then Chad said so quietly she nearly didn't hear him, "Yes, I do know."

She probed his face, noting the sincerity there, the genuine emotion for their daughter. "Chad, why did you bring me flowers?"

The question was out before she had a chance to think about it, before she had an opportunity to stop herself from asking it. Rather than feeling imprudent, though, she felt relieved that it was out.

Chad didn't even blink. "Did you read the card?"

Hannah felt her cheeks heat again. "No. I..." She what? Her reasons for not crossing that room, not picking up those roses, were as sound as ever, but she didn't feel up to sharing them. The hurt was too fresh.

Chad awkwardly got to his feet, twisting his body this way and that until he was standing. Hannah looked up at him. He appeared to be trying to get something from his jeans pocket, but couldn't quite manage the task, what with his hands being secured to a railing post above waist level.

His gaze met hers, then he almost uncertainly looked away. "Do you think you can reach my pocket?"

Hannah mimicked his movements of moments ago until she stood next to him.

"No, not that one. The other one," Chad said, swiveling his hips to give her access to his front pocket.

Trying to ignore the soft denim of his jeans, the

slight scent of soap that clung to his warm skin, she slid two fingers into his pocket, then slid them out again. A small, dark blue velvet pouch fell to the carpet between their feet.

Hannah stared at it, her heart beating heavily in her chest.

"I should have done this a long time—I mean, if I'd had a brain in my head—I should have offered to do the right thing the moment I saw Bonny."

Thunderstruck, she watched him struggle to get his point across, his thick throat convulsing around a swallow.

"Aw, hell, Hannah, if you had read the card on those flowers…"

Somehow she found her tongue, though lack of air refused to allow her to speak above a whisper. "What did it say, Chad?"

His gaze caught and held hers. "Marry me."

Hannah's gaze riveted to his face. In her chest, her heart seemed to cease beating. Her lungs refused air. And if she didn't restart both posthaste she would surely pass out.

Carefully lowering herself back to the floor before she fell down, she stared at the velvet pouch and the ring it likely held.

Chad's chuckle held an undeniable measure of nervousness. "That's not the response I was looking for, Hannah."

She tried to work her mouth, but in order to do so, she had to actually have words to fill it with. "I—I don't know what to say, Chad. I…didn't expect this…."

"If you had, it wouldn't have been a surprise now, would it?"

She looked up at him, attempting to wrap her mind around his proposal. Slowly her heart began pumping at a normal rate of speed and her breathing evened out. She bit down hard on her bottom lip. She'd give everything, anything to be able to say yes. To accept his proposal and take the ring she couldn't even see. But she couldn't. Not without knowing the motivation behind it.

"Why?" she whispered, holding his gaze.

Chad blinked once, then again. "Why?"

She shrugged, watching as he sat back down next to her.

"Because you love me," he said.

Warmth coursed through every inch of her veins, bringing to life the fluttering butterflies in her stomach. Yes, she did love him. With every cell of her being. More than that, she had fallen back in love with him. Completely, utterly, irreversibly. That he knew that made her feel an even stronger connection to him. She tugged her gaze away from his face. "That's not what I meant, Chad. I—" She blindly groped around her spinning head for the right words. "What is it about you that I should agree to spend the rest of my life with you?"

Please, please, say it, her heart pleaded. *Just tell me, I can say yes, then we can have the happily-ever-after I've been dreaming about all my life.*

"Marry me because we have a daughter together." Chad spoke the words clearly and calmly.

Her hopeful gaze moved from his right eye to his left.

"Marry me for Bonny's sake. The rest can come later."

The hope that had ballooned in her slowly deflated.

She tucked her chin into her chest and closed her eyes, wondering if he could hear the quiet breaking of her heart. "No."

She couldn't believe she'd just said that. Couldn't believe she was turning down the chance to spend the rest of her life with the only man she'd ever loved.

"I thought—I mean, didn't you—"

Tears threatened to choke Hannah, but she managed to ask, "Why did you ask me? Why now?"

"Are you saying it's too late?"

The confusion on his handsome face was all too adorable, all too heartbreaking. "Why, Chad?"

He stared at the concealed ring still between them, his cuffs clanking as he shifted. "Because it's the right thing to do."

"Then my saying no is the right thing for me to do."

"But I—"

She swallowed hard. "Look, Chad, I appreciate the offer. I do, really. But to get married for Bonny's sake alone...don't you see? It's wrong. It would never work." *Because every moment of every day I'd see you and know you didn't love me.* "If you want to play a role in Bonny's life...I have no objection to that. Even if I did, you could get a court order—"

"I don't want to play a role, Hannah. I want to be her father. Full-time. Not a weekend dad. Not like my father was."

"Then we...then we can work something out in that regard. Maybe you can come by for an hour every other day. Every day if you want. I don't know."

And she didn't know. She didn't know what the future held for them as parents to Bonny living in separate households. In fact it was very hard to see the future at all right now. All she could focus on was the here and now.

She looked at him, trying to read his thoughts. The confusion on his face slowly turned to resigned acceptance. Disappointment, perhaps.

"You have to quit," he said absently.

"What?"

He turned to her as if surprised he'd said the words aloud. "Skip-tracing. You should quit. For Bonny's sake. I'll support you both."

"And as Bonny's father you have the right to make that demand?" she quietly clarified.

He didn't say anything.

Hannah tried to grab on to indignation with both hands, but the emotion slipped through her grasp. Instead she felt an odd sort of gratitude that he cared that much for their daughter.

Hannah leaned against the wall and briefly closed her eyes. "If it helps any, one of the reasons I was so reluctant to take this trace was because I was hanging up my bounty hunter cap for good. Next week I open the door to Seekers."

His silence was unbearable. She opened her eyes to find him staring at her. "You're opening Seekers?"

Her cuffs clanked as she moved to nervously tuck her hair behind her ear. "Yeah. I rented a place in Manhattan. Bought a sign and everything. From here on in I search for others' lost loves instead of the state's missing lawbreakers." She cleared her throat. "You know, with Bonny to think about and all, I had to start doing something else. Skip-tracing is not exactly a nine-to-five job."

She glanced at him and found him grinning at her. His reaction caught her off guard. He wasn't the least bit upset to hear that she alone was starting a business they had once talked about opening together?

"I'm happy for you, Hannah," he said.

His words brushed her heart. She looked away, suddenly self-conscious. She battled a small part of her that wished he had been upset by her announcement.

"And you?" she asked. "As Bonny's mother I think I have the right to ask you not to involve yourself in risky activity."

Her question went unanswered, leaving her to consider the possibilities.

His long sigh broke the silence that had settled between them. "I really screwed this up, didn't I, Hannah? I just can't seem to get this marriage thing...this father thing right."

Her heart went out to him. She wished she could reach out and touch him. But since she couldn't, she leaned toward him and gently pressed her lips against his.

The look in his eyes was one of shock. But slowly it shifted to longing. She began to pull away, but he groaned softly and sought a more solid contact. Testing the limit of the cuffs, Hannah melted against him, wishing for all the world that she could touch him with more than her mouth. Wanting to fit into this one kiss all the things she might never have the chance to tell him again.

A flurry of activity outside the front door caused them to stare at each other then pull away.

"FBI," a commanding voice shouted. "We're coming in!"

Chad stared at the ceiling. "Randy always had the worst timing."

A dozen men with cold expressions, weapons in hand, and phone cord-type wires disappearing into their ears spread throughout the house, barely giving Hannah and Chad a glance. Hannah shuddered.

"Are you okay?" Chad asked her.

She glanced to find him a little too close for comfort. The moment the voice outside yelled "FBI," and the wooden door splintered as the agents busted their way into the house, she must have snuggled against Chad for protection. She stared at where her legs were twined with his and her breasts pressed flush against his chest. Her breath froze in her lungs. Quickly she wriggled away.

A lone figure pulled away from the pack. His movements were noticeably slower and more assured than those of his co-workers. He pulled a cellular phone away from his ear and punched a button.

"Oh, no." Hannah didn't know whether to feel anxiety or relief as the dark-haired FBI agent studied them. Out of the corner of her eye, she spotted the plastic sample tube of the stolen microprocessor chips and easily moved her leg, covering the tube with her skirt.

Stuffing the phone into his jacket pocket, the agent pulled out his billfold, flashing a twin of the identification Chad had stowed somewhere. "Special Agent Randall McKay of The Federal Bureau of Investigations." He tucked the ID away. "Now that I've showed you mine, let's see yours."

Chad splayed his hands where they were bound. "I'd really like to help you out, Randy, but as you can see I'm kind of tied up at the moment."

Randy? Hannah stared at Chad. She vaguely remembered him saying the agent's name in New York when they were running from McKay in PlayCo's parking garage. She had assumed he knew it from having run into the agent under similar hapless circumstances.

As if reading her thoughts, Chad looked at her. In his eyes she read a mixture of regret and gravity she couldn't quite explain but hoped he would.

"What's going on here, Chad?" she asked. "I feel like there's something I'm missing."

"That's because you are." He grimaced, then glanced at the agent hovering over them. "Hannah, that FBI ID I used? Well, it wasn't fake. Maybe no longer valid, but it wasn't fake. I used to be with the FBI."

Now she was even more confused. She moved to rub her face, but the cuffs prevented her from it.

"Can you get these things off us, McKay?" Chad asked.

The agent waved for another junior officer nearby. The cuffs were immediately removed.

Hannah absently rubbed her wrists. "I don't know if I'm getting you here. I mean I know you were in the Marines...."

Chad's small smile was somehow sad. "That was the great thing about our relationship before. Or at least what I thought was great then. At any rate, it was what I needed. Someone who never asked questions." He threaded his fingers through the curls over her right ear, seemingly fascinated with her hair despite the agents filling the room. "You accepted me simply for who I was. To you it didn't matter what I'd done in the past. You only cared about now and the future." He sighed and dropped his hand. "I don't know why I never told you I used to be FBI. Maybe because my resignation came right after Linda and Josh were killed. Maybe because it didn't matter to me anymore."

Chad used to be FBI. Hannah tried to wrap her mind

around the information. She supposed it should have some sort of impact on the way she looked at him, but it didn't. She'd always known he was one of the good guys. That he'd officially been one didn't surprise her. It confused more than hurt her that he'd kept the detail from her.

"And no, before you ask, I didn't think that my past involvement gave me license to use the ID whenever the mood moved me. The first time was at PlayCo and only then because I'd just been hit with the news that I was a father again and I wanted to get this trace over with ASAP."

She nodded slowly, understanding what he was saying, but still needing to think about everything else behind it.

She swallowed, wondering if there would be a time when she'd ever completely understand all that was Chad Hogan.

Nearby, McKay said something under his breath. "Are you about done, Hogan?"

Chad grimaced. "Let's just say McKay and I go back a ways. A long ways. In fact, I think it would be safe for me to say Randy here owes me one for pulling him in here." He looked up at the agent, then said to Hannah, "I put a call through to him when I was away from the room this afternoon." He slanted the other agent a look. "Though it took him long enough to get here."

"You called him?" Hannah asked, glancing at where McKay stood close enough to listen in. "When?"

"Right after we...after I left you at the motel, from a mall phone booth. The same place I got Furgeson's address here." He shifted onto his feet, obviously uncomfortable. "Look, Hannah, I couldn't take any chances. Not after what happened to Persky in Atlantic City, and with those two goons at the airport. Things were getting too dangerous."

Hannah stood. Surprising even herself, she smiled. "Protecting me again, Hogan?"

"Yes, I was. And if you want to be ticked off about it, go right ahead. There's more to consider now than just you and me," he said quietly, Hannah guessed so that McKay wouldn't hear. "There's Bonny to think about. And, well...I'm not going to lose another child because of my mistakes."

Hannah's throat contracted. *His mistakes?* She couldn't bear to think that he still held himself responsible for what happened to his son.

"The only problem is that now McKay's going to take Furgeson in himself and we'll lose the bail."

Right now she couldn't care less about the bounty on Lisa's head. She only wanted this whole thing to be over with, quickly, so she and Bonny could go home, and...

And she could start repairing her broken heart.

McKay stepped forward. "Are you done now? Mind if I ask a few questions of my own? I mean, if it isn't too inconvenient."

Chad's eyes seemed to question her readiness. She silently nodded.

"Good," McKay said, giving the impression that he was used to such banter with Chad. "Where is Furgeson?"

"As you can see, she's not here," Chad said.

"Obviously." The agent looked to Hannah. "Tell me where she is."

Hannah admitted she felt a little better about their

situation, but not much. "A man by the name of Jack Stokes has her."

McKay looked at her. "You handle that Alfa of yours well, Miss McGee."

Her cheeks burned. "Thanks."

His small grin held no amusement. "I wouldn't go thanking me just yet. You and Chad here are still in a heap of trouble with the Bureau."

Chad sighed. "I'd think you'd be interested in going for the big fish rather than chasing after the guppies."

"Don't underestimate me, Hogan. You and the lady may be small fish, but you are a catch."

"I'm not underestimating you. On the contrary, I was giving you credit, thinking you would put fingering the real mastermind of this microchip caper ahead of arresting us." Chad grinned back at the federal agent.

"What is it you think you know, Hogan?"

"Obviously more than you think, my old friend." He put his arm around McKay's shoulders.

"There is one important difference, however." McKay held his hand palm up. "You broke the law in your efforts. I didn't."

Grimacing, Chad took his federal ID from his front shirt pocket and slapped it into McKay's hand. "That's because you are the law. Besides, the ID isn't entirely fraudulent. It was mine until I left the agency four years ago."

"Have you made your point yet?" McKay asked. "If you have, I missed it."

"Where do you go from here?" Chad asked in the same tone. "I know where you'll go. You'll go back to New York to wait for Stokes to bring back Furgeson. Case closed."

"Are you saying someone else is pulling the strings?" McKay asked.

The room was filled with people rushing in and out, avoiding the three of them standing as still as light poles in the middle. For long moments no one more than blinked. Then finally McKay exhaled gustily and said, "Okay, Hogan, let's get to it."

Chad winked at Hannah, the brief gesture making her fear stagnate. She fought the urge to smile.

"Agent Jones, get your men out there and block all entrances to the house."

Chad smacked his hand against McKay's shoulders. "You know what I'm up to, don't you?"

McKay shrugged him off. "You're going to use this house as the base for contact." He paused. "That means you have something somebody wants. Namely the items that were in those toy phones."

Hannah thought of the key Lisa had given her, the key to the storage locker that held the two boxes of chips. But Chad obviously wasn't playing cards with McKay just yet.

"Does it really matter? As long as you and I get what we want, it doesn't matter what I do or don't have. The important thing is that *they* think I have the items."

"And of course you want immunity from prosecution."

Chad clucked his tongue in admonishment. The moment the FBI agent had given in to Chad Hogan, he opened himself up to every demand Chad could think of.

Randy scowled. "I'm telling you right now, I'll be watching you. Impersonate a fed again, and your hide is mine, Chad."

"I'm shocked by your low opinion of me. This isn't about impersonating anyone anymore. Oh, no." Chad guided him toward the back of the house. Hannah walked beside them, striving to keep her amusement from showing.

Chad brushed lint Hannah couldn't see from the FBI agent's blue polyester lapel. "And wiping the slate clean is not all I have in mind, either. Not for what this is going to yield you. You see, once you have the brains behind this operation, McKay, you sign that we delivered Furgeson to you so we can get our bounty."

Chapter Twelve

Men roamed everywhere. Hannah watched them impassively, surprisingly unaffected by their presence. In fact, she was enormously reassured. More so since Mc-Kay had had one of his agents take her to pick up Bonny at the motel. She couldn't think of any place safer for her little girl than being in a house guarded by at least fifty FBI agents.

She finished changing her messy daughter's tiny pink T-shirt then moved her from the kitchen table to her lap. She pressed her palm to her flushed forehead. Was it her, or did she feel a little warm? Could be a result of the tooth coming in. Or maybe she was coming down with something. She looked into the baby's eyes, trying to decide.

Bonny's features instantly brightened and she reached out her hand. "Dah!"

Hannah felt her own cheeks warm. She didn't have

to look to see who had just come through the kitchen door. Bonny's exuberant reaction was enough.

"Dog, huh?" Chad said as he hauled the baby easily into his arms.

Hannah gave a small shrug. "That's what I thought it meant." She'd never even considered that her daughter would recognize her father on sight. Still didn't. It was pure coincidence, that was all. That and Chad had been the first man she'd let so close to her daughter.

Then again, Bonny hadn't called Jack "dah."

She shook off the strange thoughts and watched Chad take the seat across the table from her.

"I missed you, short stuff," he said, tapping his index finger against Bonny's nose. He wasn't quite as happy when she grasped the finger and stuck it into her mouth, giving a healthy chomp. "Ow!"

"She must have another tooth coming in," Hannah said.

Chad's grimace was altogether endearing. "Yeah, well, looks to me that she's doing just fine with the ones she's got."

"Can you check to see if she feels a little warm to you?"

His expression instantly sobered as he stared at her, then Bonny. He lifted his large hand, then pressed his fingers to several points on their daughter's face and neck. "She feels fine to me, but I don't know. Do you think maybe you should give her something?"

"No. But we should keep an eye on her just the same."

In that one instant it was all too easy to imagine that they weren't in the midst of what essentially amounted to a military state. That, instead, they were in their own home somewhere, nothing more than an average, everyday family doing everyday family things.

Her smile slowly faded.

But they weren't, were they? There was nothing normal about their current situation. And there was nothing normal about their relationship. Oh, she supposed her bond with her daughter was normal enough. And Chad and Bonny were growing more attached with every passing moment. If only the ring Chad had wanted to give her had more to do with love than a sense of outdated gallantry. "I should have offered to do the right thing the moment I saw Bonny," he'd said.

She averted her gaze, hating the tears welling up in her eyes. Didn't he understand that she couldn't marry someone only because she'd given birth to his daughter? She couldn't stand thinking for even a moment that she'd somehow trapped him into doing something he would never have done otherwise.

The door opened again and in stepped McKay.

For the most part, they'd been left on their own in the kitchen, with only an occasional nondescript agent passing through on his way to the back. She'd suspected the peace wouldn't last for long and she was right.

"Take these and see if any of them look familiar." Randy McKay tossed a pile of color photographs onto the kitchen table.

"I didn't give you enough credit, McKay." Chad reached around Bonny and picked up one of the photos. "You have been busy."

The agent gestured vaguely with his right hand. "They were gathered by one of my men. People either suspected of theft of high-tech items, or with a past of smuggling them out of the country. I'm hoping you'll identify one in particular.''

Hannah leaned toward Chad. ''You think the men from the airport this morning are in here?''

In the hour since McKay had found them, Chad and Hannah had filled the FBI agent in on everything that had happened since they had taken on the unusual case. Well, *almost* everything. Hannah warmed slightly, remembering her and Chad's respite from the chase that morning. Besides, that detail didn't matter. Not anymore.

If only she could force her heart into agreement.

''There is only one way to find out,'' McKay replied, staring in an odd way at Chad. ''Look them over. If you come up with anything, let me know.''

Hannah pulled the photographs closer. McKay walked from the room, leaving them alone again.

''Chad?''

He slowly looked at her. ''Strange change of events, wouldn't you say?''

Hannah smiled. ''Considering we were facing jail time, yes, I would say conditions have changed drastically. What surprises me is that McKay handed the reins over to you.''

Chad grimaced and directed his response to Bonny. ''He's hoping I'll hang myself with them, isn't he, Bon-Bon?''

Hannah recognized his use of her own nickname for Bonny and her heart gave a little squeeze. ''You are more likely to hang him, and he knows that.''

A slight arch of a brow told Hannah he was surprised by the compliment. She fought a smile, enjoying that she could still make him feel good.

She sifted through the pictures in front of her, pushing them toward Chad once she finished, but careful to keep them out of Bonny's reach. So many faces. She held out a picture, but Chad didn't take it from her.

"Hannah?"

She glanced at him, thinking he had found something in one of the pictures. Instead, her breath froze in her chest at the sober expression on his face.

His frown was poignantly endearing. "I know I haven't always been honest with you, you know, about my past."

She secretly bit the inside of her lip, unsure where he was headed, and not entirely certain she wanted him to go there given everything that had happened between them in the past few days. "You mean about the fact that you used to be FBI?"

His wry grin touched her in a way that reminded her of when they first met.

For the second time she realized that she had never really known Chad. Not really. From the moment she first laid eyes on him, she knew she had wanted him— for who he was at that moment. For all the promise his responding, fiery gaze had held, despite the shadow of pain that always touched his expression. A shadow she had ignored, keeping her focus steadfastly on the future. Their future. On who she believed he could be. Then came the time when she'd wanted a ring and he'd bought her an Alfa Romeo. Ironic that now that he'd offered her a ring she wanted nothing more than his love.

He shook his head. "No, Hannah, this isn't about that. Before...well, I thought I could keep everything separate. Live with you in the present, and lock the past safely away." He thrust his fingers through his hair. "But it doesn't work that way, does it?"

She ached to reach out to him, but couldn't seem to put down the picture she held.

"I was an agent for the FBI for a little over six years. I quit the day after the death of my wi—of Linda and Joshua."

She tried to imagine Chad dressed in the strict blue suits worn by the men in the other room, but couldn't. The Chad she knew was a rugged loner she had never seen in anything other than jeans. Whose golden-brown hair was forever in need of a trim, and whose eyes hinted at a wild, reckless nature she had thought inherent. And his wild nature *was* inherent. It had only found a different, more intense release after the loss of his family.

"Thanks," she said quietly. "I mean, for telling me."

He stared at her for a long moment.

She shifted, guessing he expected more from her. More questions? Probing? Perhaps anger that he had kept something from her that had been a large part of his life?

Whatever he expected, all she could offer in return was quiet acceptance.

She concentrated her attention on the picture in her hands, though she could see little more than colors and blobs.

"Is that it?" Chad asked, a tinge of amusement coloring his voice.

She slanted him a wary glance. "Yes. Unless, of course, there's some other deep, dark secret you've been keeping from me."

His ominous silence sent a chill racing up her spine. Was there something else he was keeping to himself?

She almost breathed a sigh of relief when he held

out his hand for the photo she'd tried to give him before. Until he said, "I want you to drop out of the trace. I want you to allow Randy to see you and Bonny back home...back to New York tonight. As soon as possible."

She blinked at him, unable to believe she'd fallen into what essentially had been a trap. "Don't even go there, Hogan."

"I want you out, Hannah."

Out? She swallowed hard, flinching away from the strong word. "Chad, I've told you that you don't have to protect me—"

"This has nothing to do with protecting you. In a situation like this, I'm better off working alone. I don't need anyone dogging my steps, distracting me."

"Distracting you?" she asked, hiking a brow. "Let's just see what's going to happen next, okay?"

What seemed like a long while later, Hannah finally returned to the task at hand. She stared at the faces in the photographs, nearly bending them with her jerky movements.

She dragged another off the pile. Was there even a jail big enough to hold them all?

Chad tossed a picture aside then fastened Bonny into her stroller so he could stand up. He was obviously as frustrated by the tedious task as she was. Tortured by demons she couldn't hope to ever understand, much less help him conquer. He walked a ways away, then leaned against the farthest wall. She waited for him to repeat his request for her to drop out.

"I wish something would break. I'm afraid our friend—" Chad motioned toward the door with his thumb "—won't wait long. He may decide to renege on the deal and take us to jail."

Hannah was relieved he hadn't said anything about her continued involvement in the trace. "That won't happen. The guy likes you."

There was a shadow of a smile on Chad's face when he looked at her. "McKay doesn't like anybody."

She returned her attention to the pictures. The one she held was of a strikingly attractive man who looked like he'd stepped from the cover of *GQ*. Certainly he couldn't be involved in anything criminal? She frowned, reminding herself that looks had nothing to do with a person's career. She was proof of that.

She slid the picture to the bottom of the pile, revealing the one under it. Her pulse vaulted as she stared down at the familiar face.

"Chad, I think I have something."

He pushed from his position against the wall. "What is it?"

Overall, there was nothing particularly remarkable about the man. He had dark, thinning hair. A round face. Dark-rimmed eyeglasses. He could have been any one of a hundred men she'd pass going about normal day-to-day business. In a grocery store. On the street.

Hannah tapped the photo with her finger. "I've seen this guy. He was standing across the street from Rita Minelli's place before we found Persky...." She glanced at Bonny where she threw a set of plastic keys to the floor. "Well, you know."

Chad took the photo from her. She had little doubt that he recognized the man.

"McKay?" Chad didn't say the name loudly, for he and she knew the agent was standing just on the other side of the door, probably listening to every word they'd said since he'd left them alone. The FBI agent immediately joined them.

"What is it?"

Hannah handed the photo to him. "Who is this?"

Randy took it. "His name is Robert Morgan." He paused, his attention focused on Chad. "Is he someone you recognize? Who you've seen in the past couple of days?"

Chad ran his hand through his hair. "He's the comptroller at PlayCo where Persky and Furgeson worked. He's the guy I spoke to."

"And he was in Atlantic City yesterday, suspiciously close to the time Persky was murdered," Hannah added. "I saw him."

"Are you positive this is the man?" McKay placed his hands on the table. "This is very important, Hannah. He was high on our list of suspects when we discovered the stolen chips were being circulated through the toy company, but every line we put out on him has come back clean. Too clean."

"Well, I don't know how much dirt this will fling on him, but I'm positive that's the man I saw around Rita Minelli's apartment building a few minutes after Eric Persky was murdered."

McKay knocked his knuckles on the tabletop. "I knew it."

Hannah examined Robert Morgan's photograph.

She said, "So Morgan recruited Eric Persky to do his dirty work, namely to distribute the stolen chips through toy telephones, presumably to parts outside the country. But when things went down, Lisa Furgeson got arrested, too. Why?"

McKay rubbed the back of his neck. "Probably so the trail wouldn't be traced back to him. Also, when an innocent is arrested with the guilty, the innocent is usually proven as such, getting the others arrested with them off as well. Complicated, but it works.''

A sudden commotion from the front of the house put an end to their conversation. Hannah rose from her chair, glancing anxiously at Bonny as Chad and McKay moved toward the door. She plucked her daughter from the stroller and held her close to her chest.

''What's going on out here?'' McKay demanded.

Hannah stopped next to an agent standing in front of the living-room windows. He made room for her and she peered out to find the mob of agents gathered around a shadowy figure.

''Who is it?'' she asked.

''I don't know, ma'am,'' the agent next to her replied. ''The moment he tried to cross the outer perimeter, we were all over him.''

Hannah reached out, squeezing Chad's forearm as he appeared beside her. Bonny did the same. ''Wait a minute...''

He leaned closer, his every muscle bunched. ''It's Stokes.''

For long moments she stood staring at Chad, trying to work out the possibilities.

''Is Furgeson with him?'' she asked.

Chad shook his head. ''Not from what I can see.''

''What is it? Do you two know that guy?'' McKay emerged from a conversation with one of his agents.

''Yes. It's Jack Stokes—noticeably without Lisa Furgeson,'' Chad told him flatly. ''It's only a matter of time before we're contacted for the chips.''

McKay stared at two of his agents. They immediately moved toward the front of the house.

Hannah followed them to the door. What was Stokes up to? And where was Furgeson? Shifting aside so the two men could bring Jack in, Hannah stared at him in shock. "What happened to you? You look like you got caught on the wrong side of a baseball bat."

Jack touched his swollen face and flinched, his battered leather cowboy hat hanging in his other hand. "Believe me, that's exactly how I feel."

Chad bit off a curse. "What have you done now, Stokes? And where's Furgeson?"

"I think we would all like to know the answer to that question," McKay added.

"I'm doing just fine, thank you," Jack offered in an offhand matter. "How about all of you?" He surveyed the packed house. "Aw, you're having a party and forgot to invite me."

Hannah had a bad feeling about all this. "Where is she, Jack?"

A grimace marred the Aussie's blood-caked face. "I wish I knew, Hannah." He looked at her. "I will tell you this much—the lady didn't look too pleased with the changing of the guard."

"You know, I ought to have you arrested." The stonelike quality of Chad's words told Stokes he meant it.

Jack half laughed. "Yeah, well, I would probably deserve it, Hogan."

Hannah looked at Chad in concern as McKay ushered them all into the kitchen.

Jack sank onto a kitchen chair. "There were at least three. Two who looked like these guys—" he moved a thumb in McKay's direction "—and one I couldn't see. I could only hear his voice from the back of a Lincoln." He moved a hand over his stress-lined face.

Hannah slipped into a chair across from his. She

pulled the picture of Robert Morgan toward him. "Did any of them look like this man?"

Jack squinted at the photo. "The two who worked me over didn't." He shook his head. "I didn't see the one in the Lincoln."

McKay leaned in. "Where'd they get you?"

"Outside a motel I'd booked a room at earlier."

Chad frowned at the agent. "This guy's small change, McKay. He's freelancing this bounty." He explained how Stokes was working for himself, hoping to get Elliott Blackstone to come around. "But I guess he wasn't having any luck," he said of the Australian. He spoke of Stokes in the third person, as if dismissing him. "But that doesn't matter anymore. What's important now is that we get that call."

Why was it taking so long? It seemed like forever, though it had only been an hour since Jack had showed up and shared his story. Hannah, Chad and Jack sat around the kitchen table, the telephone sitting silently in the middle of it, while Randy McKay stuck to the shadows. Bonny was safely asleep in her stroller in the corner, her thumb stuck halfway into her mouth, a blanket covering her tired little body. She was blessedly unaware of the activity going on around her.

"I don't know, Hogan," McKay said from the open back doorway where he was smoking a cigarette. "I'm beginning to think Morgan—if it is Morgan—isn't going to contact you. Circumstances have gotten too hot for him. It's my guess Furgeson has met with the fate of her co-worker and is this very minute lying in a ditch somewhere."

"Keep your thoughts to yourself, McKay," Hannah murmured.

McKay stepped into the beam of light from the ceiling fixture. "I'm considering calling off this whole farce. This isn't getting us anywhere."

"We're not going anywhere, mate." The determination in Jack's voice held a measure of threat. "If Hogan and McGee think he'll call, then he'll bloody call. So just crawl back into your hole and shut up, will you?"

McKay stood where he was for a long moment, returning Jack's scathing stare. Hannah knew the agent held the power to do as he threatened. With a wave of his hand he could place her and Chad under arrest and shut the whole operation down. She swallowed with difficulty. What would become of her and Chad and Bonny if that happened?

"That's it. It's over. I'll catch up with Morgan eventually, but it won't be today." McKay started toward the kitchen door. "We're closing up shop."

Chad immediately went after him and Hannah moved to get Bonny. The telephone gave out a short, sharp ring that stopped them all midmotion.

Chairs screeched as they urgently reseated themselves, not paying attention when McKay closed the door, backtracking to stand behind Hannah.

"Answer the thing!" Jack moved to snatch up the black receiver. Chad gave him an ominous look and he stopped.

On the fourth ring, Chad reached out and picked it up. "Hello."

Hannah felt like a rolled spool of copper wire, unable to move, unable to breathe. She saw no sign of emotion on Chad's face.

"Furgeson?" His grip on the receiver tightened. Hannah leaned forward, immediately sensing the change in his demeanor. He wasn't talking to Lisa anymore.

"I understand." Silence. "Yes." He placed his hand tightly over the receiver and mouthed to McKay, "Baker's Oil Field."

The agent nodded and quickly left the room.

Removing his hand from the receiver, Chad spoke. "Agreed. In an hour. Alone."

Chad's gaze trailed to where Hannah stood facing away from him in the open back doorway, her arms crossed over her chest. She seemed so distant somehow. Alone. Untouchable. Bonny was safely tucked away in the corner in her stroller sawing some logs, while he had three FBI rookies outfitting him for the meeting ahead at the oil field.

Since the call had come in, he hadn't had a moment to breathe, much less talk to Hannah. And despite the adrenaline flooding his veins, he wanted to talk to Hannah more than anything right now.

An agent yanked at the Velcro pulls of the bulletproof vest they'd outfitted him with, securing it tightly in place. Chad pulled down his T-shirt then shrugged into a denim shirt one of the men had supplied. Yet another agent said, "The microphone is hidden in the neck of your T-shirt here. The earpiece shouldn't be visible—"

"I know the drill, Agent. Are you done?"

The three men looked at one another, then at McKay, who stood nearby. McKay gave an almost imperceptible nod and the three men filed out of the room. Chad watched them go then looked back at Hannah, barely noticing when McKay and Jack Stokes left the room as well.

If Hannah was aware of the goings-on behind her, she didn't let on. Her posture was stiff, her fingers white-knuckled where they curved around her rib cage.

Chad swallowed thickly then moved to stand behind her, looking over her shoulder at the dark night beyond. The air blasting in through the open door was thick and sticky, making him edgier still.

"Why do you have to do this, Chad?" Hannah asked quietly.

He hadn't known what to expect. Maybe for her to demand to come along, to see this to the end as a team, a partnership. But this was miles away from that.

She turned to face him, dropping her hands to her sides. "I mean, now that Morgan has made contact, arranged for a meet, why not just let McKay and his men take over from here?"

Why not indeed? Chad's mind filled with a half dozen reasons. That Morgan had made contact with him. That he'd agreed to go to the meet…alone. That he needed to do this so McKay wouldn't charge him for impersonating a federal officer. But all those reasons lost steam when he saw the concern that shadowed Hannah's blue, blue eyes.

She pulled her bottom lip between her teeth then released it. He found the innocent movement sweet and provocative all at once. "There isn't anything I can do to talk you out of this, is there?"

It was more a statement of fact than a question. Chad glanced at Bonny's sleeping face. At the way her thumb hung halfway out of her cherub mouth. His heart gave a painful lurch unlike any he'd felt before.

There *was* something Hannah could do, he realized, just as surely as she must. She could use their child, their daughter, as an excuse for him to back out of the deal. She could hold Bonny up and say, "You don't want to put your job ahead of another child, do you, Chad?"

He dragged his hand over his face then looked at Hannah again. That she didn't say those things, that she didn't try to use Bonny to control his actions meant the world to him.

And if he did rip off the vest right now? Call in McKay and tell him one of his guys was going to have to go to the site? What would happen? Nothing on the legal end. McKay wouldn't arrest him, he was certain. What if he opened his arms to Hannah and proclaimed his love for her? He knew that was what she wanted from him, what she needed. And he was pretty sure that no matter how much pain he'd caused her, she'd slip right into his embrace without a backward glance.

But he couldn't do either. Solely because he would be the one always looking backward. Preoccupied with the baggage he even now carried on his shoulders.

"This is just something I have to do, Hannah."

She nodded once, solemnly, as if expecting his words.

It was the only thing he could do because frankly the uncertainty of where he went from there, where he and Hannah and Bonny went from there, was driving him crazy. All he knew was that the longer he delayed the end of this case, the more time he bought to keep Hannah next to him. The more room he had to make sense of the answer that seemed forever on the fringe of his consciousness, the better. Despite his request that she do just that a short time ago, the thought of her going back to New York with Bonny, leaving him behind because of his wavering, was one he didn't even want to consider.

He had to do this because it was all he knew to do.

He wanted to say more to Hannah, to try to explain all this even though she looked like she didn't expect any more than she'd already gotten.

The door swung inward. "Five minutes," McKay said.

Chad gestured him away then the door closed again.

Hannah looked at him expectantly.

Chad fought the impulse to tug up his T-shirt and rip the vest open so he could breathe. If only he thought that would help. "The truth of it is, I have to do this right now because…because it's the only thing I can do—" He abruptly turned and stepped a couple of feet away, trying to put his thoughts to words. "Aw, hell, Hannah, I don't know what to tell you. If you had said yes to my proposal earlier, taken the ring…I don't know. Maybe it would have made a difference. Maybe it wouldn't. Perhaps it would only make me doubly determined to get Morgan for having put you and Bonny in danger these past few days. I just don't know…."

He didn't expect a response so he wasn't surprised when he didn't get one.

He hadn't been surprised, either, when she turned down his uncomfortably awkward proposal, made while they were handcuffed to the stairs, of all things. Oh, yeah, that moment he'd been shocked. Isn't that what she'd wanted fifteen months ago? For them to get married?

Although in retrospect, he supposed he'd always known somewhere deep inside that Hannah would never have agreed to marry him for only the sake of their daughter. She'd never made it a secret that she wanted the whole nine yards. More than just the traditional wedding and the white picket fence. She wanted him completely, heart and soul.

His heart he had given her long ago. It was his soul he feared was no longer his to give.

After she'd said no to his proposal, he also recognized himself for the heel he was. He suspected that he'd asked her to marry him more to ease his own conscience than any real attempt to right what was wrong between them. Because to do that would mean facing down his own demons.

Perhaps that was another reason he needed to go to that oil field tonight.

He started when he felt the feather-light touch of her hand on his shoulder. He fought the urge to relax against it, to give himself over to the comfort she offered.

"This is the same thing all over again, isn't it?" he said as much to himself as to her. "It seems that I've come full circle. And I'm scared to death that I'm going to make the same mistakes all over again." He stared at the closed door. "But what scares me even more is not seeing it through." He closed his eyes. "Don't you see, if I don't go through with this, I'm afraid I'll see myself for the coward I am."

He felt the warmth of Hannah's body as she pressed her front against his back. Her arms snaked around his waist. Seeming to sense the Kevlar vest underneath, her hands stilled against his chest. She cleared her throat. "You're not a coward, Chad. There are a thousand other things I could call you, but never a coward." He heard her swallow as she rested her cheek against the back of his shoulder. "A lesser man would have run in the other direction when I introduced him to his daughter. Not you. You stuck it out. Oh, yeah, sure you said it was only for the case, but I never believed that for a second. Well, okay, maybe for a second because my mind couldn't grasp your true motivations then. But you never do anything for money, so I know you didn't stick around because of that. You weren't an FBI agent because it paid well. You didn't even choose bounty hunting because of the cash.'' She gave a quiet laugh. ''You're the guy who blew our entire savings to buy me a sports car for my thirtieth birthday, remember?''

He began to pull away from her, but she held tight. ''Hold on a minute. I'm not finished yet.''

Chad waited, his heart banging against the wall of his chest.

Hannah's arms tightened around his waist. ''I'm not exactly sure how to put this, but I just wanted to tell you that no matter what you do tonight, or tomorrow or even the next day, I know you'll do the right thing, Chad. And no, this doesn't have anything to do with your proposal. This isn't about me anymore. It's not about me and you, though I won't lie to you. I wish there were a me and you to talk about.''

She drew in a deep breath. ''I guess what I'm trying to say is that I trust you, Chad. I trust you to do what's right for all of us. Even if you don't trust yourself.''

She slipped her arms from around his waist. The sudden absence of her heat from his back made Chad want to groan as she stepped away.

The door opened and this time McKay stepped into the room. But Chad ignored him and turned toward Hannah.

He glimpsed it there in her face, her love for him. It was obvious in the brightness of her eyes, the color in her cheeks, the damp fullness of her lips. It was completely unselfish and fathomless and present, though unspoken. It hit him like a blow to the gut. And made him wonder exactly what she saw written on his face.

Before he knew what she was doing, she slowly stepped forward until mere inches separated them. She pressed her palms against his protected chest, then pressed her lips lightly against his, her eyes holding his captive.

"Time to go," McKay said gruffly.

Hannah pulled away. Chad wanted to groan and pull her to him again, kiss her in the way he longed to, thoroughly and without reservations. But he didn't. Instead he watched as she gave him a small nod.

Torn between wanting to stay and needing to go, Chad turned and followed McKay out the door.

Chapter Thirteen

Hannah sat holding Bonny in the back of a nondescript dark sedan that drove toward Baker's Oil Field. In the front, Randall drove and another agent sat beside him, passing on McKay's orders through a cell phone to Chad, who rode in one of the leading sedans driven by Jack Stokes. Hannah shivered and held Bonny a little tighter, earning her a quiet protest from the baby. Before leaving the house, Chad had demanded she stay there, well out of the way with Bonny. She had staunchly refused, and it was McKay who told an adamant Chad that he would make sure she and his daughter were kept well out of the way of danger.

Houston's night lights flickered outside the windows, but Hannah didn't see them.

Everything had changed drastically in the days since Elliott Blackstone had given her this assignment. The case had expanded from the simple task of bringing two fugitives in to stand trial, to encompass a microprocessor chip smuggling ring, a murder and a kidnapping.

Hannah pressed her lips against Bonny's sweet-smelling temple, uncaring that the baby was chomping on the chain of her necklace. Life was so much easier when all the bail-jumpers were like Eddie the Snake. The type who were habitual liars and thieves, more danger to themselves than anyone else. She had no problem tracking and apprehending people like that.

In the pocket of her skirt, Hannah fingered the plastic tube of chips she'd held on to even after she'd given the key to McKay, who'd arranged to have the remainder of the chips picked up from the storage locker and put into the trunk of the car Chad rode in.

"Do you think this will work out okay?" Hannah spoke the words into the empty air in front of her.

McKay met her gaze in the rearview mirror. "We'll be in unfamiliar territory dealing with an unknown quantity in Robert Morgan." He grinned. "Everything will be fine." His gaze trailed to Bonny and the smile left his face.

Hannah didn't appreciate his attempt at humor. But she hadn't been only referring to now. She wanted, needed to know how things would be when this was all over. The last person to answer that question for her was Randy McKay. The only man who could give her a clue rode three car lengths ahead, driving into who knew what.

Sitting in the back of that car, out of harm's way, out of the direct action, unable to help Chad, she'd never felt so utterly, entirely, completely helpless in her life.

"Mah!"

Hannah pulled back to look at her daughter's shadowy face. Had she just tried to say what she thought she had?

It was in that one moment that she realized she had been humbled only one other time. The moment when she'd given birth to Bonny. When she'd stared at the tiny, pink, wrinkled human being crying at the top of her lungs she even now held and had no idea what to do with her except love her.

Maybe that was what she needed to do with Chad. Just love him.

Bonny laid her head against Hannah's shoulder, her breath soft against her neck. Hannah closed her eyes and smoothed her daughter's hair back. A simple action. A reassuring action.

The car was silent except for the hum of the engine as they moved steadily toward the meet.

"Get Hogan on the line," McKay said.

The agent in the passenger's seat spoke quietly, then handed a cell phone to McKay.

"I want to make one thing perfectly clear to you, Hogan. You are not to give the chips to Morgan under any circumstances, do you hear me?"

Hannah discreetly leaned closer, trying to listen in. She couldn't hear a thing, but judging by the frown on McKay's face, whatever Chad had said hadn't made the agent happy.

"Don't you dare patronize me, Hogan. You kept the whereabouts of the chips from me until I had no choice but to allow you to take them to the meeting. I will not risk losing them now, do you understand? This is my behind on the line here."

McKay cleared his throat. "You should reach the site in ten minutes. My men are already set up. Remember," he said more urgently. "You must look like you are going to give him the chips. Once he touches one of the boxes, we'll have his neck, lock, stock and barrel."

McKay handed the cell phone back to the other agent.

"Why doesn't someone turn on the lights?" Hannah squinted into the inky blackness of the night, hating that she couldn't make out where Chad was some fifty yards on the other side of a small, man-made rise. With the car no longer humming beneath them, the silence was all-encompassing, encouraging her to say something to make certain she could still hear.

"Are you sure this is it?" she leaned forward to ask the other agent. McKay was outside talking on that cursed cell phone of his where she couldn't hear anything.

"This is the place."

Hannah strained to make something, anything out of the night. She couldn't see anything. She gently placed a sleeping Bonny down on the seat, covering her with her blanket, then climbed out of the car. She was careful to be as quiet as possible as she neared McKay.

"What's going on?" she whispered anxiously. The air was surprisingly dry and cool, smelling of oil and dust. She shivered, hating the fear that filled her. "Do you think Morgan's here? Waiting and watching from the shadows?"

"I don't know." McKay pushed the button to light the dial on his watch. "We're five minutes early."

"Oh, terrific," Hannah whispered. "We have a punctual crook."

The sound of Randy's footsteps as he moved to the

front driver's door caught Hannah's attention. "Tell the driver to turn the headlights on," he told the other agent.

Within a blink of an eye, headlights on the car Hannah guessed Chad had been riding in flicked on, revealing the tall rig that earned the spot its name. Hannah stared at the rig that pumped relentlessly, siphoning oil from the deceptively dry-looking ground.

"It looks so menacing."

Tires spitting up dirt and gravel sounded from a distance. McKay accepted a radio from the other agent then turned a few knobs until Hannah could hear Chad's voice.

"Don't look now, but our three o'clock has arrived."

Hannah turned to watch an approaching car. As it grew nearer, she noted it was the dark Lincoln that had followed Chad to the airport earlier.

"Here we go."

Hannah barely heard Chad's words. She could only concentrate on the twin beams of light shining directly on him in the distance.

"Chad, please don't do anything stupid," she murmured to herself. "If you have to give him the chips, do it. Don't risk your life. I...Bonny...our daughter needs her father."

"You realize I just heard you say that."

Hannah blinked, not particularly caring what McKay heard or didn't hear.

The Lincoln stopped twenty feet away from Chad's car. For long, quiet moments, nothing happened. They were terrifying moments during which Hannah anticipated the worst.

"What do you think he's doing?" she whispered.

"Making sure Chad came alone," McKay said.

Hannah's heart jumped into her throat. "What about Stokes?"

"At this point, it doesn't matter much, does it? Either Morgan wants the chips or he doesn't."

Finally one of the back doors of the Lincoln opened and a figure stepped out. From her vantage point, Hannah couldn't make out much. The blinding headlights and the darkness surrounding them saw to that. She anxiously shifted her weight from one foot to the other.

"Where are they?" a man's voice demanded. Hannah had heard that voice before—it belonged to one of the men at the Houston airport.

McKay adjusted the volume of the radio as Hannah watched Chad remove something—no doubt the plastic tube of chips—from his jeans pocket then hold his hand in the man's direction.

"Just a sample," Chad's voice intoned. "You'll see the rest after we see Furgeson."

The man motioned and another car door opened. Two figures emerged into the night.

"You're hurting me!"

"Let the girl come forward, Morgan," Chad ordered.

It was Lisa. She tried to move away from the man holding her, and was quickly wrenched back.

"Give me the rest of the chips," the shadowed man demanded.

Chad stood still for a long moment, then motioned toward his car. "They're in the trunk. Come and get them."

You have to lure Morgan to take them, Hannah silently urged. *You must get the exchange on record.* She nearly whispered the words as if Chad stood next to her rather than fifty yards away. She felt much like a rabbit trapped in the headlights of an oncoming car.

For long, torturous moments, no one moved. Even the wind seemed to cease its quiet restlessness.

Then the man stepped forward. Was it Robert Morgan? The one in the picture? The one she saw outside Rita Minelli's apartment?

Long, confident strides brought him closer to Chad, until he stood in front of the headlights from his car. The beam illuminated his face with its unkind light. Robert Morgan.

Hannah stared at the man responsible for so much. It seemed she and Chad had run into Morgan or his cronies at every turn. She shuddered.

"Bring the boxes here," Morgan said.

Chad dropped his hand to his side.

Take him the boxes! Hannah screamed silently. *Hogan, don't play games now! Take him the cursed chips!*

"How can I be sure you'll hold up your end of the bargain and let Furgeson go?" Chad asked.

Morgan shrugged his shoulders. "Putting it in writing will not allay your fears, Mr. Hogan. You will have to take me at my word. As I must take you at yours."

For long moments Chad and Morgan battled a silent duel. One that excluded surrounding warriors, yet depended on their presence.

"Let her go," Morgan ordered.

Lisa stumbled into the beams of the headlights, her hands still bound behind her, no doubt with the handcuffs Hannah had put on her hours earlier. Morgan grabbed her before she could rush forward.

"We will make the exchange at the same time," he said.

Hannah's gaze trailed Chad as he rounded to the

back of the car and hauled out two suitcase-size boxes. Morgan maintained his hold on Lisa as Chad approached.

"I hope you're getting this all on tape, McKay," Chad said under his breath, "because you're only getting one crack."

Hannah swallowed hard, caught between the urge to run forward and the need to stay behind and protect her daughter. As Morgan's hand touched the top box, the Lincoln's headlights went out.

"What the hell?" Chad shouted.

"Chad!" Hannah's eyes adjusted quickly, fear pressing in on her from all sides.

"McKay." Chad's voice started breaking up, more static than words. "Subject has the chips." There was the rustling of clothes as he moved. "Did you hear me? Morgan has the chips!"

"Get the woman!"

Hannah heard the shouted order without benefit of the radio and recognized the voice immediately as Morgan's. She strained to make out Chad's and Lisa's figures where they dove in the opposite direction.

Hannah grabbed the agent's arm. "Damn it, McKay, do something!"

McKay shouted into his radio, "Go, go, go!"

Spotlights were flicked on from every corner, it seemed, making it look like the sun had risen on Baker's Oil Field alone. Hannah frantically searched for a sign of Chad among the men storming the area. There! There he was, ripping off his wire and apparently looking for her.

Agents grabbed one of Morgan's henchmen, then ran after the other, when movement caught the corner of

Hannah's eye. She quickly looked toward the Lincoln then back at Chad. He was taking the earpiece off.

She grabbed McKay's hand and took the radio. "Chad! Can you hear me? Morgan's getting away."

Chad's hand halted near his ear and he tilted his head to the side, Hannah suspected so he could hear her better.

"Repeat, Morgan's getting away!"

Robert Morgan was disappearing into the Lincoln, escaping the attention of dozens of agents crowding the lighted scene.

Chad bit off a curse. "The subject!"

Hannah watched half the men turn toward him, but it was too late. The Lincoln roared to life, racing away from them in reverse.

Hannah started to bolt in the direction of the car next to her, but McKay's deathlike grip on her arm stopped her. "You stay out of the way and keep safe."

She returned his forceful gaze. "Like hell I—"

Her words caught in her throat as she watched Chad sprint full speed in the direction of the dark vehicle holding Morgan. It was impossible he could catch the car. Inconceivable he could stop the man about to outwit them all. The negative certainties piled up, but Chad lunged for the back of the Lincoln anyway as the car swerved around to move forward. He flung himself onto the trunk, digging his fingers into the tiny space between the trunk and the rear window.

Hannah held her breath as the Lincoln shot off into the night. She expected Chad to be thrown from the back as his long, rugged body moved back and forth. He appeared to be holding on by sheer will alone. She had to do something to help....

Behind her, Randy McKay jumped into the car. She

climbed into the back seat and gathered a still sleeping Bonny into her arms even as McKay started the engine.

"What were you waiting for?" she demanded as he pulled forward. "Chad could have been killed."

McKay's face was set into deep, angry lines. "I had to be sure Morgan made a move on the chips."

"The chips? How many people have to die for those pieces of techno-plastic, McKay? What's on those things that's so damn important?"

"That's not the point, McGee. It never was."

"Well, then, tell me exactly what is, because I can't figure it out."

McKay jerked to stare at her. "The chips are the latest in computer processing technology. Technology developed by one of our government contractors. The smartest computer brain technology to date."

"You mean all this is about how fast a computer can process data? Technology that will be outdated in six months?"

"No, you're still missing the point, McGee. This case is about whoever is trying—illegally—to get ahold of this technology with the intent to copy and mass-produce it in another country, then sell the resulting product back here. I want to get the person or persons who paid Morgan."

He glanced back at her. Spotting Bonny, he slowed his speed, but made it to the paved highway only moments after the Lincoln some fifty feet up the road.

Hannah anxiously watched Chad pull himself up on top of the textured roof of the Lincoln. Only Morgan was now aware of his presence and purposely swerved the auto back and forth along the dark, two-lane highway, trying to shake him off.

McKay pressed the button to the radio he'd taken

back from Hannah. "Hogan? Chad, can you hear me? I need to make sure Morgan's taken alive. I need him alive."

The Lincoln swerved off the road onto the gravel shoulder, forcing Chad's jean-clad legs over the side of the car. Hannah was terrified he'd be thrown. Somehow he managed not only to hold on, but to seize the handle of the back door. The shrill shriek of a car horn jerked her gaze to the road in front of them. The Lincoln had overcorrected and was racing head-on toward a car coming in the opposite direction.

The Lincoln just barely missed the other car, but the speed at which it was traveling now put a good hundred feet between the two cars. Hannah noted with a measure of relief that Chad was climbing into the back.

The Lincoln swerved violently off the road, then pulled back onto it. There was a struggle going on inside. The knowledge both relieved and scared Hannah. But at least the movement meant Chad was still alive.

The bright beams of an oncoming vehicle blinded Hannah, the tremendous sound of a horn deafening her. But this time it wasn't just a car. It was an eighteen-wheeler.

Hannah clutched a crying Bonny close to her chest as McKay pressed on the brakes, slowing the car to a stop on the right shoulder. Even as Hannah scrambled for the door handle, her gaze was glued to the scene playing out in front of her. The Lincoln swerved left...then right...then collided head-on with the eighteen-wheeler.

The loud explosion snatched Hannah's heart right from her chest.

"Chad!"

Hannah leapt out, staring at the truck and the Lincoln

that appeared to be one large ball of blue and yellow flame.

"No!"

Hannah's legs sprang to watery life and she ran up onto the road, holding Bonny. Pain and loss hit her like sharp shards of glass. She would have entered the fire itself if it had not been for her daughter, whose sharp cries deafened her even over the sound of the fire.

"Chad..." All the life seemed to drain straight from her.

Was this what it was all about? Hannah stared into the lapping hot flames. Did she and Chad make it this far for it to end like this? She bit roughly on her bottom lip, drawing blood, and pressed Bonny's damp cheek against hers. It wasn't fair. She and Chad still had so much to work out. So much to say to each other. So many more nights to spend locked in each other's arms. So many more years delighting in their daughter's growth.

Now he was gone.

Tears spilled down her cheeks and sobs racked her body. All she could think about was Chad—and how she'd lost him.

"Damn." McKay cursed, running his hand through his hair. He stood staring at her, then rushed past her toward the burning vehicles. But the intense heat and flames forced him back. Hannah could read his mind—there was no way anyone could have survived the brutal crash.

"Hannah, I want you to know I intend to honor my agreement with Hogan."

Through her tears she stared at McKay's blurry outline. "What?"

"Furgeson. I'll sign off on her recovery so you can collect the bounty."

A hand grasped Hannah's shoulder. She instantly stiffened. She didn't want any favors from McKay. She couldn't bear to think that any amount of money was capable of compensating her for the loss of Chad...or Bonny for the loss of her father. Unable to see past the tears obscuring her vision, she batted his arm away. Her fingers met with a rock hard chest...a chest too high to be McKay's. Her heart lurched.

"Take the offer, Hannah," a familiar voice murmured. "It's the least he can do."

She blinked rapidly even as Bonny's frantic crying suddenly ceased. "Chad?"

Sweet God in Heaven!

Hannah melded into his arms, their slippery, tear-soaked daughter cradled between them. She didn't know how he had escaped the crash, or even if he was uninjured. All she cared about was that he was alive. *Alive!* She alternated between clutching him as if she'd never let him go, and probing his face to verify that he was indeed there and she wasn't seeing an apparition. His face was soot-covered, the front of his hair singed, his T-shirt and jeans torn and dirty, but there was no denying that the man holding her was one-hundred lovable percent Chad Hogan.

"If I'd known I'd get that kind of reaction from a stupid stunt like that, I would have done it a long time ago," he murmured, chuckling when she kissed him once...then again...and again.

"I thought—I mean, you couldn't—Oh, Chad..."

She battled back the emotions threatening to swallow her whole and pressed her mouth against his again as if by sheer will alone she could somehow inhale him so he'd always be with her.

He grasped the sides of her head and held her mere inches away from his face. "Marry me, Hannah."

Her heart dipped low in her stomach, then rebounded until she feared it would leap straight from her chest. If he said again that he wanted to marry her solely because of Bonny, she was afraid she'd die right then and there.

"Chad, I—"

He kissed her response into oblivion, then pulled back. In his eyes she saw the love she had always seen there tenfold. The love he refused to acknowledge, to share. "Marry me. Not for Bonny's sake. Marry me for my sake." His throat worked around a swallow and it was all she could do not to stop him right there, tell him that she'd marry him in a second if that was what he truly wanted.

He chuckled, the sound nervous and uncertain. "There was a moment back there when I was in that car when I thought I wouldn't make it. A split second when I was sure that was all she wrote. And I seemed to have been given a choice. Either get out of that damn car and return to you, or stay and pay for the sins of my past."

"Chad—"

"Shh. I'm not done yet." He looked from one of her eyes to the other. "I didn't even hesitate. I got out of that car as fast as I could. I had to get back to you.

"I love you, Hannah McGee. I can't believe how difficult—I'm sorry I couldn't tell you that before. That it took all this to make me realize that the ghosts that haunted me weren't real, but ones of my own making. I regret that my stupid pride and inability to escape the past wouldn't let me." His lips met hers and he groaned. "Oh, Hannah, you had to know I've always loved you."

She stared at him, her breath frozen in her lungs. "I have," she whispered. And she had. She'd felt it when he held her. She'd seen it in his eyes. Witnessed it in the small things he did for her, like rubbing her feet, like buying her that blasted Alfa Romeo. She'd sensed it in his caress and the way he said her name when they made love. And she'd known it beyond a shadow of a doubt in her heart.

But there was a world of difference between knowing and actually being told. Hearing the words come from his lips, seeing the earnest almost fearful expression on his face, made her feel as if her heart had sprung wings and was even now soaring above the mess in the middle of the road, moving beyond the chaos of her life up until that moment, freeing her in a way she couldn't have imagined.

"I'm done," Chad said.

"Done?" Hannah repeated.

"Yes. You, um, have yet to answer my question. And I have to tell you, after earlier tonight…you know, the other time, I'm not much liking this hesitation, Hannah."

The laughter that bubbled up from her throat startled even her. Bonny looked puzzled and attempted to cover Hannah's mouth with her chubby little hand. Hannah grasped her daughter's fingers and kissed them again and again. Then she moved past them and kissed Bonny's father again and again.

"Are you crazy? Of course I'll marry you, Chad."

Relief swept over his features sure and complete, making her laugh again as he hauled her into his arms.

Then abruptly he pulled away, appearing to have forgotten something. One hand still gripping her as if afraid to let her go, he searched his pockets with the other. Hannah's smile felt like it would never leave.

He looked so utterly, thoroughly confused and wholly adorable. "Where? I had it...."

Hannah realized what he was looking for and found it nearly impossible to swallow past the emotion that clogged her throat. "You wouldn't happen to be looking for this?" She moved a squealing Bonny from her left arm to her right, then held up her hand. There the two-carat diamond solitaire twinkled on her ring finger.

She'd picked up the velvet pouch along with the tube of chips back at Furgeson's place. And in the midst of the madness that swept them all up into its whirling funnel, she'd found a measure of comfort in slipping it on.

Chad took her hand then tugged her until she was partially pinned to his chest. This time when he slanted his mouth against hers there was no humor in the move, no relief. Only one-hundred-percent love. And a huge dose of lust.

Bonny let loose a tremendous squeal. Hannah reluctantly pulled away from Chad, then watched as Bonny lunged in her father's direction. He took her, then tucked Hannah into the cradle of his other arm.

Chad's gray eyes smiled down at her. "Do you really think we should be carrying on this way in front of, you know, our daughter? After all, she's just eight months old."

Hannah slipped her hand down toward the seat of his jeans. "Yeah, well, she's just going to have to get used to it because I don't plan to stop any time soon."

Some yards away McKay cursed, then stepped away

from the inferno that had been the Lincoln and headed toward them. Chad nudged Hannah in the other direction, down the middle of the road.

"The chips. Hogan, get your behind back here. I've got to get those chips!"

"The chips are gone, McKay. And so is Morgan. You're going to have to wait for another day to get the guy behind this."

Chad grinned down at Hannah even as he rubbed his chin against Bonny's soft hair. "I've experienced about as much danger as I can take in one lifetime. I'm not doing anything but going home with my family."

Epilogue

Chad jimmied his index finger between the tight collar of his shirt and his neck. What was it about bow ties that they never allowed enough room for a good, thick swallow? The kind of swallow that went along with slick palms and a hammering heartbeat?

"It's only natural, mate. You know, the nervousness. Hell, it ain't every day a man signs away his life."

Squinting against the noon sunlight, Chad grimaced at Jack Stokes, the only one who had followed him out of the church and onto the front steps where he'd chosen to wait until everything was ready. His uncle Nash was inside, as was—surprise of surprises—his father, decked out in full military regalia. He hadn't known quite what to say when his old man virtually marched down the aisle, his cap tucked neatly under his arm, and offered him a hearty handshake.

Still, Chad couldn't focus on any of these facts for

more than a fleeting moment. Not when he was due to marry Hannah in ten minutes.

"What would you know about getting married, Jack?" he asked the Australian.

Stokes pulled at his own tie, that and a crisp white shirt his only concessions to the formal event. He seemed genuinely puzzled when Chad had gestured to his old creased brown leather jacket, jeans and trademark dusty hat. "Yeah, well, I might just know more than you think I do on that particular topic, Hogan." He flashed a grin. "But I don't think it's a story you want to hear on your wedding day."

Chad glanced toward the closed church doors. "Yeah, you're probably right. I have a story or two of my own I don't particularly want to share right now, either."

In the past two months since returning to New York City from Houston the weather had shifted from late summer to fall. He'd hung up his bounty hunter hat to open Seekers with Hannah. He'd also come to learn exactly what having a growing baby girl in his life meant, from soothing small hurts to keeping Bonny from following their new puppy's lead and trying to drink from the toilet. Rather than finding everything achingly familiar, he'd instead found it all refreshingly, redeemingly new.

Then there was Hannah....

He didn't think it was possible to love her more than he already had. Oh, how wrong he'd been. Every morning, before he even opened his eyes, he reveled in the feel of her body pressing into his. Enjoyed breathing in the scent of her wild hair. Got a kick out of watching her burn the latest of her burn-proof dinners, after which he'd pitch in and they'd come up with something together. And with each and every tick of the clock he felt his heart fill with even more love for this woman who had coaxed him back from the brink and showed him how to live again. Who had taken two single people and an eight-month-old baby and made them into a family with all the fixings, including Sunday mass—followed by dinner with his uncle Nash and her uncle Vincent and their extended families—and meat loaf Mondays. And no matter how hard they worked to get their new business off the ground, they always returned to their apartment at the end of the day and did things—family things—with Bonny that transformed the house into a real home. Even now the windows sported pumpkin decals and on their door hung an autumn wreath. And the refrigerator was covered with hideous attempts at art by a now ten-month-old Bonny.

Chad caught himself tugging at his collar again. Then why was it the prospect of making everything official made him nervous? "You know, Jack, I have a theory on men's resistance to com..." His words trailed off as he turned to find the ex-fellow bounty hunter, now prized employee of Seekers, had gone back into the church, leaving him standing alone on the steps.

So much for male bonding.

Glancing at his watch, Chad surmised that it wasn't so much his fear of commitment, or even of his past anymore, that made him anxious about getting married. It was the prospect of change.

"And what a load of horse crap that is, too," he mimicked what Hannah would probably have to say on his theory, then grinned.

Ten more minutes...

He slid his hand into his pocket and took out the ring he'd picked out for Hannah. Snapping open the box, he stared down at the simple platinum band, wondering for the fifth time if she'd find it too plain.

The church door opened behind him. Chad bobbled the ring box, nearly sending it flying down the steps.

A familiar baby's giggle tugged at his heartstrings as he turned toward the door. There stood Hannah, covered from head to foot in fluffy, intricate lace, holding a squirming and undeniably restless Bonny. Chad's breath caught in his throat. He'd never seen Hannah look so beautiful. Or so nervous.

Bonny lunged for him. He took the little munchkin, noticing the spiky dampness of her lashes. Obviously she hadn't been all sweetness and cream inside. She immediately went to work on his bow tie, nearly choking him.

"You know, it's bad luck to see the bride before the wedding," Hannah said, a smile playing at the sides of her mouth.

Chad scanned her face. Every sweet freckle stood out in relief against her white skin. "Hannah, I think we've had enough bad luck to last us a lifetime." He looked at her dress and his throat grew tight in a way that had nothing to do with Bonny's attempts to strangle him. "You, um, weren't thinking of running out on me, were you?"

The hint of a smile turned into shining reality. "Not on your life."

"Good."

She cocked her head slightly to the side, nearly toppling the gauzy veil covering her red hair. "Are you sure you want to do this? I mean, it's not too late to back out, you know. I don't want you to feel that you have to marry me or anything.''

Chad freed one of his hands then slid his fingers along the satiny ridge of her jawline. Was it possible for one woman to be so incredibly soft? ''Baby, I want to marry you more than anything in the world.''

In that one moment, every ounce of nervousness vanished, leaving him feeling confident and sure—and so much in love with the two women in his life he thought his heart might crack his rib cage.

He brushed his mouth against Hannah's and nearly groaned when she instinctively leaned into him.

''I'm pregnant,'' she blurted. ''Again.''

Her face turned the most charming shade of red as her gaze darted everywhere except at his face.

''I didn't know...I mean I wasn't sure....'' She took a deep breath. ''I bought three home pregnancy tests this morning. Every last one of them came up positive.'' She stared at him for long moments. ''Well, aren't you going to say something?''

''Sure,'' he murmured. ''I love you.'' He kissed her again. Then again. Tangling his tongue with hers until he felt her anxiety melt away and until she was kissing him back.

It wasn't until Bonny gave a robust squeal that Chad remembered exactly where they were and what they were supposed to be doing. Then he took his bride's hand in his, tucked his daughter a little more snugly against his side and went into the church to reconfirm publicly what he already knew in his heart. That he and Hannah and Bonny and the child they would soon have were a family in every sense of the word.

*   *   *   *   *

You're not going to believe this offer!

In October and November 2000, buy any two Harlequin or Silhouette books and save $10.00 off future purchases, or buy any three and save $20.00 off future purchases!

Just fill out this form and attach 2 proofs of purchase (cash register receipts) from October and November 2000 books and Harlequin will send you a coupon booklet worth a total savings of $10.00 off future purchases of Harlequin and Silhouette books in 2001. Send us 3 proofs of purchase and we will send you a coupon booklet worth a total savings of $20.00 off future purchases.

Saving money has never been this easy.

I accept your offer! Please send me a coupon booklet:

Name: _____

Address: _____ City: _____

State/Prov.: _____ Zip/Postal Code: _____

Optional Survey!

In a typical month, how many Harlequin or Silhouette books would you buy <u>new</u> at retail stores?

☐ Less than 1   ☐ 1   ☐ 2   ☐ 3 to 4   ☐ 5+

Which of the following statements best describes how you <u>buy</u> Harlequin or Silhouette books? Choose one answer only that <u>best</u> describes you.

☐ I am a regular buyer and reader
☐ I am a regular reader but buy only occasionally
☐ I only buy and read for specific times of the year, e.g. vacations
☐ I subscribe through Reader Service but also buy at retail stores
☐ I mainly borrow and buy only occasionally
☐ I am an occasional buyer and reader

Which of the following statements best describes how you <u>choose</u> the Harlequin and Silhouette series books you buy <u>new</u> at retail stores? By "series," we mean books within a particular line, such as *Harlequin PRESENTS* or *Silhouette SPECIAL EDITION*. Choose one answer only that <u>best</u> describes you.

☐ I only buy books from my favorite series
☐ I generally buy books from my favorite series but also buy books from other series on occasion
☐ I buy some books from my favorite series but also buy from many other series regularly
☐ I buy all types of books depending on my mood and what I find interesting and have no favorite series

Please send this form, along with your cash register receipts as proofs of purchase, to:
In the U.S.: Harlequin Books, P.O. Box 9057, Buffalo, NY 14269
In Canada: Harlequin Books, P.O. Box 622, Fort Erie, Ontario L2A 5X3
(Allow 4-6 weeks for delivery) Offer expires December 31, 2000.

PHQ4002

Silhouette® —

where love comes alive—online...

eHARLEQUIN.com

your romantic
books

♥ Shop online! Visit Shop eHarlequin and discover a wide selection of new releases and classic favorites at great discounted prices.

♥ Read our daily and weekly Internet exclusive serials, and participate in our interactive novel in the reading room.

Ever dreamed of being a writer? Enter your chapter for a chance to become a featured author in our Writing Round Robin novel.

• • • • • •

your romantic
life

♥ Check out our feature articles on dating, flirting and other important romance topics and get your daily love dose with tips on how to keep the romance alive every day.

• • • • • •

your
community

♥ Have a Heart-to-Heart with other members about the latest books and meet your favorite authors.

♥ Discuss your romantic dilemma in the Tales from the Heart message board.

your romantic
escapes

♥ Learn what the stars have in store for you with our daily Passionscopes and weekly Erotiscopes.

♥ Get the latest scoop on your favorite royals in Royal Romance.